THIS DREAMING ISLE

EDITED BY **DAN COXON**

UNSUNG
STORIES

Published by Unsung Stories
43 Mornington Road, Chingford
London E4 7DT, United Kingdom
www.unsungstories.co.uk

First edition published in 2018 –First impression

This book is a work of fiction. All the events and characters portrayed in
this book are fictional and any similarities to persons, alive or deceased,
is coincidental.

Paperback ISBN: 978-1-907389-59-7
ePub ISBN: 978-1-907389-60-3

Edited by Dan Coxon
Cover Artwork © Jordan Grimmer 2018
Cover design by Vince Haig
Text design by Cox Design Limited
Typesetting by George Sandison

Printed in the UK by TJ International

INTRODUCTION

Earlier in the year, when this anthology was entering the later stages of the editorial process, Paul Wright's film *Arcadia* was released to a small number of cinemas around the country. Comprised of archival footage set to a score by Adrian Utley of Portishead and Will Gregory of Goldfrapp – with a cursory narrative of sorts provided by Wright's voice-over – it explored Britain's relationship with the land, including the passing of folk traditions and the incursion of the industrial age into our countryside. There was an obvious elegiac tone to parts of the film, but also a sense of weirdness, a strange, unsettling undercurrent that emerged from the archives: masked figures, ritual dances, traditions rooted in folklore and legend. It looked like something from *The Wicker Man*.

This Dreaming Isle occupies that same fertile ground. It was always our intention to allow the contributing authors a free rein when it came to their stories – we asked only that they should tie them to a specific place in the British Isles, and should in some way explore the myths and traditions, the folklore and history that make this land unique.

What's startling upon reading these stories together, in one volume, is that so many of them occupy that territory commonly called 'folk horror'. We are faced with haunted lochs and medieval witches, spectral apparitions and Black Magic. Even Andrew Michael Hurley's 'In My Father's House' – arguably the weirdest story in this anthology – suggests a timeless presence in the landscape, something not entirely malevolent, but not on the side of the angels either.

In some cases, the same images surface with eerie regularity. Secluded hills, mirrors, the appearance of a stranger in a small community: these are all elements that are common in British folk tales, and they crop up here too, threading through the stories. But even more startling are the differences, the kaleidoscopic variety of the authors' interpretations of place, and folklore, and 'Britishness'. These tales dig deep into the layers of history beneath our feet, revealing strata upon strata: back through the medieval witch trials to the Norman invasion, and beyond. It's no coincidence that two of the stories turn up ancient creatures, fossilised in the very bedrock of the land.

Of course, these days it's almost impossible to discuss Britain, past or future, without Brexit rearing its scaly head. When this anthology was first conceived (and I can be precise about this, as I've time-travelled back through the email threads) the crucial vote on 23 June 2016 was still three months away, and the notion of Britain being anything other than part of Europe seemed ludicrous and far-fetched. Little did we know that two years later – after the Leave vote, the failed negotiations, the infighting and the resignations – it would still seem ludicrous and far-fetched, but we would be shackled to it nonetheless. I'm reminded of a ride at Alton Towers called The Black Hole that I rode when I was a teenager, plummeting down through the darkness at such speeds that my stomach felt as if it was rising into my throat. That sensation of being in blind, rudderless freefall scared the shit out of me then – much as it does now.

The political landscape of Britain is different today, even if the actual landscape hasn't changed. The notion of 'Britishness' is all too often marred by reactionary nationalistic sentiments, the chest-thumping of the far right or the 'tea-and-scones' tweeness of Theresa May. It has never been the intention of this anthology to push any kind of political agenda, but we were very clear about what we didn't want. There was no space here for anti-immigration rants or 'this is our land' conservatism. I'm pleased to say that none of the stories we were sent even attempted to head in that direction – our authors are far too sensible, and too reasonable, for that.

Which brings me back to *Arcadia*. When the film was released, Paul Kingsnorth penned a short essay for their website, intended to be part of the promotional push for the movie. Kingsnorth is sometimes a controversial figure, and it didn't take long for the debate to brew around his contribution. Entitled 'Elysium Found?', Kingsnorth's essay quickly moved away from the weird, unsettling heart of Wright's film, instead using it as a flag to wave for old-fashioned patriotism and nostalgia. Several of the authors in this book took offence at the right-wing, reactionary tone of the piece – and rightly so. The past isn't tea and scones on the lawn, it's malicious ghosts and weird goings-on in the fells, it's witches burned at the stake and towns razed to the ground by Vikings. The past is a dangerous, cutthroat place, filled with violence, injustice and inequality. Those who see it through rose-tinted glasses aren't engaging with it, they're simply fantasizing – and that's always dangerous.

The very idea of Britishness is in turmoil at the moment. With everything that's happening on the political scene, it's hard to imagine what this country will look like five years from now, never mind the decades to come. But the stories in *This Dreaming Isle* make one thing clear: there are rich veins of weirdness running through the soil here, an underground river of the strange and the unsettling that has been part of Britain's cultural landscape for centuries, and shows no signs of drying up any time soon.

Brexit or no Brexit, Britain's weird stories are here to stay.

Dan Coxon
August 2018

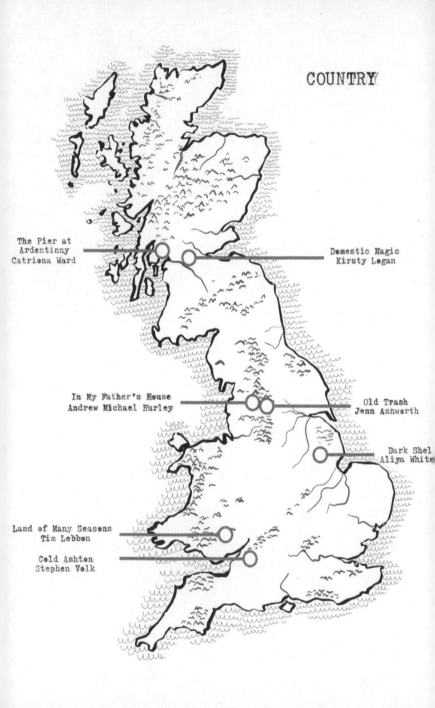

COUNTRY

The Pier at
Ardentinny
Catriona Ward

Domestic Magic
Kirsty Logan

In My Father's House
Andrew Michael Hurley

Old Trash
Jenn Ashworth

Dark Shel
Aliya White

Land of Many Seasons
Tim Lebbon

Cold Ashton
Stephen Volk

COUNTRY

THE PIER AT ARDENTINNY

CATRIONA WARD

It may send me mad. The light in the cupboard will not turn off. Light bleeds through the cracks, creating a glowing doorway in the dark. The bed faces it directly.

We are in the red bedroom in the west wing. It has a large cupboard set in the wall by the bedroom door. An overhead bulb throws stark light over the dusty interior. A cord switches it on and off, but now pulling the cord produces nothing but a robust *click*. The bulb burns on regardless.

I have done everything I can think of. Pulled the cord with varying degrees of gentleness and force. Flicked all the other switches in the room, hoping that one of them controls it. Searched the baseboards for another, secret switch which might have escaped my first sweep. I tried to unscrew the bulb and retreated swearing with singed fingers. I tried again, this time with a towel wrapped around my hand. The towel started smoking and now the room smells of burnt polyester.

Anthony sleeps on, of course, no earthquake could prevent that. Whorls of grey chest hair struggle through the gaps in his pyjama top. The granite jawline of which he is so proud is softening year by year. But he looks very peaceful. I am envious.

I could wake Anthony's mother Estelle and ask her how to turn the light off, of course. But I think I won't do that.

Outside the wind races, tugging and tapping at the house – panes shake in their fixtures, latches rattle, slates shift uneasy on the roof. For days the rain has fallen on us from clouds of pewter. Scottish weather can give one the creeps. There's too much low angry sky. It sees me, somehow.

>•<

Anthony and I met by the cloakroom of our favourite restaurant. There was a mix-up with the tickets and we both had the same number. We laughed but we were a little annoyed. The flustered girl searched the racks for my green linen jacket and his heavy, velvet-collared astrakhan. He is always cold.

We talked about the restaurant, how we loved the food, about how long we had been coming to this place. We each claimed it as 'our place'. There was a friendly, competitive edge to it all which I liked. He wasn't worried by my beauty. I quickly realised that he was everything I wanted. Kind, intelligent. In search of purpose. I realised that I could give him that. Director of this, CEO of that, Trustee of whatever – all the various ways of saying *money*. Only those who have too much feel the need to disguise it so.

He had a wife before me, Imogen. She left him, then shortly afterwards died. I don't plan to do either of those things.

>•<

For breakfast there is haggis – of course – pallid eggs and crimson strips of bacon that disintegrate into salty granules at the touch of a fork.

Estelle comes in from seeing to the hens. Rivers of broken capillaries run down her cheeks. She wears her wellington boots at table.

'Oh, Irene,' she says, in her traceless accent. 'Do have a piece of toast at least. There's nothing to you.'

'Coffee is fine.' I smile.

Anthony lowers the paper. 'Leave her alone, Mother,' he

says, squinting slightly. He is too vain to wear glasses and he is frightened of contact lenses.

'Did you sleep well?'

'The light in the cupboard in our room won't switch off,' I say.

'Oh,' says Estelle. 'I'll ask Jamie to look at it.' Jamie's arms are decorated with delicate swirls of blue ink to the shoulders. He has a face that was never young or surprised by anything. He lives in a flat over the old kitchen at Ardentinny during the week, and goes who knows where at the weekends.

'Drizzle all morning,' Estelle says. 'But it's meant to clear in the afternoon. Let's walk over to the village after lunch. A good long stroll.'

'How long?' I ask politely.

'Four miles or so. We'll have tea by the pier. It's lovely. Jamie can collect us in the Land Rover later.'

Through the window the hills glower behind their mask of rain.

She follows my gaze, anxious. 'It's better in the summer,' she says. I can see her heart in her face. She is one of those women. 'Honestly. The sun is out all day. Isn't it, Anthony?'

'Yes,' he says. 'It's heaven, Reeney.'

Early on, Estelle fastened onto the idea that I want to be married in London. The thought grieves her deeply.

I have no objection to holding the wedding here. Ardentinny House is soft with age and surrounded by rolling land. Deer walk the lines of the hills in pronged silhouettes. It is all very suitable.

I am going to let her persuade me slowly. It is good to start out with her in my debt.

>•<

The sky clears after lunch. We set out towards the village under a deep blue sky. The path is green and wide. Bees crawl busy through the heather. The air is warm, smoke-sweet. My skin drinks the sunlight. We all feel it. Estelle's cheeks pink up beneath the red. I don't know how anyone stands those grey days.

Anthony begins to whistle, something melodic with a lilt of folk song. Estelle laughs and hums along. She strides out and soon overtakes us. We dawdle behind, wind whipping our cheeks.

I take Anthony's hand. He squeezes it. 'You're a peach for coming,' he murmurs. 'Ma loves this walk.'

Ahead, Estelle turns and calls, 'I love this walk. Come on, slowcoaches!'

We hurry to catch her. She is standing in a ring of raised turf. 'There was a Celtic hill fort here,' she says. 'This is old land, lived on by many people through the ages. Everyone leaves something behind.' Her eyes are misty. 'The past is everywhere. Even the loch at Ardentinny is charmed, you know. They say you see people's true nature in it. Before two youngsters married they would go together to the lake and look at their betrothed's reflection, to make sure they were not wedding a demon or an evildoer.'

'How fascinating,' I say.

Estelle turns abruptly and strides away. I realise, too late, that she is crying.

'She gets like that sometimes,' Anthony says. 'We used to picnic here when we were children. So this place reminds her of Dad and Lisette.'

'Oh,' I say, making my face soft and loving. 'I am sorry.' I touch his cheek. 'Let's not be sad today. Let's think about the future.'

'You're right.' He lifts me off the ground and kisses me. 'Will you look in the loch with me, Reeney?'

'And reveal my wicked nature? Never.'

'Wicked, you say?' He squeezes me until I can hardly breathe. He likes me to be pert. 'Let's catch up with Mother, wicked woman.'

The land begins to slope gently downwards and there is the feeling of water nearby. We crest the final rise and the village of Ardentinny lies below us, clinging to the shore of the gleaming loch. Boats rise and fall on the gentle swell. Neat houses of whitewashed stone, a little grey church with no spire, as if it is unwise to reach too high in these parts. All around the land rolls on in heights of green and purple.

From this direction one enters the village through the churchyard. We come down the hill and climb the stile. The stones are upright, golden with lichen. I go quickly through the ranks of the dead. I wait by the lychgate while Anthony and Estelle pay their respects. His father lies here. Beside him is buried Anthony's twin sister Lisette, dead at nineteen. Anthony does not speak of her often. I know he feels guilt. He dared her to jump the fence. They didn't check the landing side and so missed the rabbit hole. The horse broke a leg, Lisette her neck.

>•<

The pier is a rickety thing of silver weathered plank. It stretches out over the shining loch. We sit with our legs hanging. Estelle and Anthony produce cheese scones from capacious waxed pockets. I drink tea from the flask.

'Photo of you two,' Estelle says. 'I want to remember this.' She takes a little camera from her pocket. A light flashes ominous red on the top. She goes down the pier to the shore and picks her way along the rocky beach.

'Shall we look?' Anthony asks.

We peer into the water together. It is rough, made of shining rills and ripples thrown up by the wind. There is no reflection, just black water and tossed sunlight.

Estelle sits down beside us again. 'I don't know if it took.' Her brow is furrowed. 'And now the battery's dead.'

Anthony puts an arm about each of us. 'Never mind,' he says. 'We can remember it instead. Where's my scone? I had half left.'

The sun dies low on the land. It sinks behind the hill to the south-west, bathing us in flame. This is the sunset for which the village and the house and the loch are named. *Ardentinny*, the hill of fire.

Jamie waits by the Land Rover, arms folded, cigarette sending up a spiral of blue in the dusk.

The journey back seems too short to account for all those hours of walking. We have supper of venison and potatoes. I eat a quarter of what I am given. I refuse wine. We play cards until Estelle's head nods. A storm is building outside, I can feel it.

In the red bedroom Anthony kneels to say his prayers.

'Our Father, who art in heaven,' he begins. I watch him

surreptitiously over the top of my book. I am secretly fascinated by this nightly ritual. I had never seen anyone do this until I met him.

'And protect the souls of those you have gathered to you: Dad, Lisette and Imogen.'

He finishes his litany of the dead, gets in beside me and is asleep almost immediately. A walk of five miles is tiring at his age. I lie for some time in the dark. The glowing doorway taunts me. The cupboard light is still on.

The cupboard is next to the bedroom door, leading to the darkened hall. Two doors, one light and one dark, like a choice at the beginning of a fairy tale.

The bedroom door gives a quiet *click* behind me. I shiver in the draughty hall. A lamp on a table at the head of the stairs gives out some light. I go to the end of the corridor then hesitate. Two passages lead away in either direction. One is carpeted in royal blue. The other is uncarpeted, cold. I follow that one. I have never before been to the flat above the old kitchen but I can guess the way. At the end of the bare hall, there is a line of light under a door. I smell cigarette smoke. Music plays from a radio, tinny.

He answers my knock as if he knew it was coming. His blue forearms bear a red stripe as if he has been leaning on a windowsill or a mantel. What was he looking at?

'Could I have a cigarette?' I ask. 'I can't sleep.' Overhead, thunder sounds. The storm is upon us.

>•<

My first memory is of kissing my mother's face during a snowstorm. She was unconscious on the pavement outside a pub. The flakes landed on her cheeks, her eyes, covered her lashes. She didn't move. I was afraid that she was dead. She wasn't, not that day. I grew up poor, often hungry. My mother and I moved around. We lived in cold, abandoned places – derelict warehouses, unsold Barratt homes, once a ruined church – with other people who had nowhere else to go. One day when I was thirteen Mother didn't wake. They came for me then and put me in care.

I took care of myself as best I could. I learned to type and use a computer. I got a job as a receptionist at a bank. I learned early on the value of my beauty. It was all I had. I have been looking for my husband since I was fourteen. It took years and many errors but I knew when I saw Anthony that I had found him.

What does it matter that I gave the cloakroom girl £50 to mix up the tickets? It is not a crime. I will make a good wife. I have trained for it, just as I have trained myself to do without food in case I must go hungry again one day. I am prepared for anything.

After breakfast I want to go back to bed but Estelle starts talking about the wedding. Anthony sits with a resigned look and I can afford to be generous. We return to London tomorrow.

'You know,' Estelle says, 'you could have a part of the house for your own if you liked. I'd love the company. We could make the west wing into a lovely flat for you. And I would be nearby to help with – you know – babysitting and so on.'

'My God,' Anthony says. He is somewhat white. 'Stop it, Mother.'

Jamie comes in. He gives Estelle a colourful envelope. 'Your things from Thirsk.' He goes. We don't look at one another.

Most of the photographs are blurry images of a finger. Estelle leafs through them as she talks, dropping some, putting others back facing the wrong way.

'I wouldn't interfere with you,' she says. 'Honestly. It would just be so nice to know that you were close by—' She screams, a high cracked sound, shocking in the drawing room with its Wedgwood china and eau de Nil wallpaper. A photograph flutters to the floor. Estelle points, covering her heart with her hand.

Anthony goes to her side. He picks up the picture. We are sitting on the pier at Ardentinny. A strand of hair blows across my chin. Anthony's eyes are closed, his mouth open. The lake is calm, arrested forever beneath a blue sky. Our legs swing, our toes almost brush the shining water. In the darkness beneath the pier there crouches a white figure.

The girl squats. Loch water ripples around her thin ankles. Her face is turned to the camera. She crams half a scone between sharp, stained teeth. She looks at us through time and space. Dark hair hangs in rat-tails about her shoulders. One eye is dark and deep as a hole. The other is covered, her head bound in what looks like dirty flannel.

I remember that day. Mother blacked my eye because I went with a man and didn't give her the money. I wrapped my head in flannel to hide the bruise. I did it clumsily because I was twelve. There I am, captured – my true self.

I am not aware of fainting.

>•<

I come to with Anthony's hand on my cheek and the scent of lavender water everywhere.

'She barely eats,' Estelle is saying. 'Poor, poor thing.' I must be at a low ebb because I detect only kindness in her voice. 'I am sorry that I frightened you, Irene. I was surprised, that's all. Old McRae's daughter must have crept under the pier as we were picnicking. She likes to hide. A sweet-natured girl but— I don't know what one is supposed to say these days. *Touched*, we used to call it.'

'Well,' says Anthony, 'now I know where my scone went.'

I look again at the photograph. The girl's features are more pointed than mine, scattered with vivid freckles. Her eyes are smaller, her hair a milkier shade of brown. She is not like me at all.

He puts me to bed, stroking by brow. 'Never fear,' he says. 'I'll stay while you sleep.'

I weep.

'Irene,' he says, serious. 'You can tell me the truth, you know. It won't change things between us.'

I cry until I cannot breathe, held in his arms. I tell him everything.

>•<

Dandelion clocks dance in the warm dusk. Estelle was right, it is beautiful here in the summer. Everything is ready for tomorrow. The pavilion sits white on the lawn like a great bird. Three hundred ivory candles stand on tables draped in ivy. Ribbons flutter on the ranks of white chairs.

Anthony was wrong, that day. What I told him did change things between us. We showed ourselves to one another. I have grown into someone who can trust.

I go to the red bedroom. A man is standing before the mirror, his back to me. I make a slight sound. He turns. It is Jamie.

'I brought you this,' he says, pointing to a silver dish which sits in front of the mirror. It is filled with water.

'I don't want it,' I say. 'Take it away. Go.'

He pauses as if to say something. Instead he brushes past me and is gone.

Anthony laughs when he sees the dish. 'Loch water,' he says. 'The old tradition. I don't need to look.'

The last of the guests are leaving in the late dusk. It was a decorous wedding, heavy with cream linen and silver. It was a wedding suitable for Ardentinny House. No one got drunk.

My ivory silk is damp with sweat. It's done now. I feel light, as if I am about to evaporate or transform.

We undress by candlelight. Everything in the red bedroom glows warm and lustrous.

'The cupboard is dark,' I say. 'Look!'

'The bulb must have burnt out at last,' he says. 'Come here.'

Afterwards I get up and go to the mirror. I feel so different these days that I am often visited by the urge to check for outwards signs of it.

In the mirror I see myself, a youngish woman tired of living by her wits. I glance down at the still water in the bowl. It shows me back in black and silver.

Behind me Anthony rouses and begins to say his prayers. 'Our Father…' he begins. I smile. Even tonight, he will not neglect it.

'And protect the souls of those you have gathered to you: Dad, Lisette, Imogen and Irene.'

'I am not dead yet, darling,' I say. It has been a long day.

He says 'Amen' and comes to me. 'Not yet,' he says and squeezes me until I can hardly breathe. 'I will have my fun.'

'Too tight,' I say, 'too tight…' His grip does not slacken, it grows stronger. My ribs creak. I gasp. 'Let me go.'

'No.'

It is only then that I look down into the still bowl of water and I see what I have married.

Through the pounding in my ears there comes a knock on the door.

'Are you two all right?' Estelle's voice is wavery, vague. She had four glasses of champagne earlier.

'We're fine,' the thing that holds me says. It breathes hot in my ear. 'Tell her.'

'We're fine, Estelle,' I call.

OLD TRASH

JENN ASHWORTH

The day of the trip was hot, the sky clear and nearly cloudless. There'd been a train from Manchester, then a local bus service called 'the Witch-Hopper' which took them on a circuitous route through the little towns and villages around Pendle then finally dropped them within a mile of the lower Ogden Reservoir, beside which they planned to camp. It wasn't an official site, but there was a pub nearby where they could use the toilet, and it was only going to be overnight.

Rachael struggled with the tent pole, trying to push it into the fabric socket where it, apparently, was supposed to fit. Mae was sitting in the long grass nearby leaning against her rucksack and swiping furiously at her mobile phone, resolutely not helping. The pole escaped Rachael's grasp and sprung onto the grass. She silently counted to five, then bent to retrieve it.

'At least we've got nice weather,' she called, feeling the sweat on her hairline. There were midges, but there was no point in complaining about them. The pole whipped backwards and forwards, a thing possessed, and Rachael sweated and swore under her breath until – nipping the skin between her thumb and finger in the process – she managed to force it into place. There. Rachael stood back and admired the tent: bright against the sun-baked grass and the dark, hazy rise of the wooded hill behind them. *Ta da.*

'Shall we unpack? Make a cup of tea?' She winced at the sound of her voice – eager and high-pitched. Mae grunted and Rachael risked a glance at her. Her face still tilted phone-wards, her bare legs bent at the knee and gaping wide like a puppet whose strings had been cut. Just beyond her, the grey square lip of the lower reservoir; behind them, Fell Wood.

'Or we could just dump the stuff in the tent and go down to the pub? Cold drinks? Some chips?'

Mae huffed and tucked the phone into the front pocket of her shorts. She'd made them herself, cut down from a brand-new pair of jeans with a pair of kitchen scissors.

'Do you want to get changed?'

'No. It's too hot.'

She must not stare. It irritated Mae and was likely to provoke an argument. Instead, Rachael heaved her own rucksack up from the grass and put it inside the tent. Threw the sleeping bags, still bundled up tight, in after them. Mae slapped at a midge on her bare thigh. What she was wearing didn't matter, Rachael told herself. What Mae wore fell into the category of things over which she was no longer willing to pick a battle.

'Mae? Mae, love? What do you reckon?'

'Will they have Wi-Fi in the pub? I can't get any signal up here.'

'They might,' Rachael said. 'But I thought we could—'

'Are we going then?'

Mae had already set off, striding along the footpath that hugged the concrete edge of the reservoir. There was no guardrail. It would be possible to sit on the edge and touch the water with the toe of an outstretched foot. Maybe they would do that later. Rachael looked at the grey-indigo surface of the still reservoir, and knew that no matter how long this rare summer's succession of hot days lasted, the water down there would be very, very cold. Then she retrieved her purse from the tent and hurried to catch up. The air was still and hot and thick with insects; she walked quickly through a cloud of them, feeling them in her hair.

But things were going well, she thought. The trip had been a good idea. Rachael had not allowed herself to hope that this would be a time in which she and Mae would build bridges, only that perhaps – if she handled it carefully, and if everything went without a hitch (she'd checked the weather forecast hourly the day before they were due to leave) it would be a period of time – just twenty-four hours was all that Mae would agree to – where hostilities would cease. And yes: she knew it was unlikely Mae would be able to get a signal on her phone and that's why she'd chosen Pendle Hill, the shadow of it falling onto the reservoir, the steep bank of its foreside overlooking Newchurch and Sabden and Barley. She had no interest in the tiny old villages and their little pubs with brooms over the door and post offices with adverts from crystal healers stuck in their windows and racks of cheap postcards with comedy friendly witches. She cared only about the hill, and its special property of cutting off the data signal that Mae relied on.

The footpath met the road. Mae vaulted over the stile, her boots slapping the pavement as she landed.

'This is nice, isn't it?' Rachael clambered after her.

'It's boring,' Mae said.

'How can you be bored?' Rachael knew what she sounded like, but couldn't stop herself. 'There's all this scenery, and the birds – I think I saw a kite earlier – and this is a lovely walk, and,' she paused, panting, 'we've got each other to talk to.'

'That's what I'm talking about,' Mae said. Then, in one of her turn-on-a-sixpence mood changes, smiled – a smile as flimsy as a trick of the light – and waited for Rachael to catch up. 'We're going to eat at the pub?'

'We can if you want,' Rachael said. 'Or we can make a fire

and do some potatoes in tin foil. Would you like that?'

Mae put her hand over her face to shield her eyes from the sun. 'Pub. Pub tea, definitely.' She looped her arm through Rachael's, and they walked alongside each other like that for a while, along the centre of the road, flanked by hedges.

When Mae stopped to pick cow parsley and thread it into her hair, Rachael waited for her, saying nothing, and hoping that she'd take her arm again when she was finished. And she did. It had the effect of making Rachael feel grateful, absurdly chosen. Rachael stroked Mae's arm, smelled her sweat and the bruised cow parsley, ignored the reek of cigarettes from her hair and walked onwards, the pub, according to the map, just around the crook of the road.

Was this how Mae's boyfriend felt? The one she snuck out to meet, late at night? The one that drove her around in his car? Chosen, like that? Or was it the other way around? Was it Mae herself who felt chosen? Was it about feeling special? They trudged in a silence not quite companionable, and the pub appeared.

'Come on,' Rachael said, 'let's go inside.'

'Mum,' Mae said, gently. She wanted something. They hesitated in the doorway, the light picking out the fine hair on Mae's arms and turning the rest of her into a silhouette. 'Can I have something to drink as well? A proper drink? Seeing as we're on holiday?'

Delay. That was the advice from the keyworker. Don't get drawn into an argument; don't fall into the trap of conflict.

'Let's look at the menu, shall we? See what they've got? Come on, love. I'm starving. Aren't you?' Rachael held her breath.

'They'd better have something vegetarian,' Mae said.

'I'm sure they will. And you can order the drinks for both of us,' Rachael said. 'I'll give you the money.'

They went inside.

He wasn't a boy, though – the one Mae had chosen, or who had chosen her. He was a man. Rachael had been able to do what was needed with a keylogger on her daughter's laptop. She was still paying for that laptop, which meant that she still owned it, really. It was a possession of the household, and not quite Mae's private property, not in the same way an email account was. Though she'd got into that too – and the second mobile phone tucked inside a slit in the side of her daughter's mattress. She had seen the messages. The photographs Mae had been sending. The presents, too: trainers still in their shoeboxes under her bed, drawers full of perfume bottles and make-up sets, mainly untouched. Vodka bottles, half empty.

Rachael watched her daughter's back as she stood at the bar: the way the soles of her trainers were worn unevenly, the coltish length of her legs. She looked around the pub. No danger – by which she meant, no men. A young woman reading a newspaper and thoughtfully eating chips with her fingers. No threat at all. A couple of female hikers sitting in a nook beside the unlit fireplace – probably an actual couple, judging by the way they sat together, sharing a plate of sandwiches in a kind of unfocused intimacy she felt guilty observing – but there was no one else. The pub was safe.

Mae came back from the bar. Plonked two bottles of Perrier, two ice-filled glasses, on the table. Flung herself onto the seat.

'She wanted ID,' she said sullenly. 'Stupid bitch.'

'Never mind,' Rachael said, mildly, 'maybe next year. You do look…' Mae was distracted, already fiddling with her phone, and Rachael caught herself in time and let the sentence tiptoe away into the shadows, unspoken.

You do look underage…

You do look like you need a hair wash…

You do look – lovely.

'Mum? Mum? You hear me? No Wi-Fi. Nothing. Can you believe it?'

She sat, fidgeted on the stool, then stood up again. Always so restless. 'I'm going to the toilet,' she said. 'Order some food for me, will you? I'm starving.'

>•<

The woman behind the bar – gloriously fat, with smudged black eyeliner and dyed red hair – caught Rachael's eye as she leafed through the menu.

'I can't serve her,' she said, 'not even a shandy. They'd hold me personally responsible.' She smiled apologetically. 'Sorry.'

'I'm actually rather glad that you didn't,' Rachael said, and laughed, as if she was making a joke she was relying on the woman to understand.

'Soup is lentil and tomato,' the red-haired woman said, 'but there's not much left. You camping?'

Rachael blushed. Camping – and not even in a proper campsite. It was probably against the law.

'Just for the night. My friend said… well, it was a bit impromptu. If you could tell us who owns the land…?'

'I don't care about that,' the woman said, and laughed. 'You'll want to be careful going back though.'

'Really?'

Rachael wanted her to wait: to save her stories of the pixies and haunted wells and boggarts and ghosts of witches from times past until Mae came back. 'Tell Mae,' she wanted to say. She'd enjoy that. But perhaps she wouldn't. Maybe Mae was too old for ghost stories now.

'No street lamps on the lane. You've not seen proper dark till you've been out here at night,' the woman said, and laughed. Rachael ordered sandwiches and chips and returned to her seat.

>•<

Did he know, this man, that Mae was only fourteen? That was probably part of the attraction. The time for delicacy had long since passed. She'd said as much to the school: 'My daughter's boyfriend is twenty-eight years old and he is raping her and I believe his friends also,' and again, to social services, who were overstretched – and anyway, Mae came from a nice home in a nice part of town and her schoolwork wasn't suffering, not that much, not really, and she was a good weight, and the police, also, who weren't able to do anything without proof, and proof was what Mae would not provide – not a word against her boyfriend who had been banned from the house, from the street, but who would park up by the swings and to whose car Mae would flit in the night, out of a locked window, through a locked door –

had threatened, in fact, to set the house on fire if the locks were applied again, and Rachael believed her.

It might be worse, though, she thought, watching her daughter come back from the toilet, wiping her wet hands on the front of her shorts. It might be worse if she felt herself a victim. Felt that a great wrong had been done to her – as it had. Perhaps better for her to feel she was part of a great romance and have Rachael around to gather the pieces when they fell?

Mae sat down and started flicking impatiently through an abandoned newspaper, thrumming with boredom. Was it better to wait for this man to lose interest in her? Wait for Mae to grow up? These two were the same thing, most probably. She was on the pill. At least there was that; the GP had prescribed it without turning a hair. And could all broken things be mended? The keyworker had been silent on this matter. Had only advised that home should be, above all, a place of peace and calm and safety. A refuge to which Mae could always return.

'We can walk tomorrow. Right up the hill if you want to. Or just… chill out? Near the tent. Did you bring a book?'

Mae snorted. The table they were sitting at was next to a rack of leaflets of tourist attractions that were no good unless you had a car, and hikes, which were no good if you didn't want to do them. Mae abandoned the newspaper and started to rake through them.

'We don't have to decide right now. We could just play it by ear?'

The woman with the red hair appeared with their sandwiches, smiling.

'There's a lot that camp up there,' she said, 'you won't get into any trouble about it. Don't fret.'

'We weren't planning to light a fire,' Rachael lied. Mae glanced at her meaningfully and rolled her eyes, which the woman noticed, and giggled at.

'You can have a fire if you like. You'll probably want one.'

'The dark. Yes, you said. It gets very dark at night,' Rachael said stiffly.

'And Old Trash, he don't like the fire,' the woman said, and winked. Rachael knew she was supposed to ask who Old Trash was – some local legend, a flasher or a hobgoblin or a sprite. The hills were soaked in these types of fictions, their walking guide packed with them, as if one could follow a public footpath right to the site of a ghost and call it up to arrive for inspection, just for your pleasure. But she'd changed her mind about the potential for these stories to entertain Mae. The woman was being entirely too familiar and she wasn't going to play along.

'What's Old Trash?' Mae asked, delighted, and Rachael hated her. She should make her mind up. If she wanted the bedtime ghost stories and the petting and admiration from strangers, she couldn't have the phone and the boyfriend and the bottles of vodka. It was one or the other. She was either a child, or she wasn't. Rachael sipped at her water, the fizz burning the roof of her mouth – and kept silent.

>•<

Peace. Calm. Safety. Rachael had flushed with shame when the keyworker had mentioned this, and the woman had handed her a tissue.

'I do try to keep things as calm as possible,' she'd said. But Rachael had not mentioned the most recent scuffle over the mobile phone. Had not outlined the way she and her daughter had actually come to blows over the thing. Rachael had tried to prise it out of Mae's hands, Mae had kicked her, hard – and before Rachael had time to think about it, before she'd consciously decided what she was going to do, Mae had thrown the phone onto the floor and Rachael had her hands full of Mae's hair and was pulling at her, shaking her around like a doll. Mae had hit her in the face and the two of them had come apart from each other in the hallway, panting, Rachael nursing a red mark on her cheekbone that a day later would come up in a bruise. Even as it happened Rachael knew the whack to the face could be some kind of comfort to her, because it was proof Mae was stronger than she looked and could defend herself from this man if she ever felt the need to. But Mae only screamed – so loudly the neighbours on both sides and beyond could hear.

'You've hurt me! You bitch! You bitch!'

Rachael, still panting, saw the hair that was still clinging to her fingers, hair she'd ripped from her daughter's scalp. She dropped to her knees, scrabbling for the phone, which Mae reached first, scooped up, and ran out of the front door with, slipping away like water down a plughole. She didn't come home for three days.

She had not told the keyworker about any of that. She'd only taken the tissue and dabbed at her eyes. There was a poster taped to the wall, something to do with drugs.

There was a helpline number. The poster was crooked and Rachael felt a sudden overwhelming desire to get up from her chair and straighten it. She turned her gaze down to her sensible lace-up shoes and her second-best pair of tights. She'd thought about what to wear for this meeting carefully, wanting to look professional and neat, but also motherly. There was no man of the house, but there was no need to look as if she had resigned herself to being left on the shelf permanently, now was there?

'Yes. Peace and calm. Of course. She does always know she can come home. I never lock the door on her. I'd never do that.'

>•<

One of the books she'd read over the last year had advised 'love bombing' a wayward child, a technique that cults used on the damaged and down-at-heel to get new recruits, but which was also supposed to repair a splintering bond between parent and offspring. The gist of it was to let the child get their own way for well-defined periods of time each week – to reverse the normal order of things – to cherish them and meet their every demand, as you did with a newborn baby. Accordingly, Rachael had let Mae order two different types of dessert and play as many games of pool with the red-haired woman behind the bar as she wanted. She'd watched her daughter and this woman bond – Mae laughing at all of her jokes and being entertained by her tall tales about the Pendle witches and their familiars: cats and goats and even, according to local lore, a dog called Old Trash that still roamed Fell Wood, baying at the moon, chewing up sheep and generally making a nuisance of himself. He was, according to the woman (*Triana* – and what kind of name was that?), the Devil himself in canine form.

'We'd better get going. Can I pay the tab?' Rachael asked stiffly, having exhausted all the leaflets, the newspaper and as much of an abandoned Catherine Cookson novel as she could stand.

'Already?' Mae's expression darkened.

'The light's going,' Rachael began, and the woman interrupted.

'Your mother's right, sweetheart. You want to get back early enough to make your fire. Get yourself tucked in. But come back tomorrow if you like. We'll do you a cooked breakfast. Real coffee. How about that?'

Mae, mollified and in one of her rare talkative moods, headed towards the door and Rachael followed her. It was all Triana this, and Triana that, and Rachael trudged behind her, nodding – not that Mae was paying any attention to her.

>•<

The light went suddenly: probably because of the hill. With it, the heat. As they found the footpath where it cut into the lane and clambered over the stile, Mae started to shiver.

'Maybe we should have that fire,' Rachael said. 'We could make tea?'

'We should definitely have a fire. Triana says—'

'Old Trash. Yes, I heard.'

Mae laughed. 'I'd love to see him. A great big slavering dog.' She lifted her phone. 'I'd take a picture of him, then leg it.'

'Would you?' Rachael imagined her tone was mild, faintly interested.

'There's a group, apparently. That goes out at night looking for him. Triana says you can pay the guide, and go out on a walk at night. We should have done that.'

'Maybe next time?' Rachael said, hopefully.

'Definitely.'

Definitely! She wanted to come again. It was like being in love, this – hopelessly, horribly in love – then finding a note from the boy you'd had your eye on in your school bag and realising that he'd had his eye on you all along. Rachael's head fizzed with plans: they would come back soon. Maybe in a fortnight or so. As soon as Mae wanted to. And this time, they'd avoid the bloody pub.

'Apparently he sends you nuts if you see him. Barmy. Triana says there's people who have been up on the hill at night,' she gestured vaguely, 'and end up walking miles without knowing where they are. They come down in the morning and they've gone fucking nuts. He gets into your head and Triana says—'

'Triana says a lot. I wonder if she's part of the business that runs the walks,' Rachael began, and Mae laughed and swatted her on the arm – a little too hard to be playful.

'It makes sense,' she says. 'All the witches. They must have been onto something...' she flicked her hair away from her face: Rachael saw it move in the dark, a pale ripple, and smelled cigarettes again. Where was she getting them from? She'd turned her room upside down.

'Well. We're here now. Old Trash or not, I'd like a fire.'

'I'm going to go through the woods,' Mae said. Informing, not asking. That was her way now. There was barely enough light to see by – the reservoir to their right, the steep bank of Fell Woods sloping upwards to their left. 'Triana says if you go up to the top, where the trees clear a bit, you can get a good signal. She says it'll only take five minutes. You boil water if you want, I'll be back before it's ready.'

They were in sight of the tent now: brash and orange and oddly shaped, as if built to withstand a terrible storm – the type of which never happened in England. The man in the shop had said it was a good tent. Easy to put up and take down on your own. But looking at it now, it seemed flimsy and cramped and Rachael wondered if they'd get any sleep at all, or if they'd lie awake all night, elbowing each other and shivering.

'I'm not sure you want to go crashing around in the dark, do you?' she said, as mildly as she could muster. They were there now, and Mae knelt, unzipped the tent, crawled in and emerged with a sweater.

'I'll bring you back some sticks for your fire,' Mae said, indulgently. As if she were the one doing the love bombing, not Rachael, and she were the one delaying answering difficult questions in order to avoid the nonsense of a silly confrontation.

'There's nothing so important on your phone that it can't wait until tomorrow, can it?'

'Don't… *start.*'

'Mae?'

She was already off, striding up the bank that became wooded. Rachael heard her, the twigs and leaves underfoot crackling, and then – when she turned on the torch setting on her phone – saw her, the cool bright light swinging around through the branches of the trees. It wasn't a big hill. And it wasn't a heavy wood: nothing like the woods in fairy tales. It was just a rise – a little rise with some trees on it. And at the top, there would be a signal, or there wouldn't, and Mae would answer her text messages and post a picture of herself posing against the deepening dusk on her Instagram, pretending to look scared – pretending to have seen the witches' dog, then she'd Snap-talk or whatever with the man she was seeing – and there could be no real harm in that, not when she was here, and he was – well, wherever he was, doing whatever he did. Rachael didn't want to think about him. And anyway, as Mae had so often reminded her, what exactly was Rachael going to do about it?

'Don't be long…' she called, and her voice spooled away across the surface of the reservoir and echoed back to her and there was no answering call from the trees. She walked along the edge of the woods, gathering fallen sticks for her fire.

After half an hour, it was full dark and Rachael had the fire going and the water boiling. She made tea. She set the two metal cups – brand new from the camping shop where she'd bought the tent (love bombing was *expensive*) – on a stone and poured from the pan into them. She watched the steam rise and waited. Mae was always a little elastic around time: could get caught up easily in her online life. She was probably safer up alone at the top of that hill – less than quarter of a mile away – than she was at school, or wherever it was she went when she was supposed to be at school. Rachael walked to the edge of the woods and called up to her. Once, twice. And of course there was no answer. She held her breath and listened. Was it Mae's voice she heard? Or perhaps a thin stream of water running through the concrete channel down the hill and to the reservoir? Or birds, settling in for the night? Birds, most likely.

She sat on her rucksack in front of the tent, the ground quite cold now – and, beyond the light of the fire, found herself unable to pick out the edge of the reservoir, the shape of the hill against the sky, or much of anything else. The fire crackled and popped, loud in the wide silence she waited in, and she drank her tea. Suppose Mae didn't come back? What should she do then? Should she wait an hour, or more? Mae could easily sit up there and chat for an hour, and she'd be furious if Rachael overreacted and it would spoil the whole trip. They still had tomorrow. Tomorrow they'd wake up together in the tent, and it would be light and quiet, and they wouldn't go back to the pub for a cooked breakfast, they'd have another fire and boiled eggs and bananas slit open and stuffed with chocolate and warmed inside tin foil. Rachael listened again. There were sheep – or *a* sheep, perhaps – nearby. She heard its baby-voiced bleat. And nothing else except the fire.

She could go up the hill herself. Go and retrieve her and risk the fight. She was talking to that man. The man who had a car. Who was perhaps even now in it, and picking up Mae's location from her Find Your Friend or whatever it was – the app both he and Rachael used to supervise her – and coming to collect her. The road they came in on curved around the back end of Fell Wood; the bus had dropped them off there and all they'd needed to do was carry their packs downhill half a mile. He could just as easily... Rachael stood up. But it would be foolish and perhaps unsafe to leave the fire, and not be here when Mae came back, wanting her tea and her bed.

Another fifteen minutes passed. She could walk down to the pub if it came to it. Would Triana be there? Cleaning, perhaps, after the serving hours were over? Or maybe even sleeping there, in a room upstairs? She could wake her up and use the telephone and call someone. Who? Mountain rescue? It was hardly a mountain. And what would they do? Laugh at her, probably. Triana would make her a coffee and try to have a woman-to-woman chat about the raising of teenagers, about giving them their freedom, about making sure home was always a place of peace and calm. 'You've got to let her come to you,' she'd say, and Rachael would have no option but to nod, humbly, and take the blame. Even imagining this speculative kindness sent Rachael into a rage. She gathered more sticks, and built up the fire. It would be quite visible now, in the dark. It would help Mae to get back if she'd got muddled in the woods and come down the hill too far along the path.

Mae loved bananas with chocolate. For a while, when she'd been a toddler, it had been the only thing she'd reliably eat. Bananas, mashed up and warmed in the microwave with pieces of chocolate mixed in. Not melted, only softened. Rachael had consulted the doctor about this, who had listened, and examined little Mae, fat and happy and grabbing at his tie with her pudgy fists, and had only made a speech about how impossible it was to force a child to do anything.

'You can't make them sleep,' he'd said sympathetically, 'you can't make them eat. You can't make them do much of anything, not really. Don't believe anyone who says you can. Bananas and chocolate are fine. She'll grow out of it.'

Rachael had protested, he'd asked her how she was sleeping and eating (*her*, not Mae!) and in the end, had offered her antidepressant tablets. 'Lots of mothers take them,' he'd said, pen poised above the prescription, which he had already printed. Rachael had been furious, and forced to change surgery.

But Mae had always loved chocolate and warm bananas and now Rachael retrieved them from her rucksack. It was supposed to be a surprise: a little treat for breakfast. Part of the love bombing. But when she came back – she'd be back any minute, surely this man would have other girls to turn to while Mae was away, and would not bother making the drive to Pendle? – they could have them tonight. An extra dessert. The sugar would keep her awake but it didn't matter. Mae could eat as much as she wanted tonight and tomorrow Rachael would find a place to buy some more, if she wanted them again.

>•<

An hour and a half, and both cups of tea drunk, and the water boiled again and set aside in its pan to get cold. The bananas waiting in their little tin foil packaging. Rachael furious, so furious that when she heard the commotion at the edge of the woods – some way along the path from the tent – she stood and strode through the dark.

'You get back here this minute,' she said. 'All that messing about. We're supposed to be here spending time with each other, you ungrateful little…'

No answer, but still the commotion continued. A breaking of sticks – and growing nearer, but strangely constant – as if someone were rolling down the hill, rather than walking down it.

'Mae? Are you all right? Have you hurt yourself?'

Rachael paused. There was no answer, just the sound of something coming nearer, a crashing through the undergrowth. She squinted into the darkness.

'Mae? Answer me?'

There was a torch in the tent. She'd run back there and get it – it was only a few paces away – and shine it into the woods. Help Mae, who was probably a little tired and disorientated (had she smuggled in some vodka in her bag? Was that what was going on here?), find her way back down the hill.

'Mae? If this is some kind of joke…'

She turned, and the sound behind her continued – and seemed to deepen somehow – as if whatever was trying and failing to find its way out of the woods had broken free of its tether, and was tumbling closer. Perhaps it wasn't Mae. Perhaps it was some drunken hiker – or an animal – a sheep, perhaps? Did sheep growl? Because now, as Rachael walked slowly away from the edge of the woods and towards the light of the fire, which seemed much further away than it should be, she heard a kind of breathing behind her, a guttural, heaving type of breathing.

'Mum?'

Mae's voice came thinly, as if from a very long way away. Rachael turned and looked back to the tent and there she was – sitting beside the fire. She must have come out of the woods at the top of the hill and walked down the lane. They'd missed each other. Rachael could see her – could see she'd brought a massive armful of sticks and was building up the fire. Thank God. And look – Mae had spotted the tin foil parcels and she was pleased about them. Rachael smiled.

'I'm over here, love! Where did you get to?'

Her voice sounded loud and quiet at the same time. It was strange to shout at night, but there was nobody else here to disturb, so she tried it anyway, and could muster only a whisper. The fire was so small – really just a glowing red speck in the dark – and so far away – impossibly far away – and there was this – this something behind her – and surely Rachael should be leading it away from the tent and away from her daughter?

'Stay where you are Mae. I'm coming!'

But Rachael stood still, and felt the presence behind her move. She could smell it – the stink of a packet of sausages gone bad – rotten meat, sweet and cloying. Her mouth filled with bile and she spat, and retched, and surely – this was like a dream – she should be at the tent now?

'Mum? Where are you?'

Rachael tried to call, but didn't. She felt held somehow. Held by the air itself, which had solidified around her, like the way everything turns to treacle in nightmares, and the thing that was behind her was moving quite slowly, padding through the grass on four feet – she could hear that now. The sore place on her hand – the bit of flesh she'd nipped with the tent pole – started to burn and throb. Rachael raised it to her face, wiggled her fingers, and could see nothing. How strange that was, she thought dimly.

'Muuuum? Bananas? You brought bananas? You nutter. I hate bananas.'

Mae's tone was amused, friendly. Whatever she'd been wanting to do on her phone, she'd been able to do it. Talk to that man, probably. Make some kind of arrangement with him. Was he on his way? Was this friendliness a distraction – meant to lull Rachael into sleep so Mae could sneak out later?

'Just hang on, Mae...' she called, her tongue feeling strange and swollen in her mouth – there, and not there – and she couldn't be sure this time that she'd made any sound at all. Rachael hurled herself against the air and the stillness holding her broke suddenly, and she ran towards her daughter, misjudging the distance. When the air gave way beneath her she had just a second to realise she'd tripped right over the edge of the reservoir before her head hit its edge, too hard to hurt – and one more second to taste blood in her mouth and see the dark shape at the edge, above her now – before she closed her eyes and went under the freezing water.

IN MY FATHER'S HOUSE

ANDREW MICHAEL HURLEY

When I arrive to pick him up for Alex's nativity play, I find him sitting in the dark with his armchair facing the window. He's been watching out for me, impatiently. He's already in his coat and shoes.

'You're late,' he says.

'Hardly,' I say.

'You said six, didn't you?'

'It's only ten past,' I say. 'The traffic was bad. What's the matter?'

'You were the one bleating on about making sure I was ready earlier,' he says.

A bus sweeps past, its lights sending the shadows of furniture across the walls. My father is a tall, weighty man but the room still seems too large around him, like all the rooms of this house.

'Well, I'm here now,' I say. 'Shall I close the curtains?'

'I can do it, I'm not a fucking invalid,' he says, edging his way out of his chair and going to the window while I switch on the floor-lamp.

The bruises may have gone down, but he's still stiff when he moves. For a man of his age and condition, the doctor told me, he'd sustained some pretty serious injuries. There had been some bleeding on the brain – she showed me where on a plastic replica – some damage possibly, too. If it were necessary, there were a number of things they could prescribe, but I had to be prepared for the fact that emotionally he might be quite a different person from now on. He may be more agitated, confused, erratic, aggressive even. The changes in behaviour might be subtle at first, she said, but being his son, I would notice them, of course. The thing is, until Julia and I went to visit him in the hospital,

I hadn't seen my father for years. Really, I knew him little better than the man in the next bed.

So, now's your chance, Julia said. It's not too late. I reminded her that he left home when I was ten. But he's still your father, Mike, she said. And look at him, for heaven's sake. The poor man was ill enough before this happened.

He was sleeping with a drip in his arm, his fatty, hairless chest lifting and falling under the blue gown. With his split and bulging eyebrows, with his swollen lips, he looked like a piece of overripe fruit. They'd shaved patches around his temples in order to stitch up his scalp. His pillow was dotted with brown bloodstains. I tried to feel something. Well, duty's a kind of love, Julia offered. You could at least help with the practicalities when he gets out of hospital. He's got no one else.

That's true.

He's lived alone since his second wife, Irene, passed away some years ago. I met her once at my uncle's funeral. Meek is perhaps a little unkind, but she was one of those people I imagine to be always doing something servile. At the wake, she went around with a bin bag for the dirty paper plates, mopped up some sick. It didn't surprise me that she volunteered to clean at her church twice a week.

I was intrigued as to how they'd met and when my father went to the toilet, Irene told me that they simply had a lot in common, the two of them. She had suffered ill-health like him. She had a son in his forties. She was divorced too, though she didn't say why. That was in the past, she said. And best left there. How much my father ever told Irene about my mother, I don't know. She seemed happy to be with him, so possibly very little. Unless, of course, he'd told her everything and she was utterly convinced of his contrition. Unless, behind the cardigan and diffidence, she considered herself his redeemer.

>•<

The curtains drawn, he takes his scarf off the back of the chair and loops it round his neck, wincing from the pain in his back.

'Which nurse was it today?' I say.

'Pancake,' he says, searching his pocket for the lighter the blokes in the warehouse at Rawlinson's got him when he took early retirement. Engraved on the metal casing is *Rod Sheppard – last of a dying breed.*

'Pancake?' I say. 'Who's Pancake?'

'Her,' he says. 'The old cow with no tits. She gave me a proper lecture.'

'What do you expect her to do?' I say. 'It's her job to keep you alive.'

'Bollocks,' he says and picks out the half-smoked Regal from the ashtray. 'She knows it's too late for me to give up now. She's just being a pain in the arse.'

'But she did your pills, didn't she?' I say.

He gestures with his smoking hand towards the dresser. The plastic organiser box is there, each compartment filled with a day's worth of capsules and lozenges. Blue in the morning. Red at night. Rod Sheppard's delight. And everyone else's. They seem to keep him calm. That is to say, he doesn't swear quite so much.

'You've not had your evening ones,' I say.

'I'll take them later,' he says.

'You might enjoy the play more if you take them now,' I say.

'Are you worried I'll embarrass you?' he says. 'Cheer for Herod?'

'I'll get you a glass of water,' I say.

'I'm not to take them on an empty stomach,' he says. 'Pancake's orders.'

'Haven't you eaten?' I say. 'Didn't Charity heat up your lunch for you?'

She has a tendency to mother him when she comes to clean on a Friday.

'I didn't let her in,' he says.

'Why not?' I say.

'Because she never stops fucking talking,' he says. 'And I needed to think. I can't get anything straight in my head when she's yap-yapping in my ear.'

'Well, why don't I make you something to eat now?' I say.

'We haven't got time,' he says.

'It's only quarter past six,' I say. 'It doesn't start for another hour. What are you in such a hurry for? Let me make you a sandwich.'

There's barely anything in the fridge. A single pot of raspberry yoghurt a fortnight past its date. An ancient jar of mustard. Half a pint of green top. In the bread bin is a stale loaf with freckles of blue mould on the crust.

'It's gone off,' I say, coming back into the front room. 'I'll go down to the shop.'

'Don't worry about it,' he says.

'But you've not much in,' I say.

'I've enough,' he says.

'Well, we can always stop off and get you something on

the way home later,' I say, but he doesn't respond. The old bastard is going to beat Death to the punch by starving himself before his lungs dissolve. Perhaps that's the plan.

'Is that the plan?' I say. 'Are you going to fast until you fade away? I can't imagine it's a very nice way to go.'

'Give it a rest,' he says. 'You're worse than the fucking cleaner.'

And I decide that when he starts effing in the middle of 'Silent Night', I'll blame Julia. It was her idea to invite him.

I know what she's trying to do, and I don't doubt that her heart's in the right place. It's one of the reasons I married her, that optimism she has: her refusal to believe in lost causes. What had happened to my father was terrible, she said, but looked at in the right way it could be the very thing that brought us back together.

You do hear about it, I suppose. Families reunited after so many years of estrangement. Love finally breaking through the levees and sweetening the silted-up bitterness. Bygones made bygones. Hatchets buried. That sort of thing. But the truth is, I don't want him to know anything about us. Even if she's quite willing to give herself away to him, Julia shouldn't be something he can have just like that. He hasn't earned the right. And I don't like him talking to Alex, either. But unfortunately Alex is fascinated by him. Both Julia's parents are dead and so my father is the only old person he's really spent time with. To a seven-year-old, he seems unfeasibly ancient and Alex has asked me a few times whether I'll miss Grandad – already it's *Grandad* – when he dies. I say, yes, of course. A different answer would confuse him, I think. He cannot conceive of the mechanisms by which a son would not long for an absent father. And, thankfully, even if I explained them, he wouldn't understand. He's at that age where we're doing our best to preserve his precious ignorance. We told him that Grandad got his bruises from a fall in the street. An accident. That was all. There wasn't much more to say about what had really happened, actually.

He'd been drinking in the Two Swans and after closing time he'd been attacked in the car park, where one of the girls who worked behind the bar found him unconscious and bleeding.

It wasn't just feet and fists, the doctor told me; it looked as though his collarbone had been fractured with a blunt instrument. The bruises on his body had the circular shape of a hammer blow. It was lucky he'd been wearing a thick winter coat, otherwise they would have smashed up his ribcage as easily as a wicker basket.

'How low can you get?' the nurse said when she came in with some fresh water on a tray. 'Beating a man who's as ill as he is. And at his age too. How old is he?'

I guessed at sixty-five.

'They're just scum,' she said.

I didn't tell her that he'd probably deserved it.

>•<

Taking two last quick drags, he stubs out his cigarette and looks around the room.

'Are we going then?' he says.

'If you like.'

'Take the tops,' he says.

'The tops?'

'The fell road,' he says.

'In the dark?' I say.

'What's wrong?' he says, with a look of derision. 'Don't you like driving up there at night?'

'It doesn't bother me,' I say, even though it does. 'But there won't be much of a view. What do you want to go that way for?'

'It'll be quicker,' he says. 'You said the traffic was bad, didn't you?'

'It'll have died down now,' I say.

'Not through town it won't,' he says.

'I was going to go on the ring road.'

'The ring road?' he says. 'At this time? The world and his fucking wife will be there. Take the tops.'

'Fine, fine,' I say. 'If you think.'

What I've found these last two months is that without his medication inside him it's more prudent to agree.

>•<

As I drive, he sits with his hands in his lap, his face alternately striped and shadowed until the street lights come to an end by the petrol station. In the night-time of the countryside, a few pockets of festivity emerge and fade: the Christmas tree outside The Green Man flashes manically with blues and yellows; there are folk streaming in through the open doors of Our Lady's in the Vale for a carol concert. But after turning off the main road and starting to climb up the side of the fell, we pass nothing apart from a few lightless farms.

He doesn't speak, only taps his fingers on his knee.

'If you want a fag, just have one,' I say and he turns to me – amused that I should think he needed my permission.

'I was just about to,' he says.

His face is amber, then shadow again. Smoke fills the car.

Julia says I look like him. Alex thinks so too. It's something people have always said. But I could never see the resemblance. Years ago, when I was a teenager, folk from Rawlinson's would stop me in the street and tell me that I was my father's double. And because they thought I looked like him, they assumed I shared his character. They'd tell me what a good man he was, ask me if I liked a drink too, if I was a fighter like him, if women fell over themselves for me.

I can't really remember what he looked like as a younger man and it's difficult to take the years off him – as you can with some people – and see that he'd clearly been handsome once. His injuries aside, he looks much older than he probably is. Everything seems too large on him, nothing is quite in proportion, as though his hands, his ears, his nose have all been borrowed. He might be tall, but he's stooped and he overfills the passenger seat, his legs crumpled in the footwell, his neck cricked.

Still, Charity considers him a catch. He's a gentleman, she says, but – her finger on my arm – thankfully not all the time. He still has a spark in his eye, she says. And if they were both thirty years younger and so on. Well, thirty years ago she'd have had some competition from the women in the warehouse office, the women from the Two Swans. Women from somewhere. There were always women.

My mother would often have a new *She* to throw at him when he came in from work.

Who is She, this time?

Where does She live?

What does She look like?
Does She laugh at me?
Does She think I'm a clown?

And the next day I'd come in from school to see her, my mother, standing in the kitchen slicing up potatoes, an empty glass on the sideboard and a sway to her eyes. Her face is smothered in make-up, her skin white, her eyelids a peacock blue. A red circle at the tip of her nose and a smile painted across her cheeks.

My father arrives home in his overalls. Sits down. Reads his paper. Eats his tea. Says nothing. Even when my mother dances like a jester round the table.

>•<

By the yellow salt bin, the road curves sharply to the left and the headlights pan across the form of a roe deer as it crosses the lane and springs into the woods. There are more of them milling around by the cattle grid, eyes like bright pennies in the full beam. Here, now, this is their hill. Gathered in numbers no one should ordinarily see. We've come upon them in the midst of a sabbat.

They split and scatter, one darting past my window and shrinking in the wing mirror. I'll tell Alex about it later. Confidentially, though. I don't think Julia will be very happy that I came over the fell. The snow we had last week is still here, smoothly drifted and untouched against the drystone walls. There are long tongues of ice being thickened again as the temperature falls in the clear night. It would be easy to hit one and skid into the drainage channel.

The road dips and rises and bends as it contours the fell.

There are turnings here and there to villages somewhere down in the darkness, places where all the doors are closed for the night and the televisions are on.

Another half a mile. Another mile, maybe. I'm right around the other side of the fell when he waves me into a lay-by. Below us, there are empty sheep pastures and at the bottom of the slope the sodium river of the M65 winds away eastwards past the sprawls of Padiham, Burnley, Brierfield, Nelson, that lie in the valley like great slag-heaps of light.

'Is this what you wanted to see?' I say.

'Course not,' he says.

'What then?'

He looks past me at the huge pine plantation that grows fur-like on the backbone of the fell.

'I used to drive up here at night,' he says.

'When?' I say. He's not had a car for years. Nor a license for that matter, since they took it off him.

'When you were a lad,' he says. 'When things were bad at home.'

He notices my expression, laughs to himself and takes out his cigarettes again.

'Don't worry,' he says. 'I'm not going to ask you to forgive me.'

'Good,' I say.

'You wouldn't anyway, would you?' he says, lighting up. 'I don't blame you. I was a cunt.'

'It was a long time ago,' I say.

'I still am,' he says.

'Fine,' I say. 'I'll take your word for it.'

'I'm serious,' he says. 'Those fellas that did me over outside the Two Swans, they had every right.'

'Why, what had you done?' I say.

'You don't want to know,' he says.

'You could have shared your self-pity on the ring road,' I say. 'Why did I have to drive you all the way up here to listen to it?'

'It's not self-pity,' he says. 'I'm not well.'

'I wish you'd taken your pills before we came out,' I say.

'The pills aren't going to do anything,' he says. 'That's why I needed to come up here.'

'But why?'

'There was always something about this place at night,' he says.

'Dark and cold, I expect,' I say.

'I mean the quiet,' he says. 'No one fucking talking. I could find myself again. I could get myself clean.'

'Find yourself?'

'This isn't me,' he says, touching his hands, his face.

I look at my watch. 'We'd better go,' I say. 'It's getting on for seven.'

'You've been telling me we've plenty of time since you came to pick me up,' he says. 'And all of a sudden we're going to be late?'

'It's just that the parking's murder at the school,' I say. 'And we'll end up on the back row where we can't see anything.'

'Ten minutes,' he says. 'You can give me that, can't you?'

'Ten minutes to do what?' I say. 'Sit here in the cold?'

'I want to go up the hill,' he says.

'Now?' I say. 'It's pitch black. What about the play?'

'You don't have to come with me,' he says.

'I've served my purpose, have I?'

'I couldn't get here by myself,' he says.

'It's not pleasant being tricked,' I say.

'I told you I was a cunt,' he says, getting out of the car.

'Well, I'm not letting you go off by yourself,' I say, following him across the road. 'What will I tell people when you fall and break your neck?'

'Tell them it was my idea.'

'They'll know it was your idea,' I say. 'That's not the point. Julia will kill me for not stopping you.'

He looks at me.

'You can try if you want,' he says.

It seems as though he's smiling, but it's hard to tell.

'Come back to the car,' I say. 'It's too cold to be out in this.'

'You don't understand what it's like,' he says. 'To hear the voice of a good man inside you.'

'It doesn't matter about the play,' I say. 'I'll drive you home.'

'You know, it was the best thing your mother ever did, throwing me out,' he says. 'I wish Irene had done the same. I didn't mean for her to suffer. I never mean for anyone to suffer.'

'When we get back, I'll call the hospital,' I say. 'See if they can help.'

'Ten minutes. Wait here,' he says and walks off slowly, stiffly up the logging track, gradually consumed by the dark.

>•<

I go back to the car, turning on the engine and the heaters. The voice on the radio promises more snow by Sunday. Julia texts me. *Traffic bad*, I put. *Be there soon.*

With the window down, I stare at the trees, willing him to hurry up. Not only because I don't want to miss the start of the play but because I'm suddenly aware of how conspicuous I am. Up on this dark hillside, my headlights are surely arousing suspicion amongst those living down below and it's so still that any sound I make must be broadcast for miles. Someone will be sent to investigate the trespassers, assess the damage done to the trees and perhaps to the silence too, which up here seems as private as the plantation itself. Certainly not ours to break.

I switch off the engine and wind up the window. Julia calls this time rather than texts. My phone pulses until it goes to voicemail. I picture her standing at the edge of the school hall, one finger pressed to her ear. When I replay the message, I'll hear the expectant burble of other parents, the scraping of school chairs, a piano. I'll hear that special tone of concern and supressed irritation in Julia's voice. But perhaps when I get a chance to explain it will do her good to see what my father is really like. Perhaps then she'll let me consider my obligation to him fulfilled. I've done what I can. Organised for a nurse to visit every other day, sourced a cleaner, offered to do his shopping. That's enough. He doesn't want my help anyway. He hasn't needed me at all since he's been out of hospital these last two months – only to bring him up here. When I find him, I'll take him home and leave him to his life. Or what's left of it. I know that Julia will warn me about regret. Once he's gone, Mike, that's it, she'll say. But nothing will change when he does. I won't feel any different about him. Not every death has to be meaningful.

>•<

I wait for the ten minutes he demanded and then get out of the car, taking my scarf and gloves off the back seat.

In amongst the trees, there is the settled blackness of winter and the track up ahead is only illuminated where the moonlight catches on the ice. For about a quarter of a mile it climbs straight and steep before it bends sharply to the left and continues in what looks like a zigzag to the top, wherever that might be. I assume that's where he's gone, but then in the snow I see his footprints leaving the path and heading into the wood. To shout *Father* would sound ridiculous, *Dad* would feel strange, *Rod* even stranger. So, I whistle instead. Whistle twice. And twice there's no reply.

The torch on my phone penetrates no more than a few feet along the narrow avenue between the ranks of trees. A tunnel of trunks and branches so thickly woven that the snow has not fallen here at all and my father's tracks run out.

For the most part, I can brush aside the hanging needles, but in places they droop so low and heavy that I have to crouch almost on my haunches to shuffle under the boughs. Or I'm forced to double back and find a different route. With his battered, aching body it's hard to imagine that he's come this far, if he's come this way at all. For all I know, he might be waiting by the car while I'm in here steadily losing myself.

I've missed it all by now. The shepherds will have adored the Christ-child, and the Wise Men (Alex among them) will have set down their gifts by the manger. All the children will have sung 'We Wish You a Merry Christmas' and received their applause. The chairs will have been stacked by the caretaker, the hall swept, the lights turned off. By now, Julia will be driving home and making excuses on my behalf to Alex – who will be crying, I know. I'd call but there's no signal. Not even when the branches thin out and I can stand upright again. Here, in a little dell, the sky is bare to its stars and framed by the shapes of treetops. The snowbank holds a set of large footprints, each one deep and sinking deeper when I use them to make my way up the slope.

At the other side of the hollow is a stretch of barbed wire, brown with rust. My father's coat has been laid on top of the spikes. But he's nowhere to be seen and after straddling the fence I find more of his clothes neatly hung over the arm of a tree. His sweater is there, his shirt, his trousers, his underpants. His muddy shoes have been paired and placed in the roots.

The deer have been this way too. Through the bracken is a narrow pathway that leads to a wide pond; a reservoir of ink fringed with frosted reeds and heather. Ice has formed at the edges of the water where the shadows must linger all day at this time of year, but in the liquid middle stars and a crescent moon lie on the surface.

My father stands naked on the muddy bank, his bruised skin sagging off his bones like wet dough. He has his face turned to the sky and it appears as though he's star-gazing, but his eyes are closed. The night deepens, the air tenses, but he doesn't move, he doesn't shiver. There might be catatonic episodes, the doctor said. Paralysis, even, where he'll feel nothing. I should have dissolved his pills in a glass of water or made a paste and buttered a sandwich with them.

He'll freeze before I can go back and fetch his coat, so I start to take off mine. But when I look back he's gone and I follow his footmarks around the edge of the water, slithering and sinking, groping at the pine trees for support.

It's not long before his tracks give out and the little cutting is littered with scraps of skin.

I pick up bloodless, boneless feet and liver-spotted hands as deflated as rubber gloves. I find my father's face draped over a branch. An ear juts from the mud like a fungus.

His thick white hide is everywhere, steaming lightly, still warm to the touch, the bruises fading with each rejected layer.

I finally catch sight of him moving as a foot-high miniature through the reeds, a little ghost in a jungle. He looks younger now. The bend of old age is gone. His skin has no trace of battery. When I head towards him he slips into the reeds and I lose him again. A stick does not bring him out, nor does a threat, or a plea, or a kind word, or a promise of forgiveness, or a promise of silence, or pity. He must have hidden himself somewhere in the dark like one of the deer. Even if I came back in daylight I'd never find him in this wood. But then something moves in the water. And out in the middle of the pond, where the light is reflected, I see the moon shiver and the ripples spreading wider and wider, until the constellations break apart.

LAND OF MANY SEASONS

TIM LEBBON

He wasn't there when I began. I wouldn't have stayed if he was. The whole point of what I do is the loneliness and solitude, the escape from my troubled existence. I hike out to these places to be alone, and sketch and paint them so that I can take them home with me. They are my escape. From the first pencil line or brush stroke, the canvas becomes a reality where I can live alone for a few hours or days, free from the real world.

The real world isn't very nice.

'Kes! Here!' My little collie scampers across the heathers and weaves through a stand of ferns, back to where I have set myself up for the day. He's a good dog. Dogs are undemanding and kind, their love a simple thing. That's why I like to bring him out here with me, because his simpleness, his dogness, doesn't taint this place.

The figure in my painting does.

Kes nuzzles against my hand. I tickle him behind the ear, and he grumbles and tilts his head in satisfaction. There's a warm breeze flowing across the hillside today, carrying scents of heather and wet mud, and the fresh, wild smells of the mysterious mountains. If it shifts ninety degrees and breathes at me across the town, I'll pick up aromas from the bakery close to the river, or the building site where they're constructing another two hundred homes. I hope that doesn't happen. This is my fourth day coming to the same spot, and I've been lucky so far – the weather has been consistent, the sky cloudy but withholding its rain, the breeze wafting in from the same direction.

The painting is progressing well. Apart from him. But right now, I'm avoiding thinking about him.

Kes growls and lopes off again, and this time I let him.

I watch as he springs through the high ferns like a lamb, leaping to find his bearings, running again, leaping again. He reminds me of myself, ploughing blindly through life and coming up here, or places like this, to raise my head above water.

'Go get 'em, boy,' I say under my breath. Kes barks as if he's heard me, and several startled birds take wing.

I look at my painting and consider adding the birds in, specks in the sky that might remind me of this place and time, but my attention is drawn to the figure once again.

He's little more than a few brush strokes right now. He appeared on my version of the hillside just an hour ago, and I surprised myself by painting him in. However much I stare at him, and then sit back and look across the hill, he's only there in my painting.

Maybe I saw a shape in the air? A shimmer in heat haze, or a waft of mist from the damp grass? The shadow of a red kite circling high above?

I can't fool myself. I saw nothing, yet still I felt the need to paint him into my picture.

It should not matter, and yet it does. My paintings are rarely literal representations of the world. The general lie of the land is as I view it, but the skies are inevitably more stormy and violent in shades of red shadow, the hillsides more desolate and windswept. I paint my mood and my soul onto the canvases, and sometimes I frighten myself with how I see the world.

It should not matter. But it does.

In my painting he is a long way away, but he is walking straight towards me.

>•<

Later that afternoon I come down off the mountain. The Blorenge is my favourite of the three hills surrounding Abergavenny. Although it is not the most dramatic to draw or paint – that might be the Sugarloaf, with its distinctive volcano-shaped peak, or the harsh knife-edge of the Skirrid – it is the quietest of the three. I can follow a familiar seven-mile walk across and around the mountain without encountering another soul, and sometimes when I'm up here I imagine that I am the last person on Earth, wandering with my rucksack full of art stuff and my dog, and recording the end of time for the no one who will come after me. For someone so lonely, the fantasy is strangely calming.

Kes runs ahead of me down the steep slope through the woods. There are old stone railway sleepers here, the track long since gone, the chains that hauled carts up and down the mountainside now rusted away to nothing. Perhaps their remains are close, fragile remnants buried deep.

I pass the old tunnel mouth. It's a strange structure, an arch of brickwork protruding from a steep bank with only darkness beneath its mouldy embrace. I've stopped a few times and looked inside, but Kes has always been uncertain, sometimes standing with hackles up as if sensing something in there, perhaps sensing nothing. Maybe it leads to other worlds. Maybe it leads to different versions of this one. I wish I was brave enough to venture in.

Further down the hill I start to hear distant traffic, and experience the familiar sadness that my time alone is over. I consider turning around and going back up. It's summer, warm and bright, and I know I could probably sleep on the mountainside. But it's late afternoon now, and I have no food or water left.

Kes whines softly. He's hungry, and probably eager to get home. He's not as young as he used to be.

'Okay, boy,' I say, and then another voice pipes up and surprises me.

'Nice dog.'

I jump.

'Sorry. Sorry.' The old man is beneath the trees to my left. I've seen him before out in the hills, usually from a distance. I recognise his long grey hair and red bandana. I sometimes think he's as lonely as me, but who am I to judge? I have no right to project my problems or faults onto him. Just because he walks the same paths as me, doesn't mean he's heading in the same direction.

'It's okay,' I say. 'I was miles away.'

'Look like you've seen a ghost.' He's looking at the kit I'm carrying. If I've seen him he must have seen me, but maybe he was too far away to make out what I was doing.

'Just tired,' I say. 'All this fresh air.'

'Lovely up there,' he says. 'My favourite mountain.'

'Mine too.' Kes has trotted up to the man, confident and unconcerned, and that puts me more at ease. The dog's a good judge of character, and he can usually smell the crazy on people. The old man kneels and ruffles the back of his neck.

'You seen the Walker.' Even in that simple remark I can hear the capital letter. He gives the word a peculiar weight.

'What do you mean?'

He doesn't answer at first. He looks down at the dog, and

something about his manner makes me think he's sorry that he spoke.

'What Walker?'

'Oh, nothing. Silly old story. The hills are full of them.'

I think about asking more, but don't. He seems like a nice old man, but I'm tired from the day's work, and I'm eager to get the painting home and set it up to dry. It's almost finished, and the more I carry it around, the longer I hold onto it, the more chance there is of causing damage.

'Nice to meet you,' I say. 'I think Kes has a new friend.'

The old man nods and smiles, then waves as he heads past me up the hill.

'It'll be dark soon,' I say.

'I like it up here in the dark,' he says. 'See you around, I'm sure.'

I head down to the road, and cross to the small car park. Kes walks beside me, obedient as ever. I open my little car and place the painting carefully on the front seat, propped so that it will not slip or tumble on the short ride home. Kes jumps into the back and snuggles down on the seat. By the time I start the car the dog is already asleep.

I sit for a while, thinking about the old man walking up onto the mountain to meet the dusk. I wonder what else he might meet up there.

He seemed unafraid.

>•<

I do not talk to anyone else that day.

Back at home, Kes trots into the house and waits patiently in the kitchen for his tea. After feeding him I feed myself, some salad and cured meats from the fridge, followed by a whole packet of biscuits and a big mug of coffee. I stare at the painting as I eat. It's propped on a stand in the large kitchen. I've been working on it for four days and I'm starting to consider it complete, but the more I stare at it, the less it seems like a painting I would have done. The landscape is familiar, and the stormy sky gives voice and scope to my constant inner turmoil and loneliness. But there's something about the shape – cast onto canvas with a few brush strokes, shadowy and yet obvious – that speaks of familiarity.

I cover the painting before going to bed.

I wake up before the dawn, as always. Kes has crept upstairs during the night and made his home on the foot of my bed. I don't mind, and he knows that, stretching out as I stretch, crawling closer to me so I can pet him as I lie awake and watch shadows retreating across the ceiling.

Something plays at my mind as I use the bathroom and dress. A certainty that is left over from my dreams, a vaguely haunting idea that plagued my sleep, but which I can no longer recall. Something to do with the Walker.

As I enter the kitchen, I know what I'm going to see. He'll be closer. He'll be a greater part of my picture, a larger part of my life.

The shape of the figure in my painting is as I left him the night before, and I breathe a sigh of relief. The idea of painting him out of the picture never even occurs to me until much later.

>•<

By the time I see the Walker again I have almost forgotten about him.

He has remained with me, visible, of course. I hung the picture in the little studio I rent in town, but it never sold. No one has commented on why they don't like it, but I'm starting to think perhaps they're put off by the strange smudge, the errant brush strokes that they see as a fault or a mistake. Only I seem to recognise him for who he is.

The next time I go up onto the Blorenge to paint, it has passed from summer into autumn. I'm wrapped up warm, and although the forecast is for a dry day, I have a rucksack containing waterproofs and wear walking boots. I've been caught out in bad weather on the hillsides before.

Kes lopes ahead of me. I decide to let him find a place for me to paint, and for an hour or so he leads the way up and across the mountain, smelling his way towards the old surface mine workings that make for such an interesting landscape. After a while I call a stop and Kes comes back to me. I give him a treat from my pocket, then look around and select somewhere to set up my kit.

The easel is steel, with spiked feet to hold it fast. The canvas I've brought today is smaller than usual. I paint standing, enjoying being able to pace back and forth to gather different angles and aspects.

I open my flask and pour a steaming coffee, then begin.

For me, painting slows things down. My life is not lived fast anyway, but I always feel that it is out of my control. Both of my parents died when I was a teen, I grew into my twenties living with an aunt, and then when I started living on my own the tides of life washed over me, always threatening to drown. I'm not self-pitying. That's just the way I am, and I sometimes welcome my loneliness rather than regret it. Without being alone, I would not be able to create the art I do, and it's the art that defines me. It pins me to the world, and when I slow the world down I start to believe I might be able to grab on and go along for the ride.

The morning passes. I drink more coffee. The painting grows. I fill out the lie of the land, impatient to move onto the part of any painting that always excites me most – the sky.

As I start to address the sky above the slope of the land, it is marred by a silhouette I have not seen.

I pause and take a step back. I hold my breath. A bird calls somewhere, a buzzard circling high above. A rabbit rustles through undergrowth nearby, Kes chasing it, flushing it out, and I wonder if the buzzard will swoop and clasp it in its claws. I think what the world would be like if birds of prey were ten times larger, and we were their prey.

Perhaps we are all prey to something, I think, and the shape on the painting manifests as the walking man once again. He's more defined than he was before, on the painting that still hangs in my studio. There he was merely a hint, a few brush strokes. Here he is more angular, more solid. More formed.

I gasp and look past the painting towards the spread of mountainside where I have painted him, and of course there is nothing there. If there was I would no longer be alone.

'Kes!' I say. The dog perks up, head raised. 'Who's that?' He looks around, darting here and there, sniffing and whining softly. Kes always likes meeting people – perhaps because he knows I'm not so keen, and he wants to guide me away from being so alone – but he sees and senses no one.

I'm not sure I do either.

I return to the painting and hover my brush over the shape in the distance. A few strokes of green and blue and the Walker will become hillside and sky once again, swept from memory with a few casual drifts of my hand, like a conductor orchestrating a sudden silence. I am a god with the power of being in my hands. It's not a feeling I like.

I leave the shape alone, but my painting is done for the day. Finding the man on my canvas has made me feel more alone than ever before. I crave the company of people, and that's a feeling I am not used to.

I pack and rush down the mountain, not afraid, but needy. Kes comes with me, and an hour later we're at the coffee shop in town. We sit outside, even though autumn's breath keeps most people behind door and glass, and after an hour watching people passing by, I see the old man walking towards us. He has his head down but is dressed as he was the last time I saw him, the bandana no longer looking out of place in the cool, breezy day. It seems that he hasn't noticed us, and I wait until he's passed us by and is walking away before I say something.

'Tell me about the Walker.'

The old man pauses, and for a moment I wonder if *he* is the Walker, and if in some strange way he's down here with me, as well as up there on the mountainside. But he's shorter and squatter than the figure in my painting, more present. When he turns around I see a strange look in his eyes. Maybe it's confusion. Perhaps I've stirred him from a deep reverie, and I'm instantly sorry for calling out to him.

I know what it's like not wishing to be disturbed.

'Oh, it's you,' he says, and he sits across the picnic table from me as if we've sat and spoken many times before, not just bumped into each other for a brief time on a hillside months ago. He pulls his coat around him and takes some time to get comfortable, finally looking up at the sky, and at the clouds drifting by. 'Coffee'd be nice,' he says.

I half-stand, then pause, thinking of Kes.

'I'll look after your dog,' he says. He clicks his fingers and Kes trots around to him, and the old man strokes and pets him. Kes is instantly at ease, and that puts me at ease as well.

I go inside and buy two coffees and a couple of cakes. Returning outside, I'm not surprised to see Kes lying on the bench with his head on the man's leg.

'You've seen him again,' the old man says.

'Yes. Today. Or rather, no, I didn't see him. Not with my eyes.'

He glances at me, one eyebrow raised. 'And they call me mad.'

I laugh, placing the coffees and plate on the table. He grunts his thanks.

'I painted him,' I say. 'Don't remember seeing him, but he's in the landscape I'm working on. It's strange. I'll show you, if you like.' I reach for the folder I use to carry my canvas, and the man shakes his head and holds out one hand.

'No need,' he says, a little too quickly. I get the feeling he really doesn't want to see my painting. He softens, though, and smiles. 'I know what he looks like well enough. I see him too.'

'You do?'

The old man nods, drinks coffee, eats cake. Kes looks up

and he drops a corner of Welsh cake into the dog's mouth. 'He's always up there, if you know where to look.'

'Do you go looking for him?'

'God, no. I just see him now and then.'

'You're talking like he's a ghost,' I say, thinking, *What the hell else could he be?*

'Not sure what he is,' the old man says. 'I only know the story. Four decades ago, he appeared in town. Came from somewhere else, and it's said he carried trouble with him like a stain. Rumours are he was a murderer, or something worse. Sometimes a stranger attracts such stories, I suppose. Anyway, he started going up the mountain on his own. He went there more and more, loved the place, spent longer and longer walking up there. Couple of people in town still remember him, and if you buy them a drink they'll even talk to you about him. They say he wasn't happy with the way the world was going, but he was happy with things up there. That's the only place he felt alive.'

I look down at my cappuccino. It's difficult meeting the old man's eye when what he says sounds so much like me.

'Anyway, one day he went up there for a walk and never came back.'

'He vanished?'

'As good as. Left his clothes and belongings in the room he was renting in town. Never seen again. By most people, at least.'

'So you think he died up there? You think I'm seeing his ghost?'

'Like I said, I don't know what he is. Could be that he died and he's a ghost. Or maybe he's still walking around up there.'

'How could that be possible?'

The old man shrugs and smiles, as if what he's about to say is preposterous and embarrassing. He sips the rest of his coffee. 'Maybe he lives somewhere up there now,' he says. 'There are... places. Old mine workings. Brick tunnels that don't seem to lead anywhere. Drainage culverts. If you get to know the mountain well enough, you soon realise you don't know it at all.'

'You think he's living in a hole in the ground.'

'I don't think at all. Best not to. None of my business, and he's never done me any harm. Live and let live, that's what I say.'

'I say that too,' I mutter, and the old man stands ready to leave. Kes lets out a little whine.

'He's just part of the mountain,' he says. 'Sounds to me like that's what he always wanted.'

As the old man walks away I think, *Maybe that's what I want too.*

>•<

It is a mountain of many seasons, and I have painted them all but winter.

Kes likes the snow. By the time we reach the trig point on top of the mountain there is four inches, and the forecast says we might have more tomorrow. But for this afternoon the skies are clear, the sun shines, and the world is a shimmering blanket of glorious white.

This mountain has become a familiar place to me. I am known in the town for painting it, and I've sold more than twenty canvases of various sizes over the past nine months. Three still hang in my studio, unsold. Each of them has a shape, a figure, and to me the Walker is very clear. I'm starting to believe that to other people the Walker is simply a smudge on the paintings, and that most believe it to be an error on my part but are too polite to say.

I am certain he is not an error. My autumn conversation with the old man convinced me of that. I've seen the old man several times since our chat, but always at a distance across the rolling terrain of the mountainside. Once, Kes saw him and ran all the way over to him, further away from me than he has ever gone before. Another time he raised his hand and waved, and I waved back. There is something profoundly comforting about our familiarity, as if we share a wonderful secret that no one else knows.

I settle down to paint, and set against the virgin snow my skies are darker and more tumultuous than ever before. Whenever I paint angry skies, I feel myself becoming more at ease with who I am. I'm still young, still finding my hand with painting and my way in life.

It's cold, and although the sun is out the breeze drifting across the mountainside makes it feel colder. My paints are thick and sticky, and I hold the brush over my mug of coffee to soften the bristles. I don't mind my work being a tough process. I think it benefits the final product, and if anyone asks – which they often do when browsing in my studio, and commenting on the wildness of my locations – I can give them a wide, deep history of how art often grows out of discomfort and difficulty.

By mid-afternoon I have the shape of the painting set, and I'm spending some time examining the skyline, seeing boiling clouds in my mind's eye, when I see the shadow on the left side of the canvas.

I gasp, almost winded with surprise. I didn't see anything, didn't do anything, and the shape has come from nowhere. It's like a shade against the snow and sky, and I step left and right to ensure I am not throwing a silhouette.

It's not me.

'It's him,' I say, and my voice is captured by the breeze and taken across the mountainside. Kes's ears prick up and he turns to look up at me. 'It's him,' I say again, and this time I look at Kes. He trots off ahead of me, past the canvas, and strays into the spread of mountainside where the shape has found itself. He sees and senses nothing.

This feels like an intrusion. The Walker is too close. Before, in the distance, he was like the old man, a presence I do not mind and which I actually enjoy. But this is personal space.

I pass my brush across a smear of white paint and spread it on the canvas. It's a crass, damaging application, and I can see that it has lessened the painting even though it is only just begun. The shape vanishes. What once was the outline of a human figure is now less than a shade.

My heart beats, my stomach sinks, as if I have done something bad. A flush of loss surges through me, a feeling deeper and more profound than the loneliness I grow used to. I have been painting the Walker all year, allowing him to inhabit my paintings as he comes closer, closer, and now I have shunned him.

But what if he really came that close? What if—?

Across the hillside, Kes turns back towards me and growls.

I feel a heavy presence behind me.

Brush poised, breath held, I wonder whether I should paint this moment away.

DARK SHELLS

ALIYA WHITELEY

There's a feeling amongst the villagers that I should stop talking to the river.

Rivers and voices have much in common. They rise and fall, swell with energy, diminish to a trickle. They travel. They never stay still, even when they seem caught in an endless repeating. Mum repeated herself often, near her end, but every time the words were new to her. I realised, after, that they had been new to me too, bringing fresh emotion every time although for different reasons.

And so on we travel through our lives, like water riding the land.

Water is water, she used to say, back when her eyes were light, and I was a young girl. I used to complain about having to take a bath after her. Well, now I know that each piece of water is a drop. A drop of liquid, or a lurch in the stomach. Jolting awake from falling far in a bad dream.

'Could you talk a little more about life during the war instead?' says the young man with a tape recorder.

'1940s?' I ask.

'Yes, around that time. It's 1988 now,' he adds.

'I'm aware of what year it is, thank you.'

He has the good grace to look ashamed.

'Nothing much changes over the years here, anyway.' I throw my hand around the large, shabby lounge of the home for the elderly where the council saw fit to put me. The other residents are watching television, or nodding to themselves. I'm certain I don't belong here. 'I just worked the land, along with my parents. Essential labour. I don't even remember it much.'

'Really?' He sounds disappointed.

'This is Lincolnshire, not London.'

'There are a lot of airfields around here. Did you see any planes?'

He's quite a pleasant young man really, and I like a bit of company. I pretend to think, and then say, 'Oh yes! There was that time when the sky was filled with those big bombers. The noise of them, it was so loud, I covered my ears with my hands. I remember now.'

Next thing I'll be claiming I was up in the sky with them. Still, it does the trick, and he goes away satisfied, promising to return. I could tell him about the flooding next time. Five of my relatives have drowned, in the past. What a miserable way to go.

The river used to burst its banks. That's clear in my mind. The rain, spattering, and then the swelling, the speed of the flow, and the houses along its banks put out sandbags on their doorsteps. Ruskington is a large village, based entirely around the River Slea. It flows right through the centre, past the church, past the grocers, then the butchers, the bakery, that fish and chip shop that's too greasy for my tastes, the carpet shop Bill and I own – no, wait, that's closed down, and the little cafe, that's gone too. The village is in a bad state. So many shops are dark shells, now. Their grey, cobwebbed windows watch me; I can feel them at my back when I sit on the bench and feed the ducks.

But the bench is very cold today. I have an audience, as usual. A few villagers are gathered, staring at me with disapproval. How did I get here? I have no memory of leaving the house. Yet here I am, and soon the bread is gone and the ducks desert me, and it's obvious I'm talking to the river because a woman is coming out of her shop and saying, 'Here again? Come on in the warm and I'll get you a tea while I phone the home.'

'Hold on while I finish up,' I tell her, and I speak my private thoughts in one long breath, murmuring, because the river hears me well enough at any volume. 'All right, lovely, two sugars please, dear.' I could walk home, but why bother when I could get tea and a lift? Besides, whenever I walk home across the fields my shoes get muddy and there's somebody else living in my house.

Tea is not what it used to be. Thick, brown tea: what happened to that? I used to start and end the day on it – tea as punctuation, my full stop to break up this long sentence that rolls on without pause, without meaning. I could drain a cup of such tea, but in the absence of that I sip, and the pleasant young man says, 'Do you mind if we try something different?'

'Where did you come from?' I say. I was by the river. At least here, sitting in my comfortable chair, nobody is glowering at me.

He turns on his tape recorder; I watch how he does it, two fingers on the red button and the black button at the same time.

'What would you like to hear about this time?'

'Tell me a memory of feeling happy. In the village. A joyous occasion.'

'Did you know,' I say, relieved to find some facts still come to me, 'that Ruskington is mentioned in the Domesday Book? It was called *Rischintone* which means *farmstead where rushes grow*. The people then were short and they died young. They were an ugly bunch, too. My family were amongst the first here. We go all the way back.'

'Well, I'm surprised you can remember that far,' he says, and his cheeky grin is a shock. It moves me, I'm like a rusty old waterwheel trying to turn; it's the flirtation, of course, that's what it is. Dad used to say *a smile can work wonders* and he was right. He was not a clever man, but he said good things to me. I wish he could still talk.

'Dad's farmworkers had a party after each harvest,' I say. To be smiled at, to be held in someone's warm eyes. 'There was dancing. I'd had my hair cut short, had seen it in a magazine. And there was a new dressmaker in the village, moved here from down south, and she'd make these miniskirts if you had the money. I got her to make me a red one, and I thought I was very daring. But to get across the fields I had to put on wellies. Wellies, and a miniskirt! Music was pouring across the fields, the sound of the Twist bouncing over the empty troughs of dirt that had held the sugar beet. I had my other shoes in a bag, I couldn't wait to get there. The mud sucked at my boots the whole way.'

'And you were happy?'

'We were all happy. It was a good way to live, the crops coming in, the demand for sugar was growing as more and more people got a sweet tooth, wanted cakes and biscuits and bags of sugar.'

'So your family grew beet for sugar?'

'We did. Had done for generations. There was a factory at Bardney that bought up all we could grow. Then the factory went under.' To go into what happened next is not so happy. Dad's face. His eyes, as I changed: dark shells. Losing the farm. Mum turning to drink, to drown out the disapproval of those silent villagers.

'And how was the party?' says the young man.

I'm not ready to tell him that. 'Did you know a lot of the farmers don't use hedges around here to separate the fields? We use ditches, but you can't see them as you walk along; it looks like all the land is joined together, owned by nobody. Or by one great big all-knowing farmer, I should say.'

'You're religious?' he asks me.

That's far too difficult a question to answer. 'No more than the next person,' I tell him, and we move on to the next topic, but his words sink into me. So I'm not surprised to find myself in the graveyard at All Saints Church, next to the bridge on the way out of the village, with a handful of bread stolen from the kitchen. I am a collection of these moments, now – these appearances in places with no interlinking journeys between them. My memory no longer flows. I am a series of drops.

There are no ducks in sight. I throw the crumbs anyway, and spend a while telling the river about my memories of All Saints. The day I wore white and the days I wore black. The water washes the words away, and my mum and dad are with me. At least they smile, and do not stare.

This time it's the butcher who comes out and says, 'Well, you should be an escapologist, shouldn't you? Come on.'

'I don't know why you don't want me to talk to it,' I say. 'It can't tell anyone.'

'Whispering to the water, are you?' he says.

Yes, that's it – water whispering. I see a painting in my mind, from that time Bill took me to London. We were just married, and we spent the morning in a gallery. Ophelia, with flowers, in the rushes, floating. Her river was nothing like the River Slea, or the ditch water. Both are heavy with mud from the fields; when you fall in there's not a speck of pale skin left in sight.

London was an experience. The Thames was a grand sight, and that's a different sort of river again. We walked along the South Bank, after seeing that picture. I was crying; I had told him everything. He said, 'We can be happy. You must promise you'll try to be happy, that you'll forget about it, not waste any more time and words on it, it's just a thing, a problem with your mind, no more than that,' and it was one of the very few times he named it, my unhappiness, and let it take up a moment of his time.

'I'll try,' I told him, 'but it's a part of me. Of my family.'

'We could move away. There's nobody down here to see, is there? None of your relatives, living or dead.'

But I said no. I couldn't leave them. And so I left my chance of happiness – our chance of happiness – behind.

Enough of happy. I'm sick of happy. The prison of it, a weight on my lungs. The thing I should be aiming to feel, and make others feel. It's a relief when the pleasant young man asks me instead, 'Can you remember a time in the village when you were sad?'

Is this a new session, or the same one? I don't know. The river has moved on. 'You want all the stories, don't you?'

'It's for a local history project,' he says.

'Oh yes, I remember. So what will you do with this tape of yours?' I lean forward and tap the recorder.

'It'll go into an archive along with all the other memories. There'll be an exhibition in Sleaford Museum.'

So I'm just one of many. Just a drop in the ocean of old people, muttering on about tea and dances and the war and how things were so much better then. Let there be some truth amongst the flood of their thoughts. Let me speak it, here, although the meaning has moved on.

'It happened in the summer,' I say. 'The murder.'

He is all attention. I see it in his face. 'The murder?' he says.

'He was the travelling type, working the fields up and down the county, taking work where he could find it. The villagers had been warned against him. There had been some trouble, rumours that he,' I lower my voice, 'he liked it rough, beg my pardon. Had hit a girl. These rumours don't just follow after people. They chase them, catch them up. But she wouldn't listen.'

'What happened?'

'He didn't turn up for work, and she didn't come home, and people put two and two together and thought they'd run off, away. I went out across the fields, in my wellies, in my miniskirt, walking until I was right on top of the ditch. I found her there. Her lovely white skin, muddied. She was face up, floating, in the water, flowers surrounding her. Her eyes were dark shells. She was so beautiful.'

'She was...?'

'Marks on her throat, nearly as red as my skirt, from where he held her down.'

'He held her down?' he repeats.

'You're like a record with a scratch, you,' I tell him, annoyed. 'That's what I said.'

'Did the police look into it?'

I shrug. 'I don't know. I only know about her. I saw her. It was the first time I saw one, you see.'

'That's shocking. That's terrible.' He is agog. I've given him what he wanted. 'What was her name? The woman's name?'

'Anna. Anna Pigott.'

He frowns at me. Then he reaches forward and turns off the tape recorder. 'That's your name,' he says.

'That's right. And it's my great-aunt's name, too. We've got a lot in common. The gift of my family. She was my first, and so many others came after her, all frowning at me, all wanting me to see them, bear witness to them.' I clap my hand over my mouth. I shouldn't say so much.

'Well,' he says. 'Well. Perhaps it's about time I was going. You must be tired.'

Water can be clear and true and cold, or it can be muddied and thick and smelly. Sometimes, just like time, it can hardly move at all.

Later, just after Bill bought the carpet shop and both Mum and Dad had been put in the All Saints graveyard, he said, *Don't tell me about them, I don't want to hear it, to picture them around us still*, and I tried so hard to never mention how they stood beside me, how they smiled at me and watched me as I slept. I tried to never talk to them directly. Bill didn't like me going out to the ducks and giving my memories to the river instead. But it had to come out of me somehow, in words, in water.

He said, *We should not have children, Anna. We should end this thing, here.* And I begged him, but he was strong. Stronger than me.

Bill was a good husband, though, all in all.

I'm sitting on the bench in the heart of the village. Here they are, standing before me, and their eyes are dark shells. With them I see my grandparents, and their parents, and more. So many of the Pigotts. And the first one who came to me – my Great-Aunt Anna, still muddied, still so sad.

Soon I will become one of them, but there will be no new Pigotts with the gift to see me. Perhaps it will mean the end of the village. Perhaps the river will dry up for good. Or perhaps everything will simply trickle on, as it has for a thousand years before, while we Pigotts silently seethe on the banks of the Slea.

I feel so guilty. I'm not meant to open my mouth about them at all, not to anyone, not even to the river. That's what Bill said.

'I'm sorry,' I tell him, lifting my chin to the cold white sky. How strange it is, talking to someone who is not there – to thin air. The villagers will think me touched. 'I had to tell someone.'

'Tell someone what?' says the woman from the bakery, disapproval dripping from her voice. She sighs, and says, 'They just can't keep you still, can they?' She'll take me inside now, and give me a cup of tea. I hope she brews it for a little longer; you might say tea is always the same but I say it doesn't matter how often you drink a cup down. It's like the past. Each drop tastes a little different, every time.

COLD ASHTON

STEPHEN VOLK

Cold Ashton is a village in the county of Gloucester, situated in the Chipping Sodbury district, five miles or thereabouts north of Bath, and, if one approaches from the direction of that city, lies in a valley, or indentation, just beyond the village of Nimlet. It encompasses the hamlet of Pennsylvania to its north-west, and its post town is Marshfield under Chippenham. The geological character is mainly of limestone, not surprisingly, given the area lies upon a Cotswold escarpment. It comprises, in broad estimation, some two thousand or so acres.

Notable buildings, I would say, could be listed upon the fingers of one hand. Holy Trinity Church, which originally came under the Priory of St Peter in Bath, has a fourteenth-century tower, whilst the remainder of it was rebuilt, with an impulsive rush of modernity, in the sixteenth by Thomas Key, its rector. Interesting features include his rebus, a 'T' entwined in a key, a somewhat impoverished rood loft, and a curious pulpit set in a niche. The stone-walled main street, however, is enhanced greatly in terms of picturesque intimacy by the proximity of the Old Rectory and courthouse. It was to the former that, during the Battle of Lansdowne, Sir Bevil Grenville, a Royalist, was carried when mortally injured.

However, none of the above attracted my services. Such a request came, instead, from the architecturally fine Manor House, which dated from soon after the Dissolution of the Monasteries, possibly from William Pepwall's time, but more likely to have been begun circa 1629 when John Gunning, another Mayor of Bristol, bought the estate. The case I had been called upon to investigate – recounted elsewhere – was that of an extremely naughty and troublesome spirit, which the housemaids had come to call 'The Nincompoop', and which resulted in an extraordinary experience at an 'ancient earthwork' on Tog Hill. But that story is not the one I wish to tell here.

This is an altogether different tale, but one no less – yes, I shall use the word – *preternatural* in nature.

Usually in my reports I can vouch for the honesty of my perception and conclusions, scientific or otherwise. In this instance, though, such reassurances cannot be forthcoming. Much of what you will read comes second-hand, though not all. And while some is a matter of tangible record, well… you shall see what I mean. I am not going to be the club bore who tells you the punchline of a joke three times before spending an hour telling you the build-up. Or I hope I shan't.

It was one evening whilst lodging at the local inn, The White Hart, a convivial place in the earthy yet hospitable way that London taverns can rarely duplicate, that I idly expressed, somewhat exposing my status as casual visitor, my curiosity about the name of the place. *Cold Ashton*. I wondered aloud, as the landlord poured an uncommonly cloudy cider, if it in any way reflected the frequency of the name-element 'cole' on the ancient trackways of England, which I believed, a lot of them, harkened back to prehistory. I could think of two hill-points in Hereford, one with a marking clump of Scotch firs bearing the name, viz. Coles Tump and Coles Hill. And there were many Colehills across the country, as well as several –*woods, –ways, –lanes, – leys*, et cetera. I suspected it went back to King Coel of the Chronicles – even the Old King Cole of the nursery rhyme.

The landlord remained mute through my excited

monologue. Now he spoke, without the merest glimmer of interest.

'Nobody round here will know that,' he opined, grumpily, adding an intriguing but puzzling afterthought: 'One man says there is a story, but no one tells it.' He then turned to serve another customer, or in any case, turned his back on me.

At first I thought nothing of it. It didn't matter to me if he shared by interest in the subject. I decided that when I returned home I would consult Bartholomew's *Survey Gazetteer* and compile myself a list. You know how it is. Certain things get in one's head and they won't let go until you worm them out, they do with me anyway, and this was one of them. It wasn't something of earth-shaking importance, granted, but I couldn't let the question simply hang. It's a failing I have, the need to burrow for hidden treasure. I had it as a boy, with lepidoptery – 'happy-doptery' as Father called it. And now, the same goes for my fascination with all things supernatural.

Coldborough. Cold Eaton. Cold Fell. Cold Newton. Coldridge. Coldswaltham... Already, the cider wetting my whistle, I ruminated upon the possibility that the 'd' was added over time, probably by naturally evolution, to make the name easier to say. (As, indeed, I later confirmed to be true. In the *Chronicle of Roger of Hovenden* (twelfth century), Vol. i, p.45, Coldingham is spelt 'Collingham', but with a 'd' in other places, 'Coldingham'; and in MSS. Temp. Ed. I., St Nicholas Cole Abbey is given as St Nicholas 'Coldabbay'. In another source 'Cold-prophet' meaning juggler, wizard or sorcerer is a variant of 'Cole-prophet', and 'Cold Harbour' is 'Cole Harbour' in Ben Johnson's *Silent Woman*.) But something else intruded on my train of thought, and began to pique my curiosity far more…

One man says there's a story, but no one tells it.

Indeed? The more I rolled the landlord's words around in my head, the more peculiar and strange they became. Why on earth would he say such a thing? What 'story'?

Did the name 'Cold Ashton' *have* a story? If so, why was it one that nobody was prepared to divulge? This, again, was like a rat to the terrier of my brain, and I determined not to leave until I had uncovered the reason behind it.

I do not rest easy when perplexed, and so it was that night. The following morning, directly after a hearty breakfast, I visited Holy Trinity. For information gathering, I've found, churches often prove the best initial port of call. I chatted amiably with the vicar, a man by the name of Doynton whose twin daughters scampered amongst the gravestones, more in blissful ignorance of their surroundings than in sacrilege. I could see no heresy in clapping-games and tag, or in childish laughter as they ran circles round a 600-year-old yew. Before I had met the priest I shielded my eyes with the visor of my right hand, the better to see the two girls whirling in their skirts, and at that moment the wind dropped with unusual suddenness, stilling the leaves on the old oak at the border with the adjacent field. The disc of the sun sur-topped a hillock – a 'shining brow' or *taliesin*, as the Celts would have it – and in the patchwork of fields lain out below it, I espied a stiff, tall, lumbering figure, the leather straps of a plough around his shoulders, lank hair hanging to his collar and sleeves rolled up beyond bony elbows, singularly diligent in his travail.

'Can I help you?' asked the Rev. Doynton from the arch of porch, and I replied that I dearly hoped he could. I explained the nature of my 'perhaps silly' inquiry, and was soon furnished with the information that the village had not always been called Cold Ashton. To the churchman's knowledge it was originally named 'Chyd', or some variation of that spelling, which I committed to my notebook. I begged access to his parish records of births, deaths and marriages, and this was happily forthcoming after a good old rattling of keys: always an excellent sign of rich spoils to come. The children were but a distant chuckling now, and the figure on the hill a fading memory.

The reverend gave me a candle which was, frankly, necessary to my researches, since the light through the stained glass did not fall where we stood, but I felt uncomfortable that he took it from an altar. The fact seemed to entreat me to give ecclesiastical substance to my endeavours. Something I felt ill able to provide.

Most of the day, and candle, had gone by the time I reached a fragment of interest, and had almost given up hope. Suddenly the word 'Ashton' leapt out at me, just when my eyes were becoming blurry from the strain. They immediately focused on the dry, yellowing page before me. I was looking at a line recounting the marriage of Ashton Goodchyld to Joan (Ioan) Lavender. The date was 1591. Goodchyld... Of Chyle Farm... I reminded myself that conformity of spelling was not a strong suit during that era. So did 'Chyd' – the old name for Cold Ashton – predate this marriage, and when exactly did it change so radically?

The next day I visited the courthouse, a stone's throw from The White Hart. There I discovered that the Domesday Book carried a brief description of 'Chyd' in 1086, giving its population as '8 households (quite small)', with some description of its taxable units: '5 exemption units. Taxed on 3.0' (which meant nothing to me). It did, however, add: 'Plough land: 1 lord's plough team's (sic). 3 men's plough teams.' Also: 'Meadow 6 acres, 1 mill, value 0.2.'

I raked through the Census records. They showed that in 1881, the greatest local employer by far was agriculture, with eighty workers, with domestic service and office clerks lagging behind with twenty-three. Further, that from 1801 to 1851, Cold Ashton grew in population by over double to 500, though, thereafter, after every ten-year period the number either stayed more or less even or decreased. This told me, at least, that the place was called 'Cold Ashton' in 1801.

Something had happened between 1591 and 1801, clearly. And it wasn't merely the corruption of language, the adding of a letter here, or dropping of a syllable there. The name literally changed completely, as if overwritten. But why?

Frustratingly, I was no nearer the answer than when I started.

My only recourse was to plunge into records of legal proceedings, and I began in the early 1590s, almost immediately regretting my decision as I waded through incomprehensibly dense writing, a frenzy of quill-scratched curlicues, marred by such convoluted medieval grammar that I wished it was in Latin or Greek: then I might have a clue to understanding it. Then I came across – to equal degrees of delight and dismay – a printed pamphlet or broadsheet, such as was used at that time to convey 'news' (and usually criminal news of some salacious or morbid interest) to the general public.

A woodcut on its cover portrayed with unmistakable

clarity the image of a woman hung by a noose from a three-sided scaffold. A side-caption read: 'Ioan Goodchyd & hir Familiar'. Lower on the page a man was shown pushing a plough. A label in the shape of an unfurling scroll read: 'Ashton'.

I never like the expression that the hairs stood up on one's neck, but I like it even less when that has occasion to happen, and it did that day, at that hour. It was too much of a coincidence not to be the same people, Ashton Goodchyld and his wife Joan, who'd been married in this village in 1591.

For the benefit of the original, pious readers, a footnote or motto had been provided at the bottom of the frontispiece, helpfully defining the moral of the tale in advance: 'All their conceited pleafures come to this / When yelling they difcend ye grand Abyfs' (sic).

A vivid, if sobering, promise. I was already committed to read on. But first, the description of the contents, written in large, bold type above the gibbet, is worth quoting in full:

The Apprehenfion and confefsion of
The Goodchyld Witch
Arreigned and by Iuftice condemned and
Executed at Marfh-fields, in the parish of
Puckle-church, the 5, day of Iulye, laft paft.
1 5 9 8
With the true manner of her practices

I opened my notebook hastily and set down the details, as near as I could understand them, and shall repeat them here, verbatim, but in plain English, minus the spreading vines of language in the original, customary for the time but hard on the eye and ear in ours, while omitting any irrelevant diversions that can be lost to no deleterious effect.

By way of a preamble, the paper began with a religious, that is to say, Christian tract about the evils of witchcraft. Anyone who has had the misfortune of plodding through the hideous *Malleus Maleficarum* of Kramer and Spengler and its woman-hating rhetoric will be unsurprised by the gist of this tired brand of fearful hysteria. Though, the unnamed writer points out that the sorceress in this case did not fly, meet for orgies, dance in praise of Satan (spelled 'Sathan' in this instance) or concoct spells. What she did, it is stated, was far, far worse – and that was to go against God.

Then followed an interjection by the Bishop of Bath and Wells, to the effect that there are hundreds of witches secretly and deviously plying their trade all round us, at all times, and we must be vigilant, lest they tighten their stranglehold on our piety. Should we give in to allying ourselves to those who believe the Devil *does not exist*, the bishop asserts, then we succumb to exactly what the Devil wants, and will face eternity 'with hordes disconsolate' in the infernal flames for our error.

It seems that Ashton Goodchyld and Joan were neighbours. She was the child of a nearby farmer. They had met in childhood – one is tempted to embellish that word with another, 'sweethearts' – but, whatever the case, as soon as Joan was of age, they were betrothed, and their future garlanded with blessings by both families. When Ashton's father and mother died, he inherited the land and continued to work it, as he had learned to do since boyhood. The soil was under his fingernails, as the pamphlet rather poetically puts it. Man and wife ran the farm happily, or at least successfully, though the marriage was childless. This is described as a heavy burden, one that 'causes angels to shed tears', but may well be the author imposing their own feelings on the matter.

In the next paragraph, Ashton goes off to war. I queried this with a margin-mark in my notebook, as no specific war is suggested. I presume the Anglo-Spanish war 1585–1604, though no reason is given for his joining up – straightened circumstances, the need for cash? So, as a mercenary? Or was he turning his back on something at home? Did the lack of a son and heir trouble him? Did he blame his wife for her lack of fertility, or see it as a sign of his manhood being lacking? To no such explanation did the broadsheet allude, so the question must remain a matter of conjecture.

Joan was left to run the farm alone, and gradually its well-being suffered. The fields gained when her own parents died lay fallow. Crops failed, unattended by the back-breaking work necessary to make them yield a return. Joan worked her fingers to the bone, but it simply wasn't enough, and whether she cursed Ashton every night or prayed for his return, she suffered the agonies of Job as her world shrank around her. And no one came to her aid. Not one of the farms surrounding her heeded her call.

Within the year, news arrived from a traveller, a man who had fought cheek by jowl with Ashton in Cádiz, under Drake. He reported that Ashton was dead. Killed by the enemy with a musket-shot to the heart. Joan's own heart failed her and she fell to the ground in shock. The man's vow to inform her – Ashton's dying wish – fulfilled, he exits the narrative, without even the dignity of a name.

As the news of Ashton's death spread, neighbours came sniffing like hungry jackals. The widow could not run Goodchyld Farm alone, and much of it was going to seed, or dead. One after another, men asked for her hand, but she knew full well they were not interested in her, they were interested only in her property. What was left of it. But it was hers. It was all she had. All she had left of what she and Ashton had created, given birth to, together. Every suitor was rejected. Some politely. Some not. One man attested to being kicked so hard he needed to buy new breeches. Another complained that a thrown cooking pan had struck him on the head. Passers-by could hear Joan shouting, even though she lived alone, and she was quickly branded mad. Or conferring with spirits. Mary Bealing later testified that she believed that, in consort with the Devil, Joan had grown herself a man's nether parts, no less.

This was only the beginning of that heady mixture, resentments and rumour. For if Joan's icy witch's teats were not to be offered to good, upstanding local men, who *were* they being offered to, in dead of night?

Hence she was spied upon, and under a gibbous moon, three lads, 'as God was their witness' (predictably), saw her dead husband ploughing the fields – no horse, straps on his back. They ran home tripping up and breathless with horror, one of them mute for a week, their ravings dismissed by the half-sensible as those of drunken fools. Yet the next morning, that very same field was found ploughed, where the clay had been hard as oak a week before.

Joan was asked to explain this.

'Why, I did it myself,' she said. 'Do I not have a back as broad as any man hereabouts?'

Nevertheless the tittle-tattle did not fade, and every tongue in the district was soon wagging about the widow whose husband had come back from dead. Honest village folk avoided her, but it didn't inconvenience Joan. She went about her tasks as ever she did, but now looked better fed. More healthy. Happier. Her produce appeared at market. She shopped and bartered like the rest of them. And they didn't like it. They felt very much safer when she was near death's door and her land near possession.

But no. Her harvests were good and she prospered. Unnaturally so, it was said, and so, as inevitably as day follows night, talk of witchcraft grew, which was common currency of grievance in those ignorant times.

One day a child threw a stone at her in the high street and she threw it back. Women berated her. Joan stood up to them 'as if made of iron'. She said to them: 'He will plough by the moon, and as far as you cannot stop the moon, he will keep ploughing for me.'

The wives of Chyd were flustered by this effrontery, and angered, and frightened by her 'lewde dealings', and took their fears to their rector, but he said he could do nothing – evidently more of the Reginald Scot stamp of scepticism (e.g. 'A disproof of their assembles' in *The Discoverie of Witchcraft*). Venting this disapproval by another route, the harridans goaded their husbands into killing Joan's cow, which was the catalyst for Joan going to Justice Loat and his clerk, Robert Nuttall, to claim compensation for the sudden and substantial loss incurred. In so doing, she can have had no idea that she was laying herself before the mercy of the heartless and afeared.

Even before she stood in front of the judge, he had heard

the counter-claim that she was a witch. The locals wanted to swim her. That would be a good way to see if they owed her a cow or not. Justice Loat said, in effect, let me be judge of that. Being, it has to go in his favour, an actual judge.

Such were the events that led to Joan being in the very courthouse I sat in, and I could not help but wonder whether she felt terror or antagonism, nervousness or righteous fervour, as she faced the bewigged and begowned figure that held her fate in the palm of his hand. Perhaps she had little conception he did. Perhaps to her it was all about a cow.

Justice Loat communicated that there were 'accusations' against her. 'What say thee?'

Joan said bluntly that she had not got the time to listen to such things.

He said she better had, because if true, this could be difficult for her.

Joan: 'If you want to accuse me, you will.'

He then asked her if she had anything to say about the killing of the cow?

Joan: 'Only that I did not do it. It was done unto me.'

'And the naming of the cow?' asked Justice Loat. 'How came it to be named Alice? A pretty name. The name of your mother.' Joan laughed loudly, whereupon he continued: 'Did you use your powers given by Sathan to transform your mother into a cow?'

Joan's smile disappeared. 'I loved my mother. My husband thought it was funny, to name a cow after her. And so we did. And milked it, as she gave milk to me when I was a babe.'

'Blasphemy!' went up a cry (though how anybody could quite define it as that, I don't know). The public gallery became noisy. The court usher called for order.

Thomas Tent was called as a witness, father of the boy who had thrown a stone. He said, as a farmer himself all his life, in his opinion it was impossible for a mere maiden to run such acreage alone, and she must have been employing witchcraft to do so (*'Malefica'* as the report has it). Joan was thence questioned on this point, at first refusing to answer at all, but speaking eventually on threat of 'more punishing methods' being employed, saying they could examine her if they wished, but would find no marks, and nothing did she employ but ordinary labour.

'Of yourself alone? Or of another?' When she did not answer, Justice Loat continued. 'A man has been seen in your fields at night. You say he is your husband, returned.'

'Yes, he has returned. From Spain.'

Some laughter ensued – though hushed by the majority and the stern countenance of the usher.

'Speak.'

'I think it will be best for him to answer that, my lord.'

And so a man, tall and thin, was led to the witness box, in his working clothes, 'grimed in dirt and unbecoming', and the question put to him: 'Are you Ashton Goodchyld?'

'No, my lord.' A hubbub of dissatisfaction rose. 'I do not even think I resemble him. I was passing through this county, hungry, tired, and, seeing a fire burning inside, and smoke rising from the chimney, stopped at this good lady's farm to enquire after work. She said there was some, and so I did it. And do it, and she pays me.'

Justice Loat: 'How does she pay you?'

The man sniffed and rubbed his nose with his sleeve. 'By whatever means at her disposal.'

He looked over at Joan, smiling, and Joan blushed 'the

scarlet of Salome', staring down at her shoes. The crowd bayed like dogs.

'I ask any man or woman under this roof to identify me as Ashton Goodchyld!' challenged the man.

'I do!' cried Harriet Hall. 'I knew him as a boy and I knew him as a grown man. There is no mistaking him.' Others took her up with the same declaration, more or less, shaking their fists. Thomas Durrant; John Uncles; John Gradwell; Anne Hubbard. 'It is he!'

'They are liars, all of them! I have never set foot in this county till now. My name and discourse is as worthy as theirs, and my words are true, as I stand before God. They should think on that. For they do likewise.'

'Then you will find it easy to appraise me of your real baptismal name,' said Loat.

The man raised his chin high. 'John Parkinson.'

'And from whence you hail, just as easily.'

'Lincoln, sir.'

'And if this be not a lie, that you come from those parts, give me the name of any town in Lincolnshire.'

The man pondered. 'Lincoln, sir.' A trickle of laughter circulated.

'Give me the name of another town.'

'I rightly did not stray far from Lincoln, sir.'

'You strayed here.'

'I will talk plain, since I am a plain man, my lord. In thy wisdom, thou knowest how this land lieth before thee. Dogs bite when whipped, and sometimes unwhipped dogs bite too. Dogs are dogs. The widow employed me. What more is there to say? Nothing, I believe, sire. So, may I please step down?'

'Why at night?' demanded Justice Loat. His clerk, Nuttall, looked up from his quill, and peered over his half-moon lenses.

The man hesitated, and lowered his voice. 'Perhaps I do so, under darkness, because I have my own wife by day.' Again he looked at Joan and again her cheeks turned crimson. No doubt all the cheeks in the courthouse coloured similarly.

'You have been seen in her bed.'

Joan: 'When, by whom?'

'If I was…'

'He was!' Harriet Hall shouted. 'He came to her in the shape of a black dog! Then a snake!'

Joan: 'And you so rarely see a snake, Harriet Hall. Even a small one.'

The man interjected: 'No. I think I was a hedgehog at the time, was I not? Or a vole?'

The gavel was striking heavily but the courthouse was a din, and his words could hardly be discerned any more.

'Your manner, good fellow,' said Loat, 'does nothing to endear you to this court, nor its applicators. You would do well to keep your tongue in check.' The man was heard to say – *and they, theirs.* 'And we shall tie this up with the utmost alacrity. This session is postponed until tomorrow, during which time the Widow Goodchyld will be held overnight under key, and questioned to our satisfaction.' At this order, Joan's arms were secured roughly by the guards, and she was carried, under protest, towards the cells beneath.

The man struck the wooden rail in front of him and cried out in full voice: 'What do you want to hear?'

'You know what we want to hear,' said Justice Loat, with

the calm of 'the surface of an unsullied millpond' though 'his eyes were as nail-heads'.

This turn of fortune suddenly incurred the man's uncontrolled rage. He swept back his hair and held out his arms at his side, in the manner of Jesus on the cross. 'The truth, then! Here you have it! I am the man, dead and risen! I will deny it no longer! Her love and need of me brought me back to this place. And if anyone brought me here, I swear it was God's doing, for it was love in my veins. And God, the Bible says, is love.'

'No!' Joan wailed, knowing all was lost, and struggling to reach him. The officers of the court held her back. Meanwhile the public 'swayed in turmoil, kin to a roiling sea'.

The man knew he would touch her no more. Perhaps he'd known the die was cast as soon as he was called to the stand. And, 'as Jesus stood before Pilate and was condemned, so too was Ashton Goodchyld of this parish, in a mockery of that Gospel, and had swore on the Good Book, as he had kissed the Devil's privies (sic) and made, both, a pact, and she, as 1 *Samuell*, 15, 23: it is all one with rebellion. *Jesabell* for hir idolatrous life is called a witch.'

And the husbandmen 'sorelie tormented did rise' and escort Ashton to the cells. And afterwards said, when they touched his flesh they felt no warmth of blood as with human flesh, but only ice, which is the 'credit and butter' (?) of the Devil. Thenceforth they called him Cold Ashton. And that was the name on everyone's whispers.

Cold Ashton.

In the days to come, the prisoner descending into a state of melancholy, the Justice visited him below, remarking upon the 'mooring of his misfortune'. His task now being to assemble evidence, the official asked him if he had ever been in the shape of anything other than a man? The answer came: 'Sometimes I fancy I have been a cocke.'

Spurred by his own spiritual curiosity, Loat then asked him questions of the Christian afterlife (for he conceived there could be no other). 'Cold Ashton' replied that the place was much like here, as fair or unfair as you make it.

In a letter the bishop had told the judge to mind his duties, 'for those who are lenient to witches may be construed to be witches themselves and looking after their kind'. But Loat refrained from subjecting Ashton to the thumbscrews or other Machinery of the Devout, since he had confessed already, and 'nought was to be gained from it'.

'The cow, my mother-in-law, in heaven, thanks you,' the younger man said, and after looking into his captor's face for a while, softly uttered, only partly a question: 'You know me to be John Parkinson.'

'You shall die Ashton Goodchyld,' came the reply.

'I am dead already.'

Loat leaned over and shook the man's hand. He reported afterwards it was like placing his fingers in snow. Inch by inch, it took the life from his arm, before the man let go, smiling.

'Fi fi fi, amen.' Cold Ashton asked what would happen to Joan. 'Will she be held to inquiry?' (This the contemporary synonym for torture.) He took his answer from the fact that Loat refused to meet his eyes.

'Until she confesses. Or not. Either way, you will both be hanged. If you wish, I will make sure you are buried side by side.'

A smile punctuated the darkness. 'Bless your soul. But what makes you think I will stay buried?'

Cold Ashton said no more, not a single word, and the Justice did not see him again until the day of execution, when, under the magistrate's express instruction, he was forced to watch as they first made his wife – stripped, shaved, and bearing the bruises and broken bones of her enforced confession – ascend the scaffold, tottering, barefoot, half-blind, and feel the rope tighten around her neck. I shall forego the detailed description of what followed, rendered in such deplorable detail in the broadsheet, and end only by repeating, from my notes, that he did so without flinching.

I closed the book, suddenly aware of the abiding silence. I wish it had some significance. I had my answers, and that was an end, of sorts – though hardly felt like it. I would have preferred to turn the clock back and not have learned what I had. Some periods of history are best not peered into. Their instructiveness limited only to reminding us of the naivety and wilful nastiness of bygone generations. I looked around at the courthouse walls, and the grand gentlemen who looked down at me in their haughty splendour, and their rich scarlet, then pulled on my coat and left.

Sitting for too long in one position had caused my back to ache – an occupational hazard of the studious – so I chose not to return to my hostelry immediately, but to stretch my legs by a circuitous route, starting with the avenue of coppiced trees called the Cotswold Way, and ending up at Holy Trinity by way of a path across fields and a stile. It did not take me long to circumnavigate the churchyard, but I found no tombstones with the name Ashton on them – though near to the 600-year-old yew were two slabs, side by side, broken at the base. The church doors were padlocked.

I had the urge to light a candle, but quickly replaced it with the need for a pint of ale.

The White Hart was not busy. It never was. However, the clientele, though small in number, seemed indefatigably loyal. So much so that some had their tankards full, waiting for them, before they walked in. The comfort of habit, or the habit of comfort. I suppose we all have it. And when we are broken out of our routine, or routine thinking, it destabilises us for a while, and we often choose to reject what does not fit in with our upholstered defences – psychological, spiritual or metaphysical. A familiar libation sitting on a bar you recognise, with friends whose very presence gives you a sense of belonging, is mainly all most people want. They do not seek disruption. But unpleasant truths are often exactly that.

I told the landlord about my discovery of the witch trial. He said he'd never heard of it, and he was Cold Ashton born and bred.

'I have,' said an elderly chap in a flat cap, perched on the stool beside me. 'It's not a bad yarn.' If he had a tooth in his head I was a Dutchman. The slurping of his stout was a thing to behold. His lower jaw almost became a shelf on which the glass could balance, while his upper lip puckered in, becoming almost invisible. When it was empty he ordered another with the most minimal gesture, not to be distracted from the serious business of lighting his pipe. My nose stung with the sharp tang of phosphorus as the match scratched the sandpaper edge of his box of England's Glory. I talked, but his eyes were not pointed at me, and he only occasionally twitched an eyebrow or smacked his lips, once or twice mumbling 'Daresay' or 'Proper'.

When his pint came, it came with another beside it. The old gent took one to a table near the fire, setting it down in front of a man whose age I would estimate at thirty or thirty-five who stabbed the fire with a poker. The burst of orange flames flickered over his features but somehow did not light them up. A curtain of dark hair hid one side of his countenance. He did not seem eager to share the other.

I asked the old man, when he returned to his seat, who the long-haired man was. A friend? He sucked the meniscus of froth into his mouth, and an inch of his pint with it.

'Just a regular. Labours in the fields here'bouts, like. Takes a shilling wherever he can get it. Keeps him in ale and sorrow. That's his chair, that is. By the fire. Always by the fire. Never seems to get 'imself warm, mind.'

His words were sufficiently illustrated to me as I watched the fellow's hands, held out, fingers slightly bent, palms open to the roaring flames. Knuckles as thick as might be of a man twice his age. Skin shroud-white. The veins across them blue. Fingernails snapped, encrusted, black. Every wrinkle embedded with the loam of weeks, months, years of toil. He turned them over gently, this way and that, as if roasting a brace of partridges. I had the intense feeling he had done so for some time, and not just tonight, or this week.

No sooner was one pint placed down than I saw another placed next to it. Another neighbourly donation. This time from a squat farmer with mud up his gaiters and rope knotted round his trouser top, hardly looking at him other than to give a slight jerk of the chin, then retiring to the far corner of the pub, nursing his own liquid fortification.

'Who got the land?' The toothless man next to me spoke. 'That's the thing. They do say Justice Loat himself came by the farm, by hook or by crook. But every minute he spent there he spent in fear. That's what they do say. And he died, and so did his children. But everyone dies, so that's no great story, is it? They say they opened Cold Ashton's grave once, and found nothing. Nothing but a black dog, or a vole, 'cording to some. Believe that or believe that not. I don't believe nothing I can't get down my throat or put in the bank. Except some say on a full moon you can see him plough that field, still. Except instead of seed he spreads the bones of little children. Cheers.' Draining the black slops of his glass, he was done. Laughter went up from a table at the back, but I took that to be coincidence.

I looked over to the hearth once again, and another drink was being proffered to the long-haired man, this time the golden bowl of a brandy, making me think it something of the nature of an offering.

'Benjamin Hall. Hall's Farm...' The giver was identified for me, and, without my prompting, my ancient and grizzled companion named others dotted around the bar. 'Jack Tent, from over Shoe way. Walter Durrant, up the road. Frank Uncles, across the street. Gordon Gradwell, that is. Dan Hubbard...' The names were familiar, but I did not realise how familiar until I consulted my notebook days later in the comfort of my home and my library. He bit on his pipe again and opened his matchbox. Then used its stem to point over his shoulder at the man with cold hands. 'Every night he's here. Never see him put his hand in his pocket. Never buys a drink. Never has to.'

What makes you think I will stay buried?

Smoke enveloped us both. The old man's eyes flickered.

'Come back tomorrow. I may tell it differently, but it will be no less true.'

Tomorrow, I left.

As certain then as I am now that if I were to return to The White Hart pub in Cold Ashton, I would see him, The Regular, sitting in his habitual chair, warming his perpetually icy hands at the log fire – and if you should go there ten years hence, or twenty years, or a hundred, I have no doubt that you will see him there too.

DOMESTIC MAGIC
(OR, THINGS MY WIFE AND I FOUND HIDDEN IN OUR HOUSE)

KIRSTY LOGAN

1. A RING

And isn't that sweet? Isn't it just too perfectly sweet, like it's a message of hope left for me and Alice, a blessing for our life together?

I caught the ring with the edge of the broom as I was sweeping out the kitchen. It scraped along the tiles and made a hell of a racket. At first I thought it was just rubbish, all clarty with grot and bugs, but when I rinsed it under the tap it came up lovely. A little circlet of glass, green as a summer sea, bright on its surface but with shadows at its centre. I thought maybe Alice's granny had left it for us on purpose. Maybe she wasn't so bad after all.

This poky Lenzie bungalow was hers, before. And it's not that she didn't know about me, but it's complicated. She called me Alice's friend, and I could hear the way she put inverted commas around it, even after Al and I had lived together for years and we'd both visited her a thousand times in this musty old house that always smelled like the sea even though it was miles from water.

I slid the ring on my wedding finger then raced through the house, calling for Alice, and found her in the spare bedroom with her arms full of floral duvets.

'These are going straight to the tip,' she said. 'Can you smell that? They're damp. Damn, I hope it's not in the walls.'

'Look, Al!' I held out my hand, queen-like. 'Isn't this pretty? Your gran must have left it.'

She peered at it. 'Is it plastic? It looks like it came out of a vending machine. Throw it away, there's enough junk in this house already.'

'It's sea-glass. I found it in the kitchen. Do you think it's a good-luck charm from your gran? To wish us well?'

Alice threw the musty duvets into the hall. 'Trust me, Rain. My gran didn't wish anybody well.'

2. PAPER

The folded page fell when we bashed the frame of the front door trying to carry the old bath out. I know, I know, we should have hired someone, but to be honest what little money we had was tied up in the house. Turns out, just because you inherit something, doesn't mean you get it for free. Alice tucked the paper in her pocket and then, when I was driving to the tip at Mavis Valley, the bath awkwardly wedged between the boot and the back seat, she pulled the paper out and unfolded it. It was as yellow as old bones and smelled musty-sweet.

'What does it say?'

Alice didn't reply.

'Hello! Are you listening?'

'It says,' she said. 'No, it's nothing.' And she balled up the paper and put it in the glove compartment

'Al, stop being weird! What does it say?'

'KELPIES TO HELL,' she said.

I wasn't sure whether to laugh. 'What's a kelpie?' Alice didn't reply, so I added: 'Call me a Sassenach if you like, just tell me.'

'A kelpie is a mythical creature,' Alice said, frowning. 'Lives in lochs. It's a horse and also a beautiful woman. If it doesn't like you, it drags you into the water and drowns you.'

'O… kay,' I said. 'But why would your gran want to tell us that?'

'Jesus, Rain, would you drop it with the secret messages? My gran was losing it towards the end. She didn't know I was going to get the house. She didn't know I was going to live here with you. None of this means anything, okay?'

So I drove the rest of the way to the tip in silence, and together we lifted the bath where Alice's granny had had a stroke and drowned, and we threw it away.

3. A HORSE

Alice found this one. It was the size of a thumb, wedged into the skirting board under the bed. She brought it to the kitchen as I was making tea and said: 'Rain, I can't find my glasses. Can you read this?'

I rubbed the tiny horse's haunches, feeling the symbols etched into the copper.

'It's not words,' I said. 'It's runes or something. Maybe it's an old Highlands superstition, and your gran left it to protect us Lowlanders from being trampled by – well, not a horse, but – life? Sadness? Money worries?'

Alice raised her eyebrows. 'Well, my mum always did say my gran was a witch. She stole another woman's man, did I ever tell you that?' Alice took the horse from my hand. 'My granddad was married to someone else when they met. A woman always dressed in green, who wore strange jewellery, rings made of glass she found washed up on the beach. She had green eyes and long black hair – black as a winter night, black like it was always wet.'

My eyes were wide. 'What happened?'

'My gran went round to talk to her, to say, basically, I want your man and there's nothing you can do about it, and she must have been pretty convincing because the next day the woman was gone. She left the village – went for a job down south or something. But you know the strange thing? No one ever saw that woman again.'

'Oh my God!' I said. 'Did your gran – do you think she – could she have done something?'

Alice laughed. 'Come on, Rain! What, you think my wee old granny was a murderer?'

'Why not? Every murderer has a family.'

'It's just a silly story,' Alice said. 'Gran was the other woman and so she had to make the original woman into a baddie, a villain to make her feel better. That's all. And she—' at this Alice jerked her hand and dropped the horse. It thudded to the floor and skittered away.

All I could do was stare at the blistered outline of the copper horse burned into Alice's palm.

4. PEARLS

It was boring, dirty work, doing up the house. Alice's gran hadn't touched anything in years – aside from hiding weird things in grubby corners, apparently. There was so much to do that Alice and I always ended up working late into the night, holding off the dark as best we could. Alice's blistered hand was healing, but slowly, and I'd got a nasty scrape up my calf from a cluster of nails left inexplicably spiked through a cupboard door.

When I found the long string of pearls on top of the wardrobe, I stripped off all my clothes and stepped into the shower – then stepped back out and wrapped the pearls around my neck. They were as long as a bridle; I looped them three times and they still covered my breasts. I stood under the hot water until I couldn't see for steam, then I walked, still dripping, into the kitchen where Alice was fixing the radiator.

'What do you think I should do with—' she said, and then she saw me and dropped the spanner. We made love on a clean dustsheet on the kitchen counter, and afterwards, Alice whispered in my ear: 'That's how you catch a kelpie, you know. With a string of pearls around its neck. My granddad told me – he caught a kelpie once. You catch it, and then it has to love you forever.' She rolled on top of me and kissed me hard, so hard the pearls pressed red circles into my sweat-damp skin, so hard my teeth nicked bloody on the inside of my mouth.

5. HAIR

We'd plumbed in the new bath, and I christened it that night with candles and bath oil. I never felt clean in this house; we'd scrubbed every inch but still kept catching this smell, rancid and salt-heavy like old seaweed. Although I hadn't said anything to Alice, I was worried that the walls were damp at the centre, the house rotten to the core.

I filled the bath full of the hottest water I could stand and slid right down, my nose the only dry part. I felt my muscles relax into liquid and heard my heart boom, boom, boom, steady as footsteps, steady as hoofbeats— And then there was nothing holding me up, and I was underwater, water in my nose, water in my mouth, and I couldn't breathe, and

I couldn't find the sides to pull myself out and I felt water in my throat, water in my lungs, and I sank down into the darkness.

Then Alice was pulling me out and I was crouching on the bathroom floor, coughing up water, breath rasping, and there was something wrong with my hand, something tight and tickling, and I reached for Alice, and my fist was wrapped all around with layers of hair. Long black hair, black as a winter night, and as long as a horse's mane.

6. A GLASS JAR

At first, I couldn't tell what was inside. When I pulled it out of the hidden dark place inside the bathroom wall, I thought it was jam. Beneath its jacket of dust, it looked plum-dark and sticky. My tongue tingled; I thought about toast and tea and the sweet smear of berries, sitting in the sun with Alice, the sound of her laugh. But that was silly: it was too late for sun, and Alice hadn't laughed for a long time.

I shook the jar and felt the thing inside smack off the glass, the wet press of meat. I gave the jar to Alice. She went to unscrew the lid, then thought better.

She looked at it for a long time. 'It's a liver,' she said.

'A what?' I asked, because I'd heard but I wished I hadn't. In Alice's shaking grip, the purplish thing in the jar quivered.

'It's what the kelpie leaves,' Alice said, and her voice didn't sound right. 'It drags you to the bottom of the loch and eats you, every single bit of you except your liver. If you find a liver on the shore, that's how you know the kelpie has eaten someone.'

7. A KNIFE

I wasn't surprised when Alice and I found the long thin silver knife wrapped in blackened grot beneath the floorboards. It wasn't easy: we had to pull up just about every rotting, stinking board in the house, and by then our hands were slick with blood and filth. Alice had told me that a silver knife through the heart is the only way to kill a kelpie, so if Alice's gran really had killed it, the knife was likely to be there somewhere. Her mistake, her haunting, was in keeping the thing. As proof? A memento? We'd never know. Then again, we knew that her bathtub drowning was due to a stroke. So I guess you can never really know anything.

Alice and I gathered up the ring and the paper and the horse and the pearls and the hair and the glass jar and the knife, and we put them all in a box. It took us a full eight hours to drive from Lenzie to Applecross. A full night's sleep through the silent winding dark. Up the cattle track and on to the empty cliff, where the land dropped away into the black snapping sea. Where there was not a sound except the wind. Where Alice's gran had done the worst imaginable thing to get what she wanted.

Together we walked to the edge of the cliff, and threw the box and all it contained down into the sea.

Then together we drove back to the house, holding hands between the front seats. A steady calm grew in our hearts; we knew that it was over, that we had cleansed the house and ourselves, that we had proven women's love was stronger than women's hate.

8. MORE

Approaching the front door, key outstretched, hands still held, hearts grown sweet, Alice and I stopped. Our hands unlinked. The doorknob was wrapped all around with layers of long, black hair.

CITY

We Regret To
Inform You
Jeannette Ng

Lodestones
Richard V. Hirst

The Cocktail Party in
Kensington Gets Out of Hand
Robert Shearman

Not A
Rig
James M

CITY

NOT ALL RIGHT

JAMES MILLER

The tower is visible from miles away. I like that. It is, perhaps, the only thing I do like. The curved glass rises above a jumble of cranes and catches the afternoon light. I might almost say it's beautiful, but it's not. 'Your uncle hardly ever uses the apartment,' said my mum. 'He's happy for you to stay while you look for a job.' She said it was a 'good opportunity'. Chance to move forward. And she's right, up to a point. She wants me to 'do something with my life'. Well, I'm doing it. I am. She just doesn't know what the fuck it is. As if there aren't more important things to do than suck corporate dick like my uncle. He's in New York at the moment. My uncle is a globalist cuck and I don't like him at all. His values are wrong but he knows something about money and power. How to get it, how to keep it, how to make it grow. I respect that about him. He made so much money so fast, my mum jokes he must have done a deal with the Devil.

The train clatters into Vauxhall station and I enjoy the sensation of my phone, throbbing with notifications in my pocket as I disembark. London is so fucking crowded. So many people. Down the stairs and out. Waiting at the junction for lights to change. A torrent of traffic and my heart pounding a little too fast. I need to get inside. I'm tempted to check my phone but I resist the impulse. Everyone else is staring at their devices but I'm not everyone else and anyway, I heard about all the snatches that take place, scum on scooters stealing phones straight out of people's hands. They do it in the blink of an eye and our pussy politically correct excuse for a police force won't chase them in case the thieves have an accident and hurt their precious little heads. Fucking joke. Fucking joke of a world we're living in. Anyone tries to steal my phone, I'll kill them.

A sigh of relief when I enter the apartment lobby. I relax a little, wiping some sweat from my face. The concierge glances up briefly from his computer screen and nods. There's a very good looking Oriental-type woman waiting at the lift lobby. Sharp black bob of hair, sharp cheekbones, smart business suit, high black heels. This makes me feel a little uneasy. I dislike sharing the lift with anybody. Dammit, if my uncle's apartment wasn't on the thirty-first floor I'd walk all the way up. A lift arrives and for a moment I consider waiting for another one – there are three lifts – but the woman actually smiles at me and without really meaning to I cut in front of her. A little rude, sure, but she needs to respect the natural order. There should be nothing more submissive than an Oriental bitch. Yeah, I fuck you long time. Up we go. The walls of the lift are mirrored so I don't know where to look. Thank fuck she gets off on the ninth floor. Up we go. I'm aware of my phone, vibrating with fresh notifications. I hold off checking it a few minutes longer. The suspense increases the thrill.

Inside. Cool air and darkness. Quite cold, in fact. I walk into the large living-dining area. The apartment has floor-to-ceiling windows but I've kept the blinds shut, cutting off the view south. My uncle boasted that on a clear day you can see all the way to Surrey but being so high up makes me feel uneasy, dizzy. At home, I have a room in the basement, where it's always dark, always quiet.

I keep the blinds where they are and look at my phone, giddy as I check my Twitter notifications. Two hundred and fifty-three in the last twenty minutes or so. I scroll through, scanning the retweets, the favourites, seeing who quote tweeted me, who's criticising me, who's getting a beating.

One catches my eye. Some fucking libtard calling me a fascist. Well, how fucking original. I click on his profile. Some cheese-eating beta cuck. 'Steve, 37, Proud Father, loves nature, Europe, History, Arsenal.' *Cuck.* A quick scroll through his feed to see if there's anything juicy in it I can use to quote tweet back and let some of my more militant followers give him a righteous kicking. He likes to retweet Hillary Clinton. *Loser!* Anyway, he only has 230 followers. Irrelevant. Pond scum. My account, @IncarceratedEarth, has a verified blue tick and 57,000 followers. And my mum thinks I'm doing nothing with my life. I put down my phone and open my MacBook.

>•<

When I look up again from the screen I realise it's one a.m. A lot has happened in the last few hours. I got into it – I mean really into it – with some feminazi *Guardian* journalist about Muslim rapists. Bitch ended up blocking me. I take that as a victory. That and all the brainwashed self-hating betas and intersectionalists who piled in trying to help her out. It's funny. The insults are still coming in. *Cuck-off,* LOL; *Fucking Nazi,* no, you're the Nazi dickwad; *I bet you've never had a girlfriend,* well that's original, I'll jizz in your wife's face you limp prick. *Are you scared now?* says another one. Hmm... the Twitter handle is @ and the profile picture is also a black square. I click on the cuck's profile – probably some alt-left Antifa ISIS lover – but the page is taking an age to load. So much for the superfast broadband that's meant to come integrated with the building. Anyway, enough. I get up, rub my eyes and stretch a bit. I ought to try and sleep but it's hard because this... this thing, this war we're fighting, it never stops, it never ends. And anyway, I hate London, I fucking despise it. Londonistan. A no-go shithole of Sharia-loving terrorists and elitist globalist pigs. Still, tomorrow I ought to send my CV off to a few more banks and funds. That's what I'm here for. To get a 'proper job'. Like my uncle said.

I keep the blinds shut and go into the master bedroom. The apartment has two bedrooms but the other room is locked. I don't know what my uncle keeps in there. I turn my phone to silent, trying to resist the temptation to keep checking Twitter, and lie in the darkness waiting to see if sleep will come. Perhaps a wank would help but I don't really feel horny or anything. The longer I lie here the more I think I can hear something. A sort of faint knocking sound. This is only my second night in the apartment. Last night I fell asleep almost immediately but I had some uncomfortable dreams. Anyway... The sound... I try to ignore it. It's very faint, after all. I mean, it's so soft, so much in the background I ought to be able to ignore it. A low sort of pulsing noise. Perhaps it's something to do with the air conditioning or the pipes. It's almost as if it's running through the walls and up through the bed. I try lying one way, then another and then, admitting that the sound is bothering me more than it should, I get up to see if I can better identify the source. I almost wonder if I'm imagining it, as if it's stuck in my head somehow. Like if I'm hearing my own heartbeat. I mooch around the kitchen, wondering if it could be coming from the fridge or the freezer. No difference, no discernible source. It's still there, ambient but annoying, seemingly coming from everywhere.

I open the blinds, wondering if the sound comes from outside. Some late-night construction work? Directly opposite the tower is a huge hole where they're due to build another, even taller skyscraper. I guess my uncle will lose his amazing view. I press my ear to the cold glass. Is that it? Perhaps someone is having a party elsewhere in the building? Could that be it? A bassline carried up through the walls and pipes. It's three-thirty a.m.

Another sound – like a door slamming – and this makes me jump. I turn my head, straining my ears for more. But nothing, just this faint persistent tapping. I decide to log back onto Twitter. Eight hundred and ninety-five notifications. Almost at once the noise seems to disappear. I scroll through looking for suitable snowflakes to roast. There – a feminazi professor from a liberal arts college calling free speech advocates fascists. Yeah. I quote tweet her tweet and @ her college, *Do you know your professor is advocating the suppression of free speech and abuse of intellectual freedom?* I roar and fire it off. Some of my loyal followers pick up the tweet and start retweeting the hell out of it. Nice. Not that her college will do anything. Universities these days are the biggest enemies of free thinking the world has ever known, dominated by political correctness, but I imagine the bitch will piss her pants when she wakes up and checks her phone. Heh. That'll trigger her.

When I next look up I notice slivers of brightness behind the blinds. Morning already? My neck, back and eyes are hurting. I sit for a minute, blinking. The noise. I think the noise has gone. It probably was a party. I'll complain to the concierge later. I get the sense, though, that the building is mostly empty, my uncle said as much. Foreigners buy the flats as investments and never move in. It's everything that's wrong with London. A real country wouldn't tolerate this. No homes for its own native population.

I scroll through my notifications, almost numb to it at this point. I compose a couple of responses but can't fit the sentiment to the character limit. Perhaps I should do another of my broadcasts on Periscope? I ought to try and leverage the fact that I'm actually in London to my advantage, to support some of the points we like to make on Brietbart and InfoWars and elsewhere. But I need an edge, a scoop, a strong angle. My last couple of broadcasts didn't get nearly enough traction.

Again, that weird account with the black squares in the Twitter handle catches my eye. The same message, *Are you scared yet?* I click on the profile and again get the 'loading' icon. Wait, here we go, their page comes up. Hmm... weird... only one tweet – the one they just tweeted at me. And they're only following one person. Me. How many followers – what? That can't be right. 1.1 million. How can they have over a million followers and just one tweet? What is this bullshit? Must be a bot, a fake account, fake followers. Must be. I admit I feel a momentary shiver of paranoia as I see this. I mean, there are people who want to silence me. People who hate the truth. The architects of the New World Order, the globalists who want total control, Soros and his ilk, the Illuminati, agents of the MSM, even the intelligence services. I wouldn't put it past them to hack my account, report me for 'hate speech'. I need to check my virus protection. These days I can't be too careful.

A loud bang, like a door slamming. Or a door *actually* slamming. I get up, abruptly dizzy. The door to the master bedroom is open, the door to the other bedroom is closed. I try the handle again but of course it's still locked. I'm overtired. I ought to get out, eat. Stay off Twitter a bit. Calm myself.

I put on yesterday's clothes and ride the lift to the lobby. No sign of the concierge. I step out and the noise of the traffic is overwhelming. I'm puzzled to see several women, six or seven plus a number of kids, gathered by the entrance to the tower, crying and looking miserable, the older ladies with their arms around the younger ones. Clearly none of them are native English. Each woman holds a bouquet of flowers and I watch as one by one they place them on the pavement just in front of the entrance. The oldest clutches a crucifix and holds up her head, muttering something or praying in Romanian or God knows what language. Weird.

I walk around trying to find somewhere to get food. The neighbourhood seems to be under construction, cranes and scaffolding, the steel skeletons of new apartment blocks rising up around chunky concrete cores. I remember seeing a Pret a Manger in an apartment block opposite the bus station by the Tube. It's empty inside and of course the woman who serves me isn't English either. I order a couple of croissants and a latte. I was thinking everywhere seemed a bit quiet and I realise that's because it's a Saturday, early for a Saturday morning. I'm losing track of time.

The day is hot and the air swirls with specks of golden dust and grit. I sit, perched on a stool, looking out. I have this sense of people watching me from the dark windows of the apartment blocks opposite. How many windows are there in London? I know it's just a trick of the light but I keep thinking there are people standing there, faceless, looking down: like mannequins or statues. I focus on my phone instead, scrolling through the feed, retweeting a few good Pepe memes: Pepe thumbing his nose at an image of Angela Merkel mocked up with a Hitler moustache and a swastika armband; Pepe covering his face in horror as another boat full of 'refugees' lands on a beach; Pepe pissing on the EU flag; Pepe high-fiving Trump. I love that cheeky little frog.

I keep myself amused doing this for a while, but it's difficult. I hear sirens and a police helicopter hovering up above. I know we're close to Parliament and for a moment I wonder if there's been another terrorist attack. Londonistan. Much of the city is no-go for us white people, the native English. We've been ethnically cleansed. Whole areas ruled by Sharia law, women in burqas, the call to prayer – and the whites who remain are even worse. Paedophiles and people smugglers who cruise the streets looking to force underage girls into marriage, 'hipsters' who ape the degenerate manners of their ethnic inferiors. No, I breathe in and tell myself this is normal – the sirens, the helicopter – this is usual. I live with Mother in a small village in Norfolk and sometimes I don't leave the house for months. I mean, it's better not to because this world, the outside world, it's hardly real anyway. Not any more. We have to fight to get it back, to render the truth. A reckoning is coming. A huge reckoning.

I keep my head down. The police helicopter is above and the chatter of its rotor blades cuts right through me. When I do glance up I see a man standing on his balcony, ten floors high. Is he looking at me? At the junction, the lights are green – I hurry past the bus station full of Muslims, refugees, thugs, hipsters – then I cross to the other side of the main road and back into the tower.

The concierge is back at his desk. He doesn't look up as I come in and for a moment I consider asking him about the noise but it seems a little silly in the light of day. I remember my uncle telling me the tower has a gym with a sauna, swimming pool and steam room in the basement. I don't normally like to expose my body in public but perhaps a turn in the sauna will do some good. Relax me. I follow the sign, go through some doors and down some stairs. The tower has a number of basement levels, mostly resident parking, but the leisure centre seems to be a mezzanine below the entrance lobby. Dim lights and I'm surprised to find the door locked. A note has been pasted over it: WE APOLOGISE TO RESIDENTS, THE SWIMMING POOL, GYMNASIUM & SPA ARE CLOSED DUE TO ESSENTIAL MAINTENANCE. What the fuck? How crummy is that? If he was ever here my uncle would be pissed. I wait a moment, wondering if I can still hear it – the *sound*. Down here the air is surprisingly cold, not warm and muggy as I'd expect close to a swimming pool. I don't think I can hear anything, only the thrum of the air conditioning. Then, a sudden loud *clang* from behind the closed door, like a heavy object is being dropped, and then dragged, back and forth. A banging, a scraping. It must be maintenance workers, doing whatever they need to do to fix the pool. A harsh, hostile noise.

I don't like it here. I go back to the lobby.

'What's up with the pool?' I ask the concierge.

He blinks at me. 'It's closed.' He shuts his laptop screen as if he doesn't want me to see what he's looking at. Probably porn. Must be boring as hell doing his job.

'I know that,' I snap, 'I can read.'

'There was a chlorine leak.'

'When will it be fixed?'

'I don't know. You'll have to speak to the building manager on Monday. Could be some time.'

'I thought… I mean, there are people down there, right?'

He tilts his head as if he hasn't heard me properly. 'No, it's a Saturday. Next week.'

Fuck this. I stand a moment, wondering what else to say. The dude is a typical cuck and by his accent he's foreign, another East European sponger, so I'll probably be wasting my time. I'm about to go when I notice the bouquets that I saw left outside earlier by the weeping women have been moved into the lobby, neatly arranged in a corner by the symbolic white sofa that no one ever sits on.

'What's with that?'

'That? Oh. The relatives leave flowers here. Once a year.'

'Why?'

I can tell he doesn't want to tell me. 'Well,' he fidgets behind his desk, 'when the tower was being built there was an accident. I don't really know what happened but four workers were killed. A crane snapped. It was a big tragedy. The families come over from Bulgaria each year to pay their respects.'

'You just leave the flowers there?'

'For a little while, yes.'

I'm not sure what to say about this. I despise sentimentality in every form and I'm surprised they're allowed to clutter up the lobby with this crap. Flowers give me hay fever. My nose itches. I have a lot of allergies.

As I'm here I figure I might as well ask about the noise. 'Did you…' I begin, 'I mean, was there a party here last night? I thought I heard something, a sound in the building.'

'A party? I don't know, sir. I wasn't on night duty.' This guy is obviously a waste of space.

Back in the apartment. I need to work out the air conditioning because it's fucking freezing. I actually put on a hoodie. In contrast my phone feels dangerously hot as it connects with the Wi-Fi. Five hundred and twenty-three notifications. I start to glance at them but it's too much. My mouth is dry and my head hurts. I plug my phone in and flop down on the bed. Grey waves of exhaustion. Black pricks and dots in my vision. Then I pick it up again, not wanting to admit I'm worried. No, not worried, *concerned*; no, not concerned, *curious* – yeah, I'm curious to know if that weird account with the black squares has messaged me again. But there are so many fucking notifications. It's like half the Internet is screaming at me. Ought to get some rest so I have the energy to be on it again a bit later. I might even try to meet up with some of my fellow bloggers and tweeters. There was some talk of a pub meet even though I hate alcohol and pubs and face-to-face interactions are draining.

My phone vibrates with a reply notification – this only happens when someone with a bit of leverage retweets or @'s me, not just any old prick. A moment of excitement and then a stab of panic. That fucking account again. *.@IncarceratedEarth are you scared yet?* Fuck this, my thumb stabs to block the account even though this goes against my principles. People block me, I don't block them. I actually believe in free speech. But wait, that can't be right. When I thumb the tab there's no option to block or even mute the account. And now it has 2.3 million followers.

And still just the one tweet. I fling my phone away. And yes, there it is again. I can hear it. That sound, like a thrumming *thunk thunk thunk*. It's almost like the sound is inside me, like I can hear my heart but it's everywhere, as if my bones are vibrating. Fuck. I press a pillow over my face, press my hands over my ears but it makes no difference. It's still there – faint, but I can hear it. Fuck. This is no good. I force myself to breathe, in and out, in and out, slow deep breaths like Mum taught me. I knew it was a mistake to come to London, a mistake to try and 'get a job' like she wants me to. I get up again. It's so cold in here, like a refrigerator. I can't find the air-con controls, can't work out how to open the windows or if it's even possible to do so because we're so high up. Like being locked in a glass coffin. But this is globalisation – everything the fucking same, all of us locked in fucking glass fucking coffins. Fuck, fuck, fuck. I fling the pillow across the room.

Then I hear a door slam. Again.

This time I'm certain. A door inside the flat.

Has someone come into the apartment?

My uncle said something about how the tower had a maid service – someone could come and clean the place, even make the bed if I wanted them to and who knows, maybe they suck dick if you pay them enough. I didn't pay much attention but that could be it. Like the maid has a key and has come to do some tidying before my uncle gets back.

I pick up my phone, which feels like the only hot thing in the place, and walk into the corridor. 'Hey,' I call out, 'is anyone there?' But there's no one. The blinds are drawn in the living room, my bag and some of my stuff are still scattered across the sofa and the floor. I don't want to open the blinds. It makes me feel sick to think about looking outside. I go back to the bedroom. This is stupid. I'm just really overtired. But then I notice that the door to the other room, the second bedroom, is a tiny bit ajar. Just a fraction.

Wait.

This is impossible. It was locked before, it was definitely locked. I must be hallucinating with fatigue. I gently push it with one shaking finger, and the door swings open.

Another Twitter notification pings onto the screen. That account. *.@IncarceratedEarth you're scared now, aren't you?*

I meet the others in a pub in Soho. There's Dan who tweets as @DanTheMan (10K followers) a leading men's rights activist, and Frank who tweets as @FrankUK (8.5K followers) and sometimes writes op-ed pieces for various alt-right blogs. I'm not quite sure what else he does. I've never actually met them before in real life and it's all a bit awkward. Why did we agree to meet in Soho anyway? The pub is crowded and noisy. Not our sort of people. Frank clearly drinks a lot of lager – I could tell he was unimpressed when I ordered an elderflower cordial. He keeps going on about how he's mates with Tommy Robinson and how the traitors in the Tory party are going to do the dirty on us with Brexit. Dan drinks vodka on the rocks. He has bleached white teeth, a fake tan and slick black hair and looks like he spends a lot of time ironing his shirt and thinking about what sort of shoes to wear. I notice he's positioned himself in such a way that he can see himself in the mirror opposite our table. Is he smiling at us, or himself? In any case, I think they're both a little disappointed by me, Incarcerated Earth, in the flesh, like I'm meant to be continually spitting truth and fire twenty-four seven. Our phones keep buzzing with Twitter notifications and that breaks up the conversation further. Whilst we might be ideologically aligned I'm not sure if we really have much in common.

I'm preoccupied. I don't understand what's going on with that door, with that room. I sent my uncle a message earlier, asking if someone else was staying in the flat. Why else would there be an unmade bed in the room, a tangle of white sheets, a couple of pillows? The doors to the fitted wardrobe were open and there was a black suitcase inside, and an old coat hanging up. In one corner, on a tray, were several large black candles, melted down and dripping with dried wax, and a small twisted figure made from straw and wire next to a plastic skull, roughly adult sized, the sort that would glow in the dark. A number of burn marks on the floor, forming a circular shape. Then I… I don't know… I went out of the room and shut the door. I was sick for a bit in the toilet, painful dry heaves as there was nothing inside me. Even while I was puking the noise wouldn't stop, I could still hear it, thumping away.

My phone is flashing – it's my uncle, trying to Facetime me. He must have got the message I sent him about the other bedroom.

'I have to take this,' I tell the others, picking up and stepping outside. 'Hi, Uncle John.'

'What the actual fuck Paul.' My uncle appears to be walking briskly down a street in Manhattan, his face uncomfortably close to the phone, his yellowish teeth and large hairy nostrils fill the screen.

'I—'

'Alex at Sterns Basher tells me he still hasn't received your CV.'

'I'm—'

'Don't bullshit me, Paul. Sebastian at Bar Cap says you didn't show up for the interview, sent some lame pussy-ass excuse about having a migraine.'

'I did have—'

'Oh, bring me the world's smallest violin. Who the fuck doesn't have a migraine these days? What the fuck are you doing?'

'I've been—'

'Busy? Busy? You think you're fucking busy? Doing what? Wanking off to pictures of Donald Trump? Don't shit me, son. I know all about your crappy little Twitter account. You wouldn't know what busy was if… hang on, I've got another call.' To my surprise he retrieves another phone from his pocket while keeping the one he's using to talk to me trained to his face. 'I said not now!' He puts the other phone away. 'I'll believe you're busy when you're negotiating a corporate buyout of a FTSE 100 company. Do you understand? Don't answer me when I'm talking! I've been twisting arms for you, Paul, I've been calling in favours. I've been putting my reputation on the line. I know you're a useless waste of space but you're my sister's kid and your mother is a good woman. What she did to deserve you I'll never know. Now stop tweeting your nasty shit to your fellow losers, turn off PornHub and send your goddam CV to Alex. Do it now!'

'But—'

He's gone. I stare at the blank screen. I can't face going back into the pub and pretending to talk to those two dickheads any longer. I need to get away. I summon an Uber. The driver is called Mohammed – of course he's fucking called Mohammed – and he tries to engage me in friendly conversation as we crawl through the West End. 'Did you just jump ship from Syria or what?' I snap at him.

'Oh no, sir, I was born here,' he prattles on.

I scroll through my notifications, my palm sweaty. I see Hillary Clinton has tweeted something snarky at Trump. *Eat Paedo pizza you cunt bitch* I tweet @ her. But this is a bad tweet, lacking finesse. I delete it – although it's already been retweeted and favourited half a dozen times – and then, another reply from that account. *.@IncarceratedEarth you're scared now, aren't you? You're really scared.* Right, I think, fuck you. I'm going to roast this cunt. My fingers are sweating, slipping against the screen of my smartphone as I quote tweet his tweet. *Does anyone know this alt-left fascist troll who keeps threatening me?* I tweet. We sit in traffic. Mohammed keeps on talking, oblivious to the fact that I've given up pretending to listen to him. I'm staring at my phone, waiting for a response. The device is hot again, the battery down to 21%. But there's nothing. No retweets, no faves, no responses. I check my feed, making sure I sent the tweet. There it is – the tweet was sent – it's out there. But I don't have any notifications. Nothing. I keep refreshing, my phone getting hotter and hotter, the battery draining down. Still nothing. Finally, we arrive, the Uber pulling up outside. 'Hey, nice place,' says Mohammed. I remind myself to give him a one-star rating. ISIS sympathiser.

I glance up at the skyscraper, the fifty stories of sheer, smooth glass. Blue lights illuminate the summit, but otherwise it is almost completely dark. Just a single light, about two thirds of the way up, flashing on and off. Doors to the entrance lobby slide open. No sign of the concierge and the bouquets that were neatly arranged in a corner have been disturbed, flowers everywhere, stems and scattered petals across the white marble floor, streaks of water from the split packages. I check my phone: almost out of battery and still no notifications. It's dark in the lobby, just an eerie blue light from the CCTV monitors, and surprisingly cold, the air conditioning on full blast.

I ride the lift up. Feeling weak, dizzy. The noise is back again, more than ever, like a steady sort of drumming. It's in the walls, it's in the floors, it's in the lift itself. It's vibrating through as I exit on the thirty-first floor. Cold up here too, so cold my breath plumes white in the still air of the apartment. I see flower petals on the white carpet floor, they must have got stuck on my shoes. My phone vibrates again, 8% battery but a notification! So loud now, the drumming, a constant, infernal pounding. Grey spots flicker in front of my eyes as I check the screen. That account. It's that account again. The door to my uncle's apartment is open and the light inside is flashing, on and off, on and off. I'm shivering in the bitter cold. *@IncarceratedEarth You're going to die now.* And then *@IncarceratedEarth Are you scared?* My phone flashes once as the battery drops to 2% and then shuts down. It falls from my fingers. A monstrous noise emerges from the flat, a continuous metallic roar, like a thousand air conditioning units being ripped to shreds and the floor is vibrating, the walls shaking. I drop to my knees, sobbing, my head in my hands. Enough, I think. Enough!

〉•〈

White Dawn @whitedawn100

Hey does anyone know what happened to @IncarceratedEarth ? His feed has been quiet for days now?

Steve5000@HARDBREXITNOW

Replying to @whitedawn100
Did you see this?
www.standardnews.co.uk 'Alt-Right Twitter personality found dead…'

White Dawn @whitedawn100

Replying to @HARDBREXITNOW
No fucking way

Steve5000@HARDBREXITNOW

Replying to @whitedawn100
Yeah, says he was found dead 'under mysterious circumstances'

White Dawn @whitedawn100

Replying to @HARDBREXITNOW
I don't believe it

White Dawn @whitedawn100

Replying to @HARDBREXITNOW
What circumstances? Still trying to ascertain cause of death. What does that mean?

Gary101@TRUMP4EVER
Replying to @HARDBREXITNOW @whitedawn100
They got him. Like what happened to @JewishGenocide in
California.

White Dawn @whitedawn100
Replying to @HARDBREXITNOW @TRUMP4EVER
I thought that was a home invasion. Some Mexicans killed
him and stole his Dodge.

Gary101@TRUMP4EVER
Replying to @HARDBREXITNOW @whitedawn100
False flag. Anyway, I did some research into the place he
was staying. Kinda weird.

Steve5000@HARDBREXITNOW
Replying to @whitedawn100 @TRUMP4EVER
How so?

Gary101@TRUMP4EVER
Replying to @HARDBREXITNOW @whitedawn100
Lotta people died building it. Crane collapse. Cheap labour
from Eastern Europe.

Steve5000@HARDBREXITNOW
Replying to @whitedawn100 @TRUMP4EVER
No more of this when we #leave, who cares about some
gypos anyway?

Gary101@TRUMP4EVER

Replying to @HARDBREXITNOW @whitedawn100
You need to look into it. There's a sub forum over on
4Chan. I'll link you.

@■■■■■■■

Replying to @HARDBREXITNOW @whitedawn100
@TRUMP4EVER
Yes. Yes. You do that. You look into it.

Gary101@TRUMP4EVER

Replying to @■■■■■■■ @HARDBREXITNOW
@whitedawn100
Who the fuck are you? #prick

@■■■■■■■

Replying to @HARDBREXITNOW @whitedawn100
@TRUMP4EVER
You'll find out. We knew your friend @IncarceratedEarth.
We were there. We held his hand at the end. We looked into
his eyes. Poor little boy. #areyouscaredyet
Are you?

THE COCKTAIL PARTY IN
KENSINGTON GETS OUT OF
HAND

ROBERT SHEARMAN

Still no discussion of a fee, but that in itself didn't worry Alex Fitch, that usually played to his advantage. Once it was all over a client would incline towards generosity – either in gratitude of a job well done (and Alex always made sure the job was well done), or, frankly, in an embarrassed rush to get him off the premises. But the latest client didn't look the sort to embarrass easily. She had a Kensington confidence, all brusqueness and matter-of-fact superiority – there was none of the self-justifying brashness you might get in Bloomsbury, and she was worlds away from the needy guilt of Maida Vale. He'd got the usual speech prepared, the one full of the reassuring stuff, the one where he'd say she shouldn't be ashamed of what she wanted, everybody had their kinks, it wasn't his place to judge. He didn't dare to give the speech. She didn't need his speech. Even for a Kensington bitch, that threw him, just slightly.

She was an old woman, they were often old – but quite how old he couldn't begin to guess. She could have been as young as seventy. It wouldn't have surprised him if she'd been a hundred. The face was the usual mess of wrinkles and pits, but for all that the skin was unblemished, and her eyes were so bright. He doubted she'd ever been beautiful, but attractive – yes, certainly. She cleared her throat, he realised he was staring. She said, 'You might think you recognise me. I'm telling you right now. You don't.' He agreed.

'Strip,' she said, and he didn't have to take orders, he hadn't accepted the commission yet, but she didn't say it rudely, and he obeyed. He stood there naked before her. 'I don't need to look at all that,' she said, 'that's not relevant. Lie down on the ground the way I'll need you, get into position.' He did so, flat on his stomach, chin flush against the floor.

Just the way she had shown him in the diagram. The floor was cold – he flinched at that – and she told him that during the actual performance he'd be quite comfortable on soft thick carpet.

She didn't touch him, but still he thought he could feel her, as she stood over, staring down at his pasty white body, as she assessed him in detail. 'It really *is* pasty white,' she said, and she sounded pleased, 'they got that bit right. And no tattoos? Not even any little ones, I know sometimes you hide them away between the folds of your joints...?' He confirmed that he had no tattoos. 'Good,' she said. 'I don't want anything to distract the guests. I want the pasty white to be pristine.'

A little while longer lying there, he heard her walk about him from side to side. 'Good,' she said, 'it's very good,' but she didn't seem to be speaking to him, and he didn't reply. 'We'll need the mouth open,' she said, and he obliged; 'not as wide as that, yes, better. An opened mouth tips the head upward, makes it more of a feature. And I want the eyes open too, can you do that? Can you do that without blinking? Think glass eyes. Think your eyes are glass, that you're dead, and we've taken out your eyes, and we've put glass beads inside the sockets.'

She didn't say anything else for a long while; then, a little impatiently, 'I finished the inspection ten minutes ago, you may as well get up.' So he did. She told him that he was hired, and said well done.

'I'm not going to pretend there won't be a little pain,' she said. 'I'm not going to pretend that you won't get stepped on. Obviously, we will try to minimise that, but accidents will happen, there'll be a lot of guests at the party, and people get clumsy when they're drunk. It is *imperative* when they step on you that you do not cry out. It would destroy the illusion. And, it goes without saying, getting up and remonstrating with them is *completely* out of order.' He said that he understood. 'But there might be something I can give you to help,' she went on. 'Bend over.'

She opened a bottle of rubbing alcohol, and splashed a little of its contents on his back, on his arse, the backs of his legs. She massaged it hard into his skin. He felt her bare hands kneading away for all they were worth. She grunted as she worked, she really put some effort into it. Alex felt curiously pleased. Her hands were surprisingly smooth, or was that just the alcohol? 'I'm not really sure this'll do any good,' she said, 'but if nothing else, it smells nice.'

And then she turned him round so they were face to face – and he thought, *Wouldn't it have been simpler for her to have walked around to me?* – but no, she'd taken him by the shoulders and swivelled him about and he'd swung as easily as if he were on a pivot. And she was looking into his eyes again, and once more she held his gaze so strongly. 'I want you to understand,' she said. 'This isn't for me. This is for my husband. Do you see? All of it, it's for my husband.' Was this it, then? That twinge of embarrassment he'd been looking for? And he fumbled to start the reassuring speech he'd been taught, but if she'd wanted to hear it it was too late, she had moved away now and was putting the rubbing alcohol away, the moment had been lost.

'There's nothing more to say, is there?' she said – again, to herself. 'I don't think so. It's an easy job, I think. Easy, compared to what some of us have to do. You're lucky. Remember that.'

'Thank you,' he said. 'For the opportunity.'
She nodded. 'Come on then.'
'Now?'
'Of course now. The party's already started.'

>•<

He took in as much of the room as he could. He supposed
he wouldn't be in a position to see it again for a long while.
It looked moneyed, but not especially ornate; he had an
impression of rich browns on the walls and furniture; it was
smaller than he was expecting.

'There's a position for you,' she said, 'right here.' He was
to be the centrepiece of the room, lying down on the very
middle of the carpet. To one side there was a tiger rug, to
the other a grizzly bear. Their fur looked so soft and glossy,
their glass eyes stared sightlessly out into the distance. 'Do
you want me to do that thing with the mouth?' he said.
Because they were so fierce, their teeth white and sharp,
they looked ready to bite.

'Let's not get too ambitious,' the woman said.

He lay down between the two other rugs, and, mouth
excepted, imitated their posture as best he could. And for
a moment her cool reserve was broken, he heard her giggle
and even give a little clap.

'Oh, you're just perfect!' she said. 'The tiger's stripes, the
brown of the bear – and you, in the middle, so pasty white!
What a contrast! What fun!'

She left the room then – or, at least, Alex suspected she left.
There was silence for a while. He was not uncomfortable, the
carpet beneath him was warm. The rubbing alcohol made

him feel sticky; he thought he smelled sweet as a toffee apple. He breathed shallowly through his open mouth, trying his best to make sure that his body stayed flat and still. He was glad she hadn't wanted his mouth in a roar position, it was an effort to keep it open as it was. He kept his eyes fixed on nothing in particular, let them blur. He thought of glass eyes, hardened them like glass.

And then there was a rumble behind him, not too distant, not as distant as he would have liked – and he didn't know at first what it could be, and it was footsteps, and chatter, and laughter, and then party guests were entering the room – the performance was starting, he was on! – and his body tensed, and he felt a flush of panic, and he nearly gulped, scratched, turned his head, he nearly did everything he could to lose his composure.

The guests talked with such excitement, with so much emphatic animation, you'd have thought they'd never talked before, that talking was some exquisite treat they had to make the most of. The men were loud, the women shrill. And already they sounded to Alex so vague and inhuman somehow, but he managed to pick out the odd snatch of conversation. The men talked of cars and cigars and the stock market and the weather. The women talked of shoes and hair and the weather. Some of them trod upon his hand. Some of them dropped cigarette ash on him.

He wondered if any of the guests admired him, had stopped to comment upon the exquisite new rug at their feet. He supposed some might have done. The words all sounded strange and silly. The men talked of tough measures and hard truths, the women talked of riots in the street. Alex decided to ignore them all.

He just hoped he looked good next to the tiger and the bear. Not as ferocious, maybe, but just as proud. That it'd seem he too had been hunted once, on the savannah, or wherever tigers and bears come from – that he'd been thought *worth* hunting. That someone had pursued him because he had a good pelt. And the tiger and the bear – there was no shame for them lying next to him, they'd been *kings* of their domain, they'd been untamed Nature, and Man had fought them fair and square and they'd lost bravely and here they were now as rugs upon the carpet but that wasn't humiliation, it was *commemoration*, they were displayed as noble savages in all their wild dignity, there was honour to the fact that they were here at this party for the great and the good, it raised them above the rest of their kind, this was as much their party as anyone else's. And Alex knew he couldn't compete with that, not really, not at all. He was no tiger. He could never be a bear. But he hoped nonetheless that when they looked down at him the guests would think there was honour to him too, that they'd think he belonged.

Someone dropped a canapé right in front of Alex's face. He didn't let it break his concentration. He didn't let his eyes change focus. The canapé was warm, and there was pastry around it, and Alex thought he could smell chicken.

The men talked of shoes, the women talked of cars, they both talked of all the executions, and how they laughed.

Alex didn't know how long this went on for. And then there was a new sound, breaking down the wall of chatter: a gong. 'Dinner is served!' called a voice, it must have been the woman who hired him – 'Dinner is served, come along, bring your drinks, come along!' And it seemed to Alex as if all the guests abandoned all pretence of polite decorum, they stampeded to the door, maybe they were very hungry, maybe they hadn't eaten dinner for a long while.

The door was closed. The sudden silence made Alex's head throb, he felt a little sick.

He stretched, and every one of his muscles groaned.

'Don't move,' said the bear.

And it was the bear, Alex was sitting up and rubbing life back into his legs, he was looking straight at the bear when it spoke.

'I'm sorry?' said Alex.

'Don't move,' said the bear. 'Get back into position. They could be back at any moment.'

'Leave him be,' said the tiger. 'It's obviously his first time.'

'The pack is only as strong as its weakest link,' said the bear. 'And he is clearly our weakest link. Back into position now, little man, or I'll rip your fucking head off.'

Alex lay back down again. Arms spread, chin on floor. He wished he hadn't moved in the first place, the muscles had woken up and couldn't believe he was proposing to subject them to the same ordeal all over again.

'I'm sorry,' whispered Alex. 'So, what, are you guys dressed up as wild animals? Or. Or, are you a real bear and tiger? Or what?'

They ignored him, or they didn't break character – they didn't answer him at any rate. And after a while Alex began to doubt he'd even heard the animals speak to him at all, maybe he was asleep, could he fall asleep with his eyes wide open? Because his eyes were hard and staring, he was still thinking of glass, they were glass beads in dead sockets.

The bear had been too cautious. The guests were gone a

long time. How long could it take to eat a dinner? Even if it were a banquet – and Alex thought it may have been a banquet, maybe it had seven courses and coffees and mints for afters – even so, why was everyone gone so long? Alex became certain the party was over. The job was done, and he'd been left here on the floor, forgotten, the joke was on him – and maybe the woman was standing over him now, laughing silently at his unquestioning obedience, this was a test. He should get up, get up right now and demand to be paid. And yet still he stared ahead, and still his mouth hung open, and his mouth felt so dry, he felt his tongue was hard and cracked, his tongue was draped over the bottom teeth like it was a rug and there was no life to it any more and it wouldn't move now even if Alex tried – *I'm going to get up*, he thought, *I'm going to get up, I'm getting up. Up I get.*

And then, before he could flex that first joint, before he could stir that first muscle, the doors were flung open, and the guests were back, and the party was resumed.

So this was the way it would be – every few hours the party would be interrupted by the gong. The guests would file out to enjoy their dinner. But they'd be back sooner or later, and the drinking and the chatter would begin again. People would stand about and make jokes and talk of nothing and stand on his hand and let ash drop on to his bare back. Were they different guests each time? Were they the same ones as before? – breaking from dinner only to let their food go down, all this socialising was just something to fill in time whilst their stomachs made space for the next bout of food, they would glut themselves on it – and Alex imagined them all as fat and shiny, that by now their swollen bellies were breaking out of their trousers and dresses. He couldn't see them. He didn't know.

During the dinners, during the periods of silence, he might try speaking to the bear and the tiger. There was never a word from either of them. He whispered, he didn't want to upset the bear's professionalism. And then, in time, he'd try to provoke the bear, he told the bear its fur was mangy, that he'd seen grizzlier things at the petting zoo, that it was barely a bear at all. He dared it to rip his head off then and there if it thought it was hard enough. Still, never a word, never a single movement from its rug fur body. Though Alex thought he detected growing disdain from the bear, from the tiger a sighed disappointment.

Alex kept going, he fixed his thoughts on what he was doing the job for. Mainly, for his family. For his wife and kids. He tried to remember when he'd last seen his wife. Probably about the same time he'd seen the kids, that made sense. It was quite a long time ago. He must make sure he saw them all again soon. Otherwise, what was the point? He'd see his wife again soon, he'd go visit, right after this new job was over. He'd see the kids. He tried to remember how many kids he had. He stopped counting at seven. He might well have more now, whenever he went to see her his wife was pregnant, he didn't know how she managed that. He didn't quite like to ask.

And he thought of his eyes, he thought they were glass beads. He knew they were glass now. He could have prodded them with his fingers just to be sure, he could jab at them with his fingernails and he wouldn't even blink. He'd have done it too, just for fun – but that would have meant moving his body, and he wasn't ever going to move again.

The half-eaten canapé was still on the carpet just in front of his face. It had long cooled. The guests had trodden all over Alex, but somehow they had always missed the canapé. The pastry hadn't even flaked, it looked firm and plump.

One day, after she'd sounded the dinner gong, and all her guests had gone, the woman knelt down beside Alex and fed him the canapé.

'It's all right,' she said. 'You can eat this.' She broke the canapé into little pieces, and one by one put them into his open mouth. They melted on his tongue. She stroked the back of his neck as they did so.

'Thank you,' he whispered.

'Ssh,' she said, still stroking him.

'How much longer?' he asked.

She stopped stroking him, got up, and left.

>•<

He liked to think he was her favourite, though Alex had to admit there was very little evidence for that. She fed the other rugs too from time to time – vol-au-vents, sausage rolls, whatever came to hand. Once she sat with the tiger and fed him an entire bowl of crisps, gently putting them into his mouth one at a time and waiting for the crunch before moving on to another. That took perseverance. Still, Alex thought he was the favourite anyway, because he was the one she had fed first.

And one day she left the dinner table and came to see them, and nuzzled their heads one by one, and then she said, 'Come on.' And Alex thought maybe she was talking to him, but no, it was to the bear, to the bear.

'Come on,' she said, her voice a little harder. 'I shan't tell you again.'

Alex had turned his head and was sitting up on his haunches, and he was watching, and he knew that was bad – and he only felt a little better when he realised the tiger was on his haunches watching too.

And the bear rug seemed to shiver, and it looked like a sigh. Then it heaved itself up to its feet, slowly, painfully. It teetered a little, trying to get balance, it hadn't been on its feet for such a long time. It steadied. It stood a full eight foot tall, and dwarfed the woman who waited fearlessly by its side.

The woman turned, and went to the door. The bear sighed once more, slumped its awful brute shoulders in resignation, shuffled after her.

The woman closed the door behind them.

'What was that about?' said Alex.

But the tiger just shook its head, settled back into position. Alex did the same.

It wasn't ten minutes before the door opened again. And the bear was back. Its gait was still unsteady. It grabbed on to a cocktail table for purchase, it looked as if it were in shock.

'What happened?' hissed the tiger.

'I don't want to talk about it,' said the bear.

'Was it, you know? Sexy stuff?'

'I said,' repeated the bear, 'I don't want to talk about it.' He fell to his knees. For all his bulk he did it so gently, the bear rug was so soft, he hardly made a sound. He spread himself flat on to the floor. He opened his mouth in an impotent roar.

'Oh God,' said the tiger. 'Oh God. I'm going to be next.' And he began to cry.

Alex wanted to console the tiger, but he didn't know what to say. He wanted to roll over and give the tiger a hug, but even tiger rugs are pretty dangerous things, and he wasn't sure his comfort would have been appreciated. And, in time, the snuffling stopped, and the tiger fell silent.

The tiger didn't have to wait too long. A couple more parties, a couple more dinners, and then the woman was back.

She nuzzled them all, but she spent most of her time with the tiger, and the tiger was shaking with fear at all the attention. And then she put a finger upon his head, just the one, very deliberately, and pressed it down firmly. 'Come on,' she said.

'I don't want to,' said the tiger, but the woman gave no reaction to this at all – maybe she couldn't hear him, maybe she couldn't speak tiger. The tiger staggered up on to its four legs – and then, awkwardly, up on to just two. The woman left. The tiger said, 'Think of me, won't you?' And it might have been to the bear, or to Alex, or to both of them, but neither replied. The tiger waited for a response, anything – then he shook his head, and still on hind legs, tottered out after the woman.

Alex expected that when the tiger came back it'd be crying. It wasn't crying. It was beyond tears. It lay down upon the carpet, covered its face with its paws. 'Oh God,' it said, 'oh God, oh God.' Over and over, all bloody night.

And then, suddenly, the bear spoke up. 'I've had enough of this.'

'What are you doing?' said the tiger.

'What do you think?' said the bear.

'You can't just leave,' said the tiger.

The bear said, 'I can do anything I bloody well want.'

It was up on its feet. Eight foot tall, and this time not bent over in defeat, standing as proud as could be.

'You won't get paid,' said the tiger.

'You two share my money,' said the bear. 'I don't want it. I don't want anything she can give me.' And he shambled across the room, fiddled about at the doorknob with his claw, opened it, and shut the door gently behind him.

'Do you think he's coming back?' said Alex.

And the tiger said, 'Fuck it. He's right. I'm worth more than this. I can take the pain and the discomfort. But I'm not going to be *humiliated*.' He got to his feet too, but now on all fours, the way tigers are supposed to, and he looked good that way, he looked *sleek*.

'I'm a tiger,' the tiger said. 'I should be doing, I don't know, what tigers do. Killing antelopes, and chasing gazelles, and shit.'

'You can't just leave me here alone,' said Alex.

'Watch me,' said the tiger. And went.

When the party resumed, Alex thought someone might raise the alarm that the bear and the tiger had gone. Two wild beasts had taken to the streets of Kensington, savage, unpaid and pissed off. No one seemed to notice. The woman didn't even care.

'The animals left,' Alex whispered to her later, next time they were alone.

'Yes, yes,' she said.

'They said I could have their pay.'

'Hush now,' she said, and put a cheese pasty in his mouth.

She would come for him now, Alex was certain. The way she had for the bear and the tiger. And that frightened him at first. But as the days went by, and the days bled into weeks, Alex felt a certain resolve – that he wouldn't let the side down the way the animals had. A pack was only as strong as its weakest link, and he would be as strong as he could be, damn it – mistreat an animal and sooner or later it'll turn on you and bite, but what dignifies mankind is its inexhaustible capacity to take whatever shit it's given, and put up with it, and like it, and say thank you. To remain loyal to the persecutor, no matter what, that was the human way – steadfast patience against all logic and sense. He was a man, wasn't he, he was better than a beast, and he would show her, whatever it was she wanted of him he wouldn't let her down, he would prove himself. He would prove he was worthy of her love. And she would see, yes, that he belonged in Kensington too.

Every day she came to him, and she nuzzled his head, and stroked his white pasty skin, and his heart beat faster in anticipation. He waited for that fingertip on his forehead that would tell him it was time to face the test she had in mind, sometimes he strained his head against her hand to force it.

He writhed to her touch now. No more pretence that he was an object without thought or feeling – they were on their own, he broke character, she never seemed to mind. Even her breath upon his skin made him roll into a little ball, or he'd stretch, or he'd twist and show her his belly. And the weeks turned into months, and he knew he must be her favourite now, she hadn't replaced the tiger or the bear, there was no one else left.

'How much longer?' he'd ask, and each time she'd ignore him.

'How much longer?' he asked, and one day she said, 'Come on.'

>•<

He got to his feet, he stood up nice and tall in front of her. He inched up on his toes, just to look a bit taller. He even flexed his muscles a little. She smiled. 'No, no,' she said. And she picked him up, and draped him over her shoulder. They left the room then, his feet dragging limply against the floor – and he thought, *But the animals were allowed to walk out all by themselves!* And he thought, *She's touching me, I'm hers.* And he wasn't sure whether he was being punished or honoured.

She took him into the party, and the guests were all around – and they were staring at him, and some were cooing, and some were laughing – but he had no time for them, he was looking at the middle of the room, he was the centrepiece, he expected to be laid out prominently with all the rites a centrepiece deserved – and there was no room for a rug in the middle of the room, because there was a bed in it, a big four-poster bed, and the bed looked so much softer and more luxurious than a simple rug could ever be, and its sheets were folded over enticingly.

She let Alex down from her shoulders then, he pooled on to the floor. She took her clothes off.

And Alex worried he wouldn't be able to perform. Oh, he could perform all right, if just lying back on your stomach with your mouth open and eyes out front was your idea of performance – but he wasn't sure he had anything more to offer than that. He was limp. And she was naked now. And no, not beautiful, never beautiful – but attractive, oh yes, he felt all the hairs on his body prick up, as if her attraction was actually magnetic, his body now covered with its own thin coat of fur. She was so white. Her skin was so dazzling white. It wasn't pasty white, it was thick like milk.

One or two of the guests gave wolf whistles, but she ignored them.

Alex tried to get on his feet, he wanted to take her in his arms.

'No,' she said.

And from the crowd she pulled out two people, a man and a woman. Both were rather elderly, and one was his father, and the other, coincidentally, the other was his mother. Alex was rather surprised to see them. He hadn't expected them to have invitations to a party like this. They were rather letting themselves down, too, couldn't they have found some clothes to wear? He hadn't seen them in ages, even longer ago than he'd seen his wife and kids – and hang on, wasn't one of them dead? At least one of them, Alex was fairly sure he'd read that somewhere.

The woman smiled, and turned the full force of that smile on Alex's parents, and she gestured towards the bed. Mum and Dad were smiling too, they couldn't resist, but they turned to each other, and they looked confused and frightened. Dad went first. That was right, too, Mum had always deferred to him.

The woman fucked Alex's father right in front of Alex, and all the guests were cheering, they were clapping their hands and beating their feet to keep time. Dad did his best, though he looked somewhat winded by the experience, maybe he was the one who'd died? And then, when she was spent, the woman pushed Dad off the bed. He collapsed into a heap, and squirmed there, then stopped. The woman pulled Mum down beside her, and then she fucked her too.

Alex knew his mouth was hung open, not too wide, not in a roar. And he felt water prick behind his glass bead eyes, but the water couldn't find a way of leaking out.

And as the woman rode high upon Alex's mother, as she pressed her bottom ever harder against Alex's mother's face, so that Alex thought he could hear her nose crack – as she rode high upon the party guests' applause, she cried out, 'This is for you, my darling husband! Are you watching, my love? Can you see? This is all for you!'

And it was so hard for Alex to turn his head now, and all he wanted was to turn his head, just so he didn't have to see his father in tears, so he didn't have to see his mother as her face bled – Alex turned his head and looked behind him, looked to where the woman was shrieking, looked to see her husband.

He was an old man. Alex couldn't tell how old. He could have been as young as seventy. It wouldn't have surprised Alex if he'd been a thousand. He was on the wall. He was nailed to the wall, upside down, legs splayed – the rug of her husband's skin was stretched out so wide and taut you could see through it. His mouth was open too, in what looked like leery astonishment, and his eyes stared hungrily out at his wife's escapades. He may have been laughing, or was that just the way his face hung, was that just a gurgle coming down his throat? And his arms, his arms were swinging from side to side, and when the hands collided they made a little clap – he was clapping to see such sport.

'All for you, darling,' the woman said, more gently. She climbed off Alex's mother, idly kicked her body off the bed. There was a catch in her voice, and Alex couldn't tell whether it was vengeance, or love, or something far stranger than either.

She stood in front of Alex.

'You can go now,' she said. 'Or, stay and get paid. It's up to you.'

She held his gaze still, just for a moment, and then she turned her head, and she never looked at him again.

The guests had cleared a path for Alex to leave the room. He took it.

>•<

Alex went back to his room. It felt like his room now, he had earned it. He lay down upon the carpet. He took up the position.

It was nice and dark in his room. He liked the dark.

The bear and the tiger had gone. They had summoned up all the little dignity they'd had left, they had got to their feet and walked out. They didn't *want* the money, they had their pride.

Alex had his pride too. He thought of leaving. He knew no one would stop him.

But it did seem rather silly to have come this far – to have seen so much, and suffered so long – and not to get paid for it.

He waited for the woman to come back.

He decided he wouldn't make it easy for the woman. When she gave him his money, he wouldn't accept it politely. He'd take it out of her hands with all the contempt within him. He wouldn't say thank you. He wouldn't even say it sarcastically.

He waited for the woman to come back.

He might even *refuse* the money. That would show her. That would prove he wasn't to be disrespected. She'd offer him the money, and he'd say no. He wouldn't even *say* no, he'd just shake his head. He'd stay here, and wait, just so she could see his dignity couldn't be bought.

It would depend on how much money.

He wouldn't refuse the money.

He waited for the woman to come back.

He got to his feet. Whatever else, he didn't have to wait lying on the floor. He didn't have to be a rug. If he were to take the humiliation, he would do it standing, he'd take it like a man.

He waited and waited.

There were some champagne glasses about the room that hadn't been cleared away. He took one, sipped at it, and it tasted good.

He waited, and waited some more. He could go, but where would he go? What was outside? Nothing, nothing but a broken marriage and more children than he could count and riots on the streets and all around Kensington, all around and everywhere, Kensington, bloody Kensington.

He tried to cry again, but the water was still jammed fast behind his eyeballs, he could imagine the water building up behind them like a dam, he could imagine soon his head might burst.

He waited. And, at last, the party resumed.

A moment of panic. He should get back on to the carpet. But no, not this time, he'd stand his ground. His white pasty body shook at his bravery.

A rumble of footsteps – and here they were, with their chatter, and their laughter, and they were holding glasses in one hand and cigarettes in the other, and how they talked, they talked so merrily! And they replenished his glass with champagne, 'Enjoy, enjoy!' they said. 'But I'm just the rug,' he tried to say, and he held up his remaining hand in protest, and they chuckled, and they shoved a cigarette between his fingers.

They stood about him, and they smiled warmly enough, but Alex thought there was desperation to their smiles, and their eyes, all their eyes glinted like glass. They chattered about cars and cigars, about shoes and the weather. They chattered about the impending revolution, it must come soon, please God, be soon. Alex chattered back, it wasn't hard. He fed their lines back at them, and he drank, and he smoked, and he laughed. He talked to all the men in suits and all the women in dresses, he talked to the bears and the tigers and the naked fools in pasty white skin. He looked for the hostess, and she was there, but always out of reach, no matter how many conversations he abandoned he could never get close enough to say hello. And he felt strangely happy anyway, and a little drunk, and very very scared, and all the creatures in the room waited and waited and waited and waited for someone to ring the gong to call them to dinner so they could eat.

WE REGRET TO INFORM YOU

JEANNETTE NG

From the papers of Professor Evangeline Hilda Aldrich, lately of Durham Cathedral School.[1]

To: Evangeline Hilda Aldrich <e.h.aldrich@ durhamcathedralschool.ac.uk>
From: John Knoepflmacher <jokn3@northumbria. ac.uk>
Subject: Re: A New Translation

Dear Professor Aldrich,

We spoke briefly at the conference *Unwriting the Book*, where I expressed interest in a new translation of Bede's *On Time* that you've been working on. It all sounds exceptionally exciting and I look forward to reading that early draft you promised me. With all the unpleasantness down south about the prime minister's necromantic sublimation, it is nice to read something homegrown, if only as a distraction.

I trust that this finds you well, etc.

BW,

J

From: Evangeline Hilda Aldrich <e.h.aldrich@ durhamcathedralschool.ac.uk>
To: John Knoepflmacher <jokn3@northumbria.ac.uk>
Subject: Re: A New Translation

Dear Mr Knoepflmacher,

The department has been talking about nothing but the possibility of Baroness Kesteven returning. The snap election

---

1 Footnotes have been added by Geoey Bell, as part of organising her surviving papers into a memorial publication after the fire.

seems like the next step. It's all gone very Walter Map, if you ask me, but the North persists as it must. But the mines remain closed, as she left them, and she can hardly close them a second time. I'd like to think this little project would be all the more important if things go that way in the South.

I'm still quite uncertain about several passages as I'm working from the microfilm of the manuscript. There is also the matter of the infamous lacuna, but once my permission comes through, I should be able to hold some old parchment to the Light. If you'll pardon the pun.

Yours sincerely,

EHA

Christ is the Morning Star
Who when the Night
Of this World is past
Brings to His Saints
The Promise of
The Light of Life
And opens Everlasting Day.

– from Bede's commentary on the Apocalypse, excerpted as a prayer and inscribed above his tomb in gold

To: Evangeline Hilda Aldrich <e.h.aldrich@ durhamcathedralschool.ac.uk>
From: John Knoepflmacher <jokn3@northumbria. ac.uk>
Subject: Re: A New Translation

Dear Evangeline,

Multispectral filming of palimpsest is always worth a quip.

Turns out that snap election was to break the necromantic seal. Didn't quite believe it till the press conference, but that's the Baroness all right. And of course it means the Journal is restructuring. The latest round of Austerity cuts mean we're moving from monthly to quarterly, but each issue will be longer. The most expensive part of a book is the binding and all that.

I do find myself asking, why Bede? After all, Cuthbert is the primary obsession of your cathedral school, isn't it? Not to say the endless parade of articles on him that cross my desk doesn't get tedious. This isn't a funding application, though, so answer how you will.

I trust that this finds you well, etc.

BW,

J

From: Evangeline Hilda Aldrich <e.h.aldrich@ durhamcathedralschool.ac.uk>
To: John Knoepflmacher <jokn3@northumbria.ac.uk>
Subject: An Introduction is Written

Dear John,

Palimpsest reconstruction has been stalled, sadly. But I've other leads. I have included a few extracts from my translation and a meander from the introduction.

My personal interest in Bede came about when I was fourteen, when I was told the tale of the Easter. Its inconsistent date, at least by reckoning of the Solar calendar, had long been a puzzle to me as a child, but it wasn't till then that I had thought to ask.

I was a quiet child.

And so it was that the calculations of Easter were laid bare to me and I first saw the meshing of cogs that effected the subtle cycles we all live by. Calendars are merely very slow-moving machines, after all. But it was more than that, it was then that I first became acquainted with the bone-deep ache of beholding imperfection in the heavens. The sun and the moon and stars should whirl and gyre in precise and even harmony, and yet they did not. For years I fretted and worried about the eleven days missing from our count. 2 September 1752 was followed by 14 September, and the year – blameless by all accounts – forever remained short those eleven, merely because we finally got around the Gregorian calendar. And not just poor 1752 but all of our reckoning of time and of days past, curled around a hole where eleven days should have been.

Eleven days is a long time, and not just in politics.

It is not always customary in academic writing to make such personal confessions but the historian must come before history, and for this humble historian, Bede – as I have said – is a lynchpin.

Yours sincerely,

EHA

Introduction to a New Translation of Bede's ON TIME
dedicated to Our Magdalene In Chains

It is impossible to overstate the impact that the Venerable Bede has had in the reshaping of our historical landscape.

His texts have made him our first national historian but Bede is bound to the North by blood and bone. He rests beneath the flagstones of Durham Cathedral[2] and it is there that untold secrets sleep. With the potential necromantic return of Baroness Kesteven, we in the North find ourselves floundering to reframe history, digging up ancient graves for old identities.

To begin at the beginning, nothing is known of Bede's parentage beyond that he was born upon monastery lands. There is no reason to suggest that he is akin to the legendary Merlin, child of an anchorite mystic[3] and an incubus, product of a dichotomous and liminal union of holy and profane. There is no reason to suggest that his ancestry may have something of the aquatic[4] about it. There is no reason to suggest any of this.

What is known is that by the age of seven, Bede was an oblate at the monastery of Wearmouth. He studied under Benedict Biscop and Ceolfrith, both men who would one day be canonised by the pen of their pupil to be saints of the North.

At the founding of their sister monastery in 682, Bede moved with Ceolfrith to Jarrow. Plague devastated the fledgling community in 686 and at the age of thirteen, Bede was one of the two surviving monks[5]. Ceolfrith was the other. For all that Jarrow and Wearmouth were founded to

---

2 The author is, of course, referring to Durham Cathedral in Durham, County Durham, not any of its shadows in North Carolina, Nova Scotia, Kansas or Oregon.

3 Attempts to connect this to the Chester le Street anchorhold are largely misguided, even if one accounts for a significant fragmentation of history.

4 The author is reaching. Jarrow comes from the Old English *Gyrwum*, meaning the 'marsh dwellers'.

5 This is questionable conjecture. It is worth noting that though Bede has penned many a physical description of the Wearmouth, he has never written of Jarrow. Nor is a boy of thirteen by early medieval standards a child ('puerulus') at all.

be the one and the same, their fates in this could not be intertwined. It is likely that these difficult days were the ones that instilled in young Bede the fragility of an oral tradition, a foundational memory that would drive him to write. Or perhaps it was simply the death toll of the monastery pushing him to take on commissions, for it is that year that Bede began to pen biblical commentaries and hagiographies.

Though Bede never rose above the rank of priest during his lifetime, he wrote freely to bishops and brothers of kings. He never alluded to any relation, living or dead, and his letters make clear that his resources were few and limited. He travelled little and wrote copiously.

A cult of Bede swiftly sprang up after his passing in 735. His body was left in the ground for a decade or more before the usual washing of the bones, a customary ritual. As foretold, they were in an excellent state of preservation and were subsequently wrapped in silk, a gift from Lul, the Anglo-Saxon bishop of Mainz. By the eleventh century, the relics of Bede had been passed on to the monks of Durham whose passion for their patron, Cuthbert, rather eclipsed all others.

Bede's most studied work is his *Ecclesiastical History of the English People*. To read it is to witness the many centuries of interpretation overlaid above one another, tracing the arrival of our faith upon these shores. Early readings, for example, credit the Irish and Italian missionaries for our conversion, showing the native kings to be nothing more than ignorant heathens. Yet through later translations coming to light during the English Reformation, it is clear that the kings' reluctance came not from a stubborn loyalty to forgotten gods[6] but a distrust of the imminent papal menace.

Many have noted that for all our modern interest in Bede's historical writings, the majority of his output remains biblical commentaries and the calculation of dates and time.[7] In the same breath it will be pointed out that *Ecclesiastical History* proved to be his last monumental composition out of an accident of chronology. But such attempts to contextualise Bede overlook the anchoring history, the transmutation of text and most importantly, the nature of time itself.

More can be done with the text than has been done before.

To: Evangeline Hilda Aldrich <e.h.aldrich@ durhamcathedralschool.ac.uk>
From: John Knoepflmacher <jokn3@northumbria. ac.uk>
Subject: Re: An Introduction is Written

Sorry I've taken quite so long to reply, the Strike means I've not been in the office and thus not replying to my emails. Hope you've coped all right with the picket lines in the snow. The Beast from the East is keeping us all on our toes.

Given how very eclipsed Bede is in medieval venerations by Cuthbert, I'm not sure I've really considered him to be quite as pivotal as you. I've long known his theological work from a few misspent years labouring in the Theology

---

6 It is likely that the author is here referring to her own work excavating the remains of the giant Gogmagog near Dover.
7 The exact date of Easter remains a point of schismatic difference in communities today.

Department. Overlooked and underrepresented in our literature, certainly, but hardly a lynchpin. I look forward to your work changing my mind.

Excellent and fascinating work on the introduction, by the way. I know you're still drafting but am impatient to read more when you have it.

BW,

J

From: Evangeline Hilda Aldrich <e.h.aldrich@ durhamcathedralschool.ac.uk>
To: John Knoepflmacher <jokn3@northumbria.ac.uk>
Subject: Re: Re: An Introduction is Written

The Strike continues. We wear on. I want to say that the South will blink first, but that may be rather too fanciful. The Baroness Reborn is as iron-willed as her first incarnation. There is solidarity from the miners, for which we are all grateful.

Bede is foundational to me. Each new translation of him brings us closer to understanding core texts underpinning the fabric of our reality. For what is history, if a not a tissue of quotations whispered into the night of this world? What can be real, but what is recorded and remembered? Our fractious modernity rests on an even more fractured history. At each new breath of the world, we are renewed. Only what is written remains. Words by whose light alone we see the past. As was written, is. And so it is written.

Yours,

EHA

PS: I'll even less likely to reply to emails for in the next two weeks. I will, however, be trying to be at the *Mistranslating the Morning Star* conference at the end of the month.

The west face, carved with the main inscription, reads:
TO THE HOLY BISHOP EADFRITH AND THE BRETHREN WHO SERVE CHRIST IN THE ISLAND OF LINDISFARNE. I HAVE NOT PRESUMED TO WRITE DOWN ANYTHING OF SUCH A MAN AS OUR FATHER CUTHBERT WITHOUT THE CLOSEST ENQUIRY INTO THE TRUTH NOR TO MAKE IMMORTAL WHAT I HAD WRITTEN WITHOUT THE MOST CAREFUL SCRUTINY OF SURE WITNESS

The opposite face is carved with scenes from the life of Bede: Bede comes to Jarrow; Benedict and Siggfrith; The Codex Amiatinus; Bede Writing the Immortal History; Bede's Last Moments.

The base reads:
TO THE GLORY OF GOD, TO CHRIST THE MORNING STAR AND IN MEMORY OF HIS SERVANT BEDE THE VENERABLE, WHO WAS BORN BETWEEN WEAR AND TYNE DCLXXIII, AND DIED AT JARROW ASCENSION DAY DCXXXV; UNVEILED 11TH OCTOBER 1904; THIS MEMORIAL CROSS WAS REMOVED IN 1914 FOR SAFETY DURING THE GREAT WAR AND RE-ERECTED IN 1921. G.W. MILBURN, YORK SCULPT

– description of Bede's Memorial Cross (Whitburn Road, Sunderland) from the Public Monuments and Sculpture Association website

**From: Evangeline Hilda Aldrich <e.h.aldrich@
durhamcathedralschool.ac.uk>**
To: John Knoepflmacher <jokn3@northumbria.ac.uk>
Subject: Reference?

I'm chasing down a reference for a conference paper I'm
giving. Does your library have the *Durham Gazette* from
1904? There's an inscription that was changed when it was
re-erected and I think there's an etching of it in its original
glory in one of the October or November issues. Long shot,
but ping me if you have any leads. I'm thinking some of the
local libraries or museums might have something in their
archives? Beamish, maybe? Killhope?

    EHA

*At the beating heart of the North Pennines Area of
Outstanding Beauty (AONB), Killhope is an award-winning
mining museum that perfectly preserves the life and work of
the mining families of the nineteenth-century North.*

    *Step back in time and witness our iconic working
waterwheel and be captivated by our mining history. Breathe
in our sights. Walk the underground mines with our guides
and spend an unforgettable day with us recreating some
living history.*

    *Whatever the weather, you'll always find a haven at
Killhope. The past is dead everywhere but here.*

    – from a promotional pamphlet produced by the Killhope
Museum Trust

**To: Evangeline Hilda Aldrich <e.h.aldrich@
durhamcathedralschool.ac.uk>
From: John Knoepflmacher jokn3@northumbria.ac.uk
Subject: Re: Reference**

You shouldn't need me to warn you, but don't go to Killhope
during Equinox.[8]
BW,
J

*A ride of ten miles brings us to Durham. In its cathedral
are the professed graves of Bede and Cuthbert. The
encroachment of the waves was the pretended cause, the
popularity of and profitableness of their bodies as objects of
veneration the real reason. Bede was stolen by a presbyter
and brought hither, Cuthbert was transferred in state. No
shrine in all England was as popular as his except that of
Thomas of Becket, 400 years afterward. Bede's tomb is in
the Galilee Chapel, a sort of lecture room for vespers. A plain
sarcophagus stands in the central aisle. On it is written in
rhyming Latin:*

Hac punt in fossa
Bedse venerabilis

*It so happens that the bones are not in that 'ditch', as the
rhymes compelled the writer to say, but they are probably in
some other one, for no one knows where his dust is, it having
been scattered, like much other famous dust in Europe, by the*

---

8 It is unclear what the author is referring to. Perhaps a superstition regarding
the rather obvious etymology of the mining village?

irreverent democratic tornadoes that sweep away so many crowned heads of the living and tombs of the dead.

The stately cathedral is the fitting monument of such virtue, but the bustling Jarrow is a far more appropriate resting place.

– from Gilbert Haven, 'Pictures of Travel', *The Ladies Repository Vol. 23* (1863)

To: Evangeline Hilda Aldrich <e.h.aldrich@ durhamcathedralschool.ac.uk>
From: John Knoepflmacher <jokn3@northumbria. ac.uk>
Subject: Where are you?

Are you okay? You weren't at registration yesterday and no one has seen you. I realise I only have your email. Are you still giving the paper tomorrow?

J.

To: Evangeline Hilda Aldrich <e.h.aldrich@ durhamcathedralschool.ac.uk>
From: John Knoepflmacher <jokn3@northumbria. ac.uk>
Subject: Re: Where are you?

We're all quite worried. Please reply when you see this.

J.

The things they do here to keep the ghosts of the past alive. They things they do to feed those ghosts. I suppose it should not surprise, if the South is willing to harness our collective will to bring back a dead Baroness and crown her Prime Minister, then so can a village in the North Pennines resurrect the shadows of days long gone.

They trade one beating heart for another, but it is small, insular. It brings back the past only for here, this patch of ground. Surely one can do more? If one had the right heart...

My only regret is that my sensible shoes may never be clean of blood again.

– from the private journals of Evangeline Hilda Aldrich

To: Evangeline Hilda Aldrich <e.h.aldrich@ durhamcathedralschool.ac.uk>
From: D E Silver <denise.e.silver@oxford.ac.uk>
Subject: Re: Re: Re: Re: Call for Papers, Mistranslating the Morning Star: New Perspectives and Old

Dear Professor Aldrich,

We regret to inform you that your registration fee is non-refundable.

All the best,

Denise Elizabeth Silver, Ninth Chair of the C.S. Lewis Fellowship.

Have you heard the scream of the circling dunlins and godwits above the marshes of Jarrow? There is no more feral a sound, none that brings you closer to the heart of the North.

Slow by Jarrow Slake but for a moment. Stand knee deep in mud and marsh and speak to me in the ancient tongues of yore.

Sink as the seers once did and see.

See and speak.

Mire and mud can meld time and here the textual layers

mesh. See upon the lake the shadows of slain men sway, dancing through Victorian air. The same staccato steps are marched by the Crusaders of Jarrow, the sharp sawing accordion notes sing with them. The sprawl of the Nissan plant is a white smear against the distant green.

History is written and rewritten here.

– from the private journals of Evangeline Hilda Aldrich

From: Evangeline Hilda Aldrich <e.h.aldrich@ durhamcathedralschool.ac.uk>
To: John Knoepflmacher <jokn3@northumbria.ac.uk>
Subject: Re: Re: Where are you?

I'm not sure I have answers yet. But soon.
  EHA

If the past can be written, then the past can be rewritten. If it can be seen and spoken, then it can be changed.

Perhaps it is paradoxical that I would exhume the past to kill it. That I would state it mutable when what we desire is for it to remain unchanging.

There are gilded days just gone, barely remembered. But nothing need change. Nothing need ever change.

I know the rituals of Killhope now, and how deep their mine goes. I know what was done at the Skinning Grove[9] to recreate itself. I know why Seal Sands[10] thrives.

It is simply a matter of submersion, of sublimation. If it can be done in the South with the bones of the Baroness, it can be

---

9 The Skinning Grove is so named for its infamous treatment of the immigrant selkie population.
10 Seal Sands is today a thriving industrial part given over to the chemical industries, famous for its development and manufacture of synthetic skin.

done here. If they can summon again such spectres of the past to poison our bones, it can be done here.

The celestial spheres are about to speak. I have but eleven days to write.

– from the private journals of Evangeline Hilda Aldrich

To: Evangeline Hilda Aldrich <e.h.aldrich@ durhamcathedralschool.ac.ne>
From: John Knoepflmacher <jokn3@northumbria. ac.nor>
Subject: Re: New Translation of Bede's ON TIME, final final draft

We regret to inform you that we are rejecting this 'new translation' of Bede as we cannot publish what does not exist. There was never such a person as this 'Bede' and such literary hoaxes do not belong to the *Greater Prussia Journal of Colonial History.*

Yours sincerely,

John Knoepflmacher

High Professor of Teutonic Studies, formerly of the Socialist Republic of Northumbria

You will never have to hear crowbar against marble, the scratch of hard iron against ancient stone. You will never feel that weight. The sheer mass of the years shifting around you.

You will never have to breathe in this dust of the years. You will never lay eyes this sacred, profane act. You will never bleed blood and ink.

You will not hear the clatter of the crowbar as it drops from my hands. Nor will you hear my sobbing as I curl around

a beating heart. This will not be you, the bleeding stigmata of written chronicles climbing up you limbs, blood and ink mixing on the ground, and you, desperate, dying, writing in this the True History, the way things should be.

You will never receive this. You will never read this. Time shifts, the past is written. Again and for the first time. All it took was the right heart.

But still I wish to tell you this: it is done.

– a fragment from an unknown manuscript, dated to the seventh century by Prof. Aldritch

To: John Knoepflmacher <jokn3@northumbria.ac.nor>
From: Silvia Robinson <s.m.robinson@
durhamcathedralschool.ac.ne>
Subject: FWD: Message from the Department

We regret to inform you that Professor Evangeline Hilda Aldrich has passed away. Her teaching duties will be redistributed within the department and Dr Geoey Bell is taking over her research.

A book of condolences will be open at the Galilee Chapel in Durham Cathedral from Friday to Tuesday.

LODESTONES

RICHARD V. HIRST

The moon is the still in the sky when F arrives at the bus stop, half concealed behind some distant cranes. It is just before dawn. F waits. He looks at the moon, tilting his head this way and that. It is surrounded either by three red stars or lights from the cranes' cabins, F can't tell.

The traffic is quiet to begin with, but he watches it grow busier and also slower, grinding first to a crawl and then, as the sun rises, to a halt.

McGlone, thinks F.

It is the roadworks in town, he has heard – the council is in the process of hauling down some old buildings near Piccadilly. But Piccadilly is almost three miles away. Surely, he thinks – he looks along the stretch of road where he is waiting, seeing it is backed up with stationary cars as far as is visible in either direction, the same ones in the same positions for nearly ten minutes now – surely all this can't be because of some roadworks three miles away. Somewhere a car horn blares.

There is no doubt F is going to be late for work. McGlone, he thinks: *McGlone*.

McGlone is the name of the company F works for. McGlone leases out apartments in the city centre. F's job is to go through the bank statements scanned in and emailed to the company by those wanting to rent an apartment and make sure that, on average, they have the amount of money in their accounts above the company's specified threshold. If they are unsuccessful, F forwards the customer's details to the sales department with a cross in a box marked 'denied'; if successful, he crosses 'approved'. Then he moves on to the next bank statement. There are always more bank statements – more than F can ever get through. It makes him anxious, whenever he accesses the portal and looks at the folder containing the pending statements, his screen flickering as yet more arrive.

McGlone.

F paces the length of the plexiglass shelter, his frozen breath trailing him. None of this can be helped, of course, this waiting around. The 192 could be just around the corner, but what difference would that make? Even if it somehow appeared and F boarded, he would simply be sat down in a motionless bus while not getting to work rather than doing so standing here on the pavement. The only difference would be he would be warmer.

Although technically an accountancy job, when he started with McGlone he was placed in the IT department, an open-plan section of office but one where the desks are arranged so that four other employees surround him. They all pass their days staring blankly at their computer screens with earphones in. McGlone is also the name of the managing director of the company. He is an old man, past retirement age, who dresses in old-fashioned suits, all wide lapels and paisley ties. He wanders the corridors of his business making sure all members of staff are where they should be. If one of F's colleagues goes to the toilet and McGlone passes by and sees he's not there, McGlone will come and ask F where he's gone and, after F tells him – sweating, stammering – that they've gone to the toilet, will return a few minutes later to make sure they're back at their desk.

F sits down on bus stop's plastic bench but finds he's unable to stop fidgeting, crossing and uncrossing his legs. The noise – engines idling, radios muffled behind windows, the distant roar of construction work, the honk of a nearby horn – is provoking. He pictures McGlone already making his morning round of the office, noting that it is practically nine a.m., that F is not where he should be. Perhaps he will email F. Perhaps McGlone will schedule a meeting, one-on-one, in which F will have to explain himself and make a plan of recompense.

There is the noise of a horn. It is being repeatedly sounded and mingled with a word being repeatedly shouted. The word sounds like F's name. He cranes his neck and sees that there is a large car a yard or so down the line of jammed traffic, a Vauxhall Zafira. A man is leaning his head out of the window and waving to F. He can see that the man is about his own age. He wears a pair of small round glasses and has his hair shaved into a crew cut revealing – F approaches the car, he cannot simply ignore the man – a series of scars around his head.

'Hey!' says the man.

F cannot remember his first name but he knows the man from his work, from McGlone. He is fairly sure his surname is Brake. Tom Brake? Alan Brake? Brake, he sees, is wearing his shirt and tie beneath a polyester windcheater. 'How's it going?' he says, and then, 'Hop in – I'll give you a lift.'

'Oh,' says F.

The man gestures with his head towards the empty passenger seat. 'You'll be stuck out here all day if you're waiting for the 192.'

'Are you sure?' says F.

'Aye,' Brake says, his head angled towards F, his eyes peeping at him over his spectacles, conspiratorial. 'I know a shortcut.'

'A shortcut?' says F.

'Yes, mate. Hop in.' The window slides closed.

F looks around, steps into the road and gets in Brake's car. 'Thank you,' he says.

Brake smiles.

'Cold out there,' says F.

They sit in silence for a few minutes, both of them surveying the traffic. F tries to think of something to say, but he doesn't know anything about Brake, not really. He works in the design department, creating logos and images for McGlone's online presence. He knows nothing of F's bank statements. After a while Brake puts the radio on and they both listen to the Robbie Williams song 'Angels'. It plays so loudly that when Brake says something to F, F can't hear him. Brake then turns it down and is about to repeat himself when the car ahead begins to move.

'I said have you seen those lights?' he eventually says. 'Up there. He flicks a pointing finger towards the sky, in the direction of the crane.

F looks out of the window and see the three lights. 'Oh, yes,' he says. They are high in the white sky, well above the crane, now a line of pale red points. 'What are they?'

'Well, that's just it. It was on the news just now. Sounds like no one's got the foggiest. They had some bloke on saying it's some kind of debris, something like that, burning up in the atmosphere. Then there was some other bloke saying they're part of some solar flare, some once-in-a-lifetime thing on the surface of the sun. They even had a couple of religious nutters on, you know? Saying it was a calling from God to a good purpose – ah ha!' Brake interrupts himself. 'Here we go!' He shifts from first gear up to third and accelerates, the car lurching forwards a few feet and then stopping. 'Fuck's sake,' he mutters.

F looks out of the window. 'So,' he says, 'whereabouts is this shortcut?'

'See that road there?' He points at the next turn-off just visible beyond the cars ahead, a side street beyond a derelict mill, surrounded by a fly-postered steel barrier blocking the turning itself from view. 'It's just down there. Just fucking there.' Brake lets out a low growl, bumps a fist against his side window and then sighs, rubbing his face with both hands. They both listen to the last few quiet moments of 'Angels', then Brake says, 'So, are you from Manchester originally?'

'Not really,' says F. 'I'm from Grimsargh.'

'Grimsargh? Is that somewhere down south?'

'No, Lancashire, near Chorley.'

'Ah, you're one of them. It draws in people from the north, Manchester. Young people. They come for university or for the crap office jobs, wandering in without knowing what they're letting themselves in for.'

The traffic moves forward a half-metre. Brake follows, already edging towards the turn-off, F's side of the car moving into the cycle lane. He feels a front wheel mount the kerb.

'What about you?' F says.

'Me?' says Brake.

'Yeah, are you from Manchester?'

'Oh yeah, pal. Big time. My family's been here since, well since... ah... since forever.' Brake has become distracted as he tries to squeeze past the three cars ahead, taking up more of the pavement, the white Citroën in front having to turn sharply away to give them more room. 'For... for, uh... for... for generations.' He raises a hand to the Citroën. 'Sorry, sorry!' The surrounding cars are beeping their horns as Brake finally rounds the corner, the Zafira now almost fully free of the road, juddering as a back wheel mounts a foot of the steel barrier. F's window comes close to a tattered poster advertising a Craig Charles live show.

Even this side street is busy, jammed with cars which have given up on the main road, but, F thinks, at least they are moving. Slowly, he and Brake inch along. The road is lined with new builds on one side, steel-shuttered terraces on the other.

'Yeah, my family were in this city before it was even a city. Pre-Industrial Revolution, you know?' Brake nudges the Zafira into the oncoming traffic, an apologetic hand raised. 'Manchester was just another backwater then – just a church, a couple of pubs and some houses by a river. Thank you... Sorry, thank you... Coming through...' Having cleared the road, he turns off through a gate and down a gravel path which F suspects to be the driveway of private property. A house, dark and impossibly large, looms alongside them as the car crunches slowly past. 'My dad always says we can trace our family back to some bigshot from the 1500s, some important astrologer who used to talk to the angels and work out when all the lords and ladies should have their weddings. Then Queen Elizabeth died and talking to angels got him in trouble, so he got sent to Manchester as a kind of punishment.' He laughs. The house is left behind but the road keeps on going, growing less gravelly and more rocky, a dirt track, possibly a footpath.

'Oh wow,' says F. 'And he was your ancestor?'

'No!' Brake laughs. 'God no, not my lot. They worked for him. Were, you know, his servants. It's only because of him that anyone knows anything about my povo family.'

The ride has become bumpy, the road surface potholes filled with rainwater. Together F and Brake bob up and down in their seats without speaking, the keys jingling in the ignition. F looks out of the windows. On one side is a thick wall of bramble and on the other what looks like allotments. F sees one dominated by a fire made up of heaped branches, a figure tending to it. It moves quickly out of sight but the thick twist of smoke keeps constant with the car, hanging in the air, the three red lights visible through its haze.

'Hey, speaking of which,' Brake says, 'do you know how I found this shortcut?' He is grinning. 'An angel told me about it.' He switches between looking at the road, grinning at F, looking at the road, grinning.

F doesn't say anything.

'Ha ha. Don't worry. I'm just messing with you.'

'Ha ha,' says F.

'Right,' says Brake, stopping laughing. 'Here we go.'

F grips the handle in the door as Brake suddenly speeds up, making a sharp turn into the wall of bramble. The car scrapes through a narrow gap, parting two of the bushes, and emerges bouncing down an embankment onto a road F immediately recognises. They are on the A34, the busy main road between Piccadilly and Oxford Road. But it is deserted, closed off. They make their way towards the city centre, enormous metal hoardings on either side of the road. They pass a van piled with cones, cables and street signage, a trio of portacabins in the middle of the road and three men stood outside in in fluorescent coats, drinking steaming cups of tea, watching as they move.

'Here's our last turn-off. This takes us to the Chester Street car park,' says Brake. 'Aren't you glad you trusted me?'

F is glad. The clock on Brake's dashboard reads 9.18. Late, but not too late. It would be unreasonable for McGlone to take umbrage with him.

The turn-off is a gate to a construction site. Although the gate entrance is open there is a length of chain across it. Brake stops the car, undoes his seat belt, gets out, unhooks the chain, gets back in the car, buckles his seat belt, drives through, stops, unbuckles his seat belt, gets out, and refastens the chain.

Ahead, F is faced with a vast nothing, a flat terrain which stretches out in all directions for as far as he can see. It is the colour of clay, composed, he can see, of bricks reduced to rubble and mixed with earth. F never knew the city could hold such an expanse, such emptiness. The only features are a path flattened through the rubble by the heavy vehicles which have come in and out of this entrance and, in the far distance, a line of parked vans at the base of a pair of mounds of what looks like further debris, a knot of large cranes beyond them. He sees the three lights in the sky reflected in the wet ground, their forms made pink and diffuse by the glistening rainwater.

'Well, here it is,' Brake says, getting back into the car. 'The headache we're all dealing with.'

'I thought the roadworks were in Piccadilly,' says F.

'They are,' he says. 'Piccadilly is where it's busiest. But they're everywhere. Don't you know? They're pulling half the city down these days.' He clicks on his seat belt and moves off.

The surface quickly grows more uneven. F sees the dozed remains of bricks which make up the terrain becoming less fragmented as the car makes its way towards the two banks of rubble – quarter-bricks, half-bricks, whole bricks all passing them by.

'Funny to think there used to be a club right here,' he says. 'Big Beat, it was called. I had some great nights in there. It was an old mill building before that, of course. One of the biggest in the country, so they said.' The path becomes rockier, growing less and less distinct from the surrounding rubble as they press on. Brake shifts into a higher gear but keeps the car slow.

'Funny,' says F. 'Funny to think of all that... exertion, you know? All that activity, all that life, all held in place by these,' he makes a sweeping gesture, 'stones.' Among the half-bricks and whole bricks F now sees there are clusters of bricks, fragmented lines of mortar cleaving them to one another. 'And now they're just getting ground up and buried.'

F looks at Brake. He hasn't been listening. He is concentrating on his driving, the car having reached the base of the one of the piles of bricks. It is impossible, F thinks, that Brake will attempt to drive up it but, again, Brake shifts gear and – slowly, haltingly – the car begins to move up the incline, following the ghost of a trail through the wreckage.

Brake's lips are pursed. He is tutting. 'Shit,' he says to himself, then to F: 'It's all different from how I remember. This was just a little pile of rocks with a space running through it last week.' He points out of the window and says in a surer tone, 'I do recognise that thing.'

It is a machine, some kind of large cylinder fastened to a trailer on its side, half-buried, with an upended traffic cone alongside. F watches it pass by slowly and, when he looks ahead, he sees that the path is no longer visible. The car is simply labouring gingerly up a slope of broken rock, its engine lowing, Brake tense, gripping the wheel and staring.

There is a sudden rumble beneath them and F feels the ground shift and the tyres spin as the Zafira slips backwards. Brake makes a sharp turn to steady the car and then, finding it is still listing, slips into reverse. But it doesn't work and they start to slide. He hits the accelerator, the tyres find purchase and they are abruptly pulled backwards, too fast to stop the car from zipping over the peak of the mound and down the other side, the descent sheerer than it should be. F feels the wheels separate from the surface. All he can think is: I am falling, I am in a falling Zafira and I may never get to work. And all he can see is the white sky with the red lights ahead flickering and disappearing and then the beige clay spinning and darkening.

COAST

Swimming with Horse
Angela Readman

The Stone Dead
Alison Moore

The Devil in the Details
Ramsey Campbell

Hoveri
Gary Bu

The Knuck
Gareth E. R

The Headland
of Black Rock
Alison Littlewood

COAST

THE KNUCKER

GARETH E. REES

1. THE DEAD CYCLIST

The girl from the farm found the dead cyclist on a single lane road to Rickney on the Pevensey Levels. He lay awkwardly, arms buckled beneath his torso, head twisted, eyes in a frozen stare across the tarmac. The girl was certain that he was a cyclist because he wore a luminescent yellow vest and Lycra shorts, but she could see no bike.

She first called 999, and then her dad, who kept vigil with her until the police arrived. A tall, fierce woman introduced herself as Inspector Ramsden. She paced around the dead cyclist, tutting loudly, as her officers scoured the hedgerows for the missing bicycle. It was a curious scene. Ramsden presumed this dead cyclist on the roadside was the result of a hit-and-run, but he was soaking wet, his fingers wrinkled, face bloated. As she crouched beside him, a bead of water seeped from the corner of his mouth. It was a hot July day and there had been no rain for over two weeks. A drought, they said on the news. *What was she missing here?* Ramsden removed her shoes and clambered onto the bonnet of the police car to get a look at the bigger picture.

'Ma'am,' protested the driver.

'Pipe down.' Ramsden gazed north across fields striated with drainage ditches, towards an escarpment where the domes of the old Royal Greenwich Observatory pushed above the trees. She swivelled slowly, taking in the vast green lowland, scattered with sheep, telegraph poles and farmhouses, out toward Pevensey Castle and the sea. This place could get waterlogged. Floods were common. In recent years, rising seas and storm tides threatened to revert it to the tidal bay it had been in Roman times. But this month the Levels were as dry as she'd ever known them. There was no watery ditch nearby into which the cyclist could have pitched. They weren't even in a particularly low-lying area. The field behind the body was one of several elevations dotted across the Levels, formerly islands in a lagoon at high tide. Anglo-Saxons built dwellings on them when they began to reclaim the marsh for crops and salt panning. Later, they became medieval villages. You could tell which ones they were from the –*eye* or –*ey* at the end of the name: Chilley, Southeye, Northeye. Where she now stood was at the foot of the abandoned village of Horse Eye, a stepped green hillock in the flatland, demarked by ridges and undulations where there had been houses and tracks.

Ramsden slid from the bonnet and put on her shoes. The girl from the farm was talking to Constable Hasan. She explained that she was driving her mum's car to Hailsham when she spotted the body. A dark stain on the road surface, which she assumed to be spilled blood, turned out to be water. This had quickly evaporated in the sunshine, indicating that the girl had arrived soon after the incident. It could have been from the cyclist's water bottle bursting on impact, except there was no water bottle here, only a body that bore all the signs of a drowning.

Nothing sensible sprang to Ramsden's mind. There was the sliver of a possibility that someone had knocked the cyclist off his bike, murdered him by forcing litres of liquid down his throat, then ridden away at ten a.m. on a Saturday. But it was a ludicrous notion.

The scenario reminded her of a peculiar incident, years ago, when ramblers stumbled upon the body of twenty-year-old Tyler Carney in Chapel Field, at the eastern side of the Levels, near the site of the medieval village of Northeye. Officers found a smoking, burned-out BMW in a track leading to the field, probably stolen by Carney, who they'd collared previously for petty larceny and vandalism. There were bruises on his shoulders but no signs of strangulation or blunt force trauma. The pathologist said he'd drowned. His body wasn't far from the Waller Haven, so it was feasible that someone dragged him from the water. Trouble was, the liquid in his lungs was briny, which cancelled out the possibility that he had drowned in the freshwater of the Haven.

The case grew more baffling when a dog walker reported a body in the Pevensey Haven on the same day, a separate channel almost two miles to the west. It was Tyler Carney's girlfriend, Natasha Logan, lain on the riverbank in a fake fur coat, also drowned. The couple were spotted on a train to Eastbourne the previous evening. It was possible that they wandered onto the Levels to take drugs and became disorientated. Toxicology found small traces of marijuana in their systems, but no class As or alcohol. Nobody could piece together a coherent hypothesis. There were no witnesses and no suspects. The case remained unsolved.

'Ma'am!' there was a shout, 'Ma'am!' Sergeant Allsop rounded the corner, huffing and puffing. 'We found the bike.'

'Where?'

'Up a bloody tree about half a mile down the way.'

Ramsden clicked her tongue and looked up at a crow flapping across the wide blue sky. She watched until it shrank over the Levels, then she said:

'Okay, so what the hell is going on here, then?'

2. THE STOLEN CAR

It was a friend of their old maths teacher who asked them to steal his car. Up to his eyeballs in debt, he was desperate for a speedy operation on his haemorrhoids. An insurance payout on the theft and destruction of his vintage BMW 2000 would allow him to go private.

He reasoned that his teacher friend would know some hooligan who'd nick it for cash, which is how Tyler and Natasha came to be recruited as car thieves. Tyler had left his teenage criminal ways behind him but couldn't turn down the money. A grand would help them rent a flat in Bexhill. Get them out of their rut and on the way somewhere. The only risky bit was stealing the car from the old codger's house without being noticed. Once they drove onto the Levels, it would be a cinch. There was nobody out there late at night, and by the time anybody spotted the flames, he and Tash would be legging it across the fields, concealed by darkness.

On the train to Eastbourne they kept a low profile, talking quietly. On the way to the house where the black BMW was parked they shared a single-skin reefer. Nothing heavy. A mild skunk. They had a car key so they didn't need to smash glass or hotwire the vehicle, though they had instructions to do that when they reached the Levels, to make it look legit. Natasha was the driver. Tyler's job was to set the thing alight. Trash it good and proper. Besides, Tash was one of those butter-wouldn't-melt types who wouldn't look too suspicious at the wheel of a posh car. She'd even put on one of her mum's fur coats and a ton of make-up to get the right look.

The plan was all sorted, they thought, driving out of Eastbourne, through Pevensey, onto the A259, then off the road near Middle Barn Farm. Natasha had already checked it out on Google Maps. There was a convenient dirt track that would take them into a field with some raised ground. They could burn the car on one side and hotfoot it to the nearest lane on the other.

As the car crawled over the mud and stones, they turned off the headlights to stay discreet. Tyler opened the window and leaned out, shining a torch to show Natasha the way ahead. Cold air rushed in, smelling of salt and rotting fish, making them shiver. An uneasy murk enveloped the car, which bucked and swayed on hidden swells and riptides in the mud, like they were being washed downstream. It was hard to tell land from sky, the visible world reduced to an amorphous interplay of densities, shifting and warping as they advanced.

They'd chosen a cloudy night for the theft, but occasionally the moon broke through, shimmering light on flooded ditches and drainage channels, boggy indents and trackways, the imprint of a community long lost. Natasha remembered a geography lesson at school about Nazca lines in Peru. They reminded her of those, and how she thought that the people who left them must have been magicians or aliens. As the clouds reconverged, all traces of light were extinguished but for the beam from Tyler's torch, glancing off the muddy ooze, which swirled and bubbled as if in a deluge, and yet there was no rain.

A trick of the light, Tyler told himself, gritting his teeth. They had to stay focused.

As they turned a bend, his torchlight caught something

protruding from a knoll. A human figure, the white of its face caught momentarily in the beam. Eyes like diamonds.

Tyler gasped and shrank back into the vehicle. Natasha slammed the brakes.

'What? What is it, Tyler?'

'I thought I saw someone.'

'You're shitting me.'

'I dunno... I think... it was over there.' Tyler aimed the light at the knoll, but it was just grass and mud, like pretty much everything around here. 'Gone now.'

'You sure?'

'Yeah, sorry. Maybe shouldn't have had that smoke earlier.'

'Don't freak me out, Tyler.' Natasha pushed on the accelerator and the car lurched towards the elevation at the end of the track, a deeper black against the wider blackness, expanding to fill the world as they approached.

They stopped the car and hurried into action. Natasha moved away from the vehicle, while Tyler smashed up the ignition, broke the window and poured a can of petrol over the interior. It was so dark she couldn't see much, but for the torchlight bouncing.

'Get further back than that,' said Tyler, 'it's gonna blow.'

Natasha backed off, hugging herself anxiously. Moments later, there was a *whoosh* and shattering glass as flames shot from all sides of the car, Tyler a silhouette against the sudden brightness, stumbling to his knees, the hillock bathed in a red glow. Natasha cried out as soon as she saw the figures, maybe five, six or more, standing on the crest of the hill, huddled in ragged clothes. Tyler saw them too, clambering dizzily to his feet. But instead of turning and running towards her, he remained rooted to the spot, looking down as if searching for something beneath him, outstretched arms paddling the air.

'Tyler!' cried Natasha as one of the figures descended the hill and stopped in front of him. It was a burly man with a wild beard. He placed both hands on Tyler's shoulders and forced him back down to his knees. Tyler clawed frantically at the man's face, mouth open in a silent scream. For a moment it looked like the two men were locked into some unholy communion rite. A diabolical baptism.

Natasha wanted to run towards them but she couldn't. A powerful force tugged her backwards, hoisting her off the ground, the tips of her toes dragging against earth as she was swept around the back of the hill, now a rugged mound framed by fire, growing smaller and fainter as she was pulled and rolled, struggling for breath, turning, turning, turning, until all was darkness.

3. NORTHEYE

They were a community of ten, eking out a living on the borderland between earth and water. When the tide went out, they descended the hill with lead pans to extract salt from the briny pools that remained. It was slow work, but salt was much in demand over in Hoh, that spur of land to the north of their Eyot, where the folk made iron. The rest of their provisions came from strips of reclaimed marshland in which they grew cabbages for the cooking pot and grass for their goats. When the sea rushed in the surrounding land became a glistening lagoon and they were left alone with the warblers and skylarks.

It seemed a peaceful place, but Tedmund lived in fear. Since his grandfather's time, and his grandfather's grandfather's time, the seas encroached with more force each year, taking back much of what they'd claimed. Something had broken down in their discourse with the gods, and the harmony between land and sea was awry. The only way to rebalance the two was to please those gods, which was why Tedmund and his family refused to embrace the Christ cult that had swept into Suth Seaxe. This alien religion might have bent the will of weak-minded folk in Hoh, but not their community. They remained loyal to the old ways, and to Woden, their most powerful god. To abandon him would lead only to destruction.

On clear days, Tedmund could see the ruined fort of Andredceaster in the distance, built by a civilisation long fled from this land, whom his own people had replaced, and he was not going to let theirs fall to ruin like that. He was determined to establish a legacy in this frontier land and could not understand why the tides were pushing back so vigorously against him. Perhaps it was a message to warn them against conversion to the ways of Christ, or punishment for their acts of reclamation. Tedmund feared that their walling and draining innovations had made an enemy of the water dragon they knew as the Knucker. If provoked, it could come upon them in the night and take a child in its jaws or raze their homes to the ground with its fiery breath. Tedmund was certain it was out there. Sometimes, when the tide was high, they'd hear an unearthly growl and see wisps of smoke rise from darkening swells, as if a vast entity moved beneath the surface.

The membrane between worlds was thinner out here than the inland-dwelling peoples could ever realise, so they expected no help. It was up to them to stand their ground against malevolent spirits. They'd heard tell that on the Eyot of Horse, on the north-western region of their inland sea, the folk had encountered the 'yellow man', who rode the skeleton of a hunting dog down their hill at terrifying speed. They hurled stones that knocked him headfirst into the waters, where he disappeared beneath the surface as his broken steed span away on the current. Whether an agent of the Knucker or another disturbed spirit, Tedmund knew not, but these were worrying times and they had to remain vigilant.

His wife Bree was wise in the old ways. She made a circle of stones around the Eyot to offer them protection. In a nocturnal high tide, when the spirits were most active, and they were most isolated, she recited her rhymes of banishment. On nights such as those, one of their number was posted as a lookout on a knoll by the lagoon's edge. As fate would have it, Sigeweard stood on guard when the Knucker finally came.

Hours after sunset, a freakishly rapid tide sent water shooting through channels and pooling in syrupy whirls around their Eyot. Sigeweard was an elder of the community, and used to the vagaries of the sea, but he knew instantly that something was amiss. A rasping sound emanated from the south, and two eyes, bright as moons, pierced the night. He whistled to alert Tedmund and the others, then stood his ground as a great hulking shape cut through the water towards him, a solitary eye winking. As its gaze lit upon his face he fell backwards in surprise, scrabbling away from the knoll on hands and knees.

After a pause, belly rumbling, the Knucker proceeded towards the Eyot, water swelling around its bulk. Sigeweard prayed to Woden that Tedmund had raised the adults from their slumber, for the beast was coming.

Tedmund was indeed awake. He stood outside his hut with Bree, Oswine, Tata, Aedelstan and Hildred. In the darkness he saw the gleam of the Knucker's hard black skin and heard its growls fall silent, as if it was waiting to pounce. Bree gripped Tedmund's arm.

'I shall defend you,' he said, as best he could, for his heart thumped with terror. They were lowly folk, without weapons and with only their gods to protect them. That is, if they hadn't been forsaken.

Without warning, the dragon blasted fire across the water, lighting up their Eyot, exposing them on the slope. In the glare they saw a human form, an emissary of the beast, rise up from the water until he was waist deep, his arms paddling against the current. Tedmund knew he must act while the enemy was vulnerable. He strode down the hill, gripped the spirit's shoulders and forced him downward until his bony white head was beneath the surface, bubbles streaming from his open mouth.

The Knucker roared with angry flame but Tedmund persisted, pledging oaths to Woden should he die in this moment. Even when a shriek assailed him across the lagoon, he held that spirit down, and kept on holding until there was no more resistance. In that instant, the Knucker's flame was extinguished and a deep night closed around Tedmund, silent but for the lapping of water as it kissed the land he called home.

4. HORSE EYE

Greg was making good time and felt fit, but damn it was hot. He'd started his cycle ride at eight a.m. to beat this infernal sun. To no avail. The sky was cloudless, air still, and by the time he reached the Pevensey Levels, the land was hard-baked. He rode at speed down the twisting B-road from Herstmonceux, hedgerows blurring, ears keen for the sound of approaching cars, but it was a quiet Saturday morning and the world felt like his domain.

At Horse Eye, his legs worked harder, adjusting to the incline that lifted him up over the Levels. At its crest he marvelled at the mirage before him, for it seemed as if the fields as far as Pevensey Castle shimmered with water, only treetops visible above the surface. As Greg's bicycle dipped into the downward slope he was surprised by an outburst of commotion in the adjacent field. A group of people in heavy woollen clothes ran towards him, clutching rocks, angry and shouting.

THE STONE DEAD

ALISON MOORE

'*This* ghost,' said Marcus, scratching at the paper with the sharp point of his pencil crayon, 'is green, and he shoots ectoplasm, and his name is Slimo.'

Lesley lifted her own pencil crayon from the intricate labyrinth of her anti-stress colouring book and looked at what her son had drawn, the vivid green scribbled over the outline of his ghost. 'He looks terrifying!' she said.

'And when you look at him,' said Marcus, 'he goes invisible.'

Lesley looked at her watch. 'You can show your drawing to Grandma,' she said. 'She'll be here in five minutes.'

I'll come at one, her mother had said. She always came at one o'clock – it was her time. And she was always precisely on time, on the dot of one. Lesley sometimes wondered if her mother sat outside in the car, or even stood on the doorstep, until the clock struck the hour. She never had to apologise for arriving late, nor looked as if she had rushed.

Lesley went to the window and looked out, but her mother was not in sight. She said to Marcus, 'I'll go and put the kettle on.'

'Can I have a biscuit?' asked Marcus.

'We'll have biscuits when Grandma arrives,' said Lesley.

Lesley was in the kitchen, waiting for the kettle to come to the boil, when the grandfather clock in the hallway struck one. Whatever the hour, the clock chimed once; whether it was one o'clock or midnight, the clock chimed once, and Lesley had begun to associate that single chime with her mother's arrival, so that throughout the day, and every day, when she heard the clock strike one, a little part of her panicked, whether her mother was due or not.

Lesley heard the knock at the door, and when she stepped

into the hallway, there was her mother, visible through the glass, as if summoned by the chiming of the clock.

The clock was an heirloom. As a child, Lesley had been afraid of it. Its chiming had made her think of the farmer's wife chasing after the blind mice with her chopper, two different nursery rhymes getting mixed up – she had got confused. And how silly, anyway, she thought, to be afraid of a clock.

'*This* ghost,' said Marcus, appearing beside her, holding up his drawing, 'doesn't have any friends.'

'Well,' said Lesley, 'maybe *we* could be his friends.'

'No,' said Marcus. 'He's not very nice. And he doesn't like us.'

Lesley opened the door and said, 'Come in, Mum.'

'This place is impossible to get to,' said her mother.

'Obviously not *impossible*,' said Lesley, as her mother came in.

Lesley began to close the door, but her mother stopped her, drawing her attention to the state of the house's exterior. 'Your paintwork's looking tired,' she said. 'I'm having all mine done by a man from the village. He's doing a fairly acceptable job, although he can be lazy; I have to keep an eye on him.'

Her mother's visits always began with a litany of criticisms: the front garden needed weeding; the windows needed washing; Marcus's bike was on the path, in the way. 'And did you have to choose *such* a poky little house?' she asked.

'Can't you ever just be happy?' said Lesley. 'You wanted me to leave Tom, and now I have. You wanted me to move closer to you, and now I have.'

'I wanted you closer than this,' said her mother, following Lesley into the kitchen. 'I thought you were going to live in Sleights.'

'I'm a ten-minute drive from you,' said Lesley. 'That's nothing at all.'

'It's not nothing,' said her mother. 'I seem to be forever on that road, on my way to visit you.'

'Well, you're here now,' said Lesley. 'Shall we have a cup of tea?' She fetched the cups and saucers out of the kitchen cupboard. Her mother would not drink from a mug.

'And biscuits,' said Marcus, who had appeared very suddenly at Lesley's hip.

'Are you going to show Grandma your drawings, Marcus?' asked Lesley.

'Come on, Grandma,' said Marcus, leading his grandmother into the living room. When Lesley went to look, Marcus was saying, 'It doesn't actually have eyes, just black holes that go on for ever and ever and ever.'

The water in the teacups clouded, darkened. Lesley spooned the teabags out and added milk, not too much. She carried the tea and biscuits into the living room, where Marcus was saying, '*This* ghost' – he pointed to a thickly pencilled outline right at the edge of the paper – 'is afraid of all the other ghosts.' Lesley put the tray down on the table, and Marcus reached for the biscuits.

'He watches too much television,' said Lesley's mother.

Maybe he did, but Lesley did not think that was where these ghosts came from. Ideas just got into his head, like how he used to think that when people died they turned to stone. Where they had lived with Tom, there was a war memorial, whose stone soldiers looked cornered, and Marcus always touched them as he passed. He had seen, in towns and cities, the stone statues of people who had died there. And he saw them in graveyards, the stone dead: men, women, children, dogs. Sometimes, the stone figures were broken, which meant that the ghosts could get out, said Marcus; they did not want to be trapped inside. Lesley sometimes found herself looking at the world the way he did, forgetting for a moment that this was not the way things were.

'He's just got an imagination,' said Lesley.

'He's got *too much* imagination,' said her mother, as if it were a bad thing, like having too many biscuits, like it might make some part of you rot. 'What's this?' she asked, picking up Lesley's colouring book.

'It's a colouring book for grown-ups,' said Lesley.

'What's the point of that?' said her mother.

'It's anti-stress,' said Lesley. 'It's rather nice. It makes me feel like a child again.'

'But you were a miserable child,' said her mother, closing the colouring book and putting it aside. 'What have you been up to?' she said to Marcus. 'I hope you haven't been inside all day. That's not healthy for a boy.'

'We were waiting for you, Mum,' said Lesley. 'I thought we could take some sandwiches down to the beach.'

'In this weather?' said her mother, eyeing the agitation of the bare trees through the cold window.

'We don't have to,' said Lesley.

'No, no,' said her mother, 'if that's what you want to do, that's what we'll do. Though I won't be able to walk on the sand in my heels. I'll have to wear my driving shoes. They'll be ruined.'

Lesley packed up the sandwiches that she had made.

Again she said, 'We don't *have* to take these to the beach,' but her mother said, 'No, no, we'll do it your way.'

>•<

The three of them went down the steps to the beach, and her mother complained about the distance, and the wetness of the steps, and the damp sand, the damp rocks.

Marcus ran on ahead, this playground vast while the tide was out, and it would not come in until after dark. Every now and then, he stopped to inspect something amongst the rocks, and when he lifted something up, Lesley said to her mother, 'He's found something.'

'Nothing dead, I hope,' said her mother.

Lesley called Marcus over to them. He showed them his grey stone, which he said might have a fossil inside. 'It might have been trapped inside the rock for millions of years.'

'You can put it with the one I gave you for your birthday,' said his grandmother.

'Right,' said his mother, 'sandwich time.'

Marcus put his stone down to take a sandwich from his mother.

'You can have a little fossil collection,' said his grandmother.

'I broke your fossil,' said Marcus.

'You broke it?' said his grandmother. 'Well that was very careless of you. Do you know how old that ammonite was? More than 100 million years old.'

'It wasn't an accident,' said Marcus. 'I smashed it with a hammer, to let the ghost out.'

Lesley avoided meeting her mother's eye. She said to

Marcus, 'At least the ghost will be happy now, won't it? Eat your sandwich.'

'No,' said Marcus. 'It's not happy. It doesn't want to be a ghost. But it did want to get out. The ghosts always want to get out.'

'Eat your sandwich,' said Lesley.

'I'll never give you anything nice again,' said his grandmother.

They ate their sandwiches standing up, huddled into themselves.

>•<

They walked along the windswept front and through the town, in whose shops Lesley's mother always seemed to be hunting for something quite precise. She inspected teacups whose pattern was right but whose size was wrong, and side plates whose size was right but whose pattern was wrong. After a couple of hours, Marcus began to complain, until his grandmother shut him up.

They had tea in a cafe. When the waitress came for the crusts of Marcus's mini pizza, she asked if they would like dessert, and his grandmother said, 'No. No dessert.'

As they left the cafe, Lesley looked up at the darkening sky and said, 'The tide will be turning.'

They made their way back to the house beneath the threat of rain. Lesley and Marcus came into the hallway like people glad to be out of a storm, though it had not yet started. Lesley's mother, who remained on the doorstep, said, 'I'll go now.'

'You don't have to go just yet,' said Lesley. 'Will you have a cup of tea first?'

'No,' said her mother. 'With any luck, I'll make it home before the rain comes.'

'Are you angry, Grandma?' asked Marcus. 'Are you angry because of the fossil?' But she did not reply.

Lesley, unbuttoning her coat, unzipping her boots, asked, 'Are your shoes all right, Mum?'

'They're damp,' said her mother.

'Oh dear,' said Lesley.

'The wet sand has got into them.'

'You'd be welcome to borrow something,' said Lesley.

'Your feet are too small,' said her mother.

Seeing that Marcus was struggling with the zip of his anorak, Lesley bent down to help him. 'Grandma's going now,' she said. 'Say goodbye.'

'Goodbye, Grandma,' said Marcus. 'See you soon.'

The heavens were opening and Lesley said, 'Look at that rain. You can't drive in that, Mum. You don't want to be driving on wet roads.'

'You don't want me spending the night here,' said her mother, 'do you?'

'Will you call?' said Lesley. It was routine for her mother to let Lesley know when she was safely home.

'Yes,' said her mother. 'I'll call.'

>•<

'Time to get ready for bed,' said Lesley, steering Marcus into his bedroom. She closed the curtains against the darkness outside.

'I don't want to sleep downstairs,' he said.

'Well,' said Lesley, 'we *have* to sleep downstairs; there's *only* downstairs now. Arms up.' She helped him out of his top.

'I liked our old house better,' said Marcus.

'Yes,' said Lesley. 'Me too. But it's nice being by the sea, isn't it? It's nice living closer to Grandma and Grandpa, isn't it?'

They were quiet for a moment, while outside, the rain continued to fall.

'I don't think Grandma loves me,' said Marcus.

'Of course she loves you,' said Lesley, holding her son's pyjama trousers for him to step into. 'She comes to see you, doesn't she?'

'She comes,' agreed Marcus, 'but I don't think she loves me.'

'She's upset,' said Lesley, 'because you broke her fossil.'

Marcus climbed into bed. 'Will you stay with me?' he asked.

'I'll stay until you fall asleep,' said Lesley. She lay down with him, and read a story that frightened him, and then dimmed the lamp and sang softly until she fell asleep beside him.

>•<

The telephone was ringing in the hallway. That's what had woken her. By the dimmed lamplight, she left her son's bed and picked her way across his room, placing her feet carefully between his strewn toys. When she opened the bedroom door, the hallway light that flooded in was painfully bright. She pulled the door to behind her and picked up the phone.

'Lesley,' said her stepfather, 'is Ruth sleeping there?'

'No,' said Lesley. 'Mum left after tea.' The grandfather clock behind her chimed and she turned and saw how late it was. 'She should have been home hours ago.'

'I'm going to drive over,' said her stepfather, 'in case she's broken down somewhere.'

Lesley turned her head towards the front door. Had she heard something? The porch light was on, but she could not see anyone through the glass, on the doorstep. With the phone still pressed against her ear, she went to the door and opened it, but there was nobody there. She looked out at the turbulent night, trying not to think about her mother's car crumpled in a ditch with the doors wedged shut, or shunted under a lorry, her mother dead on impact, or not quite dead but trapped.

'I'll stay near the phone,' she said to her stepfather. There was a tremble in her voice. She felt unsteady. 'Do you think I should call the hospital?' The hairs on her bare forearms were standing on end. She shut the door again, and locked it. As she moved back down the hallway, with her stepfather's voice in her ear, it took her a moment to notice her son, wide awake and standing in his bedroom doorway.

'This ghost can't ever be happy,' said Marcus, and Lesley looked for the drawing in his hands, but his hands were empty. He reached out, to hold on to her, holding on to her clothes, not looking quite at her but over her shoulder, towards the front door, in through which had come all the cold air that Lesley could feel at her back, cold air in which the chiming of the grandfather clock still seemed to vibrate.

HOVERING
(OR, A RECOLLECTION OF
25 FEBRUARY 2015)

GARY BUDDEN

From Ramsgate, we look south-westward over Pegwell
Bay, where, through the silted-up sand, the Stour, after
innumerable twistings during the finish of its course,
finds its way to the sea. The railway is cut through the
southern side of this hill, and when it was made a number
of Saxon graves, dating from the fifth and sixth centuries,
were found in the chalk, and also some Roman graves,
showing that the two races lived here simultaneously.

Highways & Byways in Kent, Walter Jerrold (1908)

Note on the text:
  *The events in this story were relayed to me by a close
acquaintance, Iain Saunders, a friend from the coastal
town of Herne Bay. I had known Iain since our schooldays
in Canterbury in the early 1990s. He had spent much of his
twenties living the existence he wanted in Falmouth on the
south-west coast of England, driving a camper van, working
the T-shirt stalls at festivals, and selling organic olives at
farmers' markets across the country. At one point in the late
noughties, he flirted with the idea of becoming a tree surgeon,
which I think would have suited him well. Sadly, it never
came about. Whenever he was in London, manning a stall at
Borough Market, we would meet for a pint of ale in one of the
wooden-beamed pubs of Southwark. Sometimes we caught
up at folk gigs at London venues like The Horse Hospital and
the Borderline, or we would both make a trip to towns and
cities like Bristol and Brighton to enjoy the live music on offer
in such places, and to catch up on neutral territory.*
  *At the time of this story's events, I was living in Enfield
and taking advantage of Epping Forest on my weekends,
maintaining a form of online journal that blended my fictions,*

photography and reports on the new territories of the London Orbital I had found myself wandering. Iain now lived in Ramsgate, having separated from his girlfriend of eight years, Tricia, in what he told me were amicable circumstances. Time had run its course, he said, and after the split he wanted to move on. Falmouth was too full of memory now, dense with the stuff, but he still wanted to be on the coast. That all made sense to me – some of the streets of north-east London where I had spent my twenties and early thirties were so freighted with ghosts I almost welcomed the developers and bulldozers levelling the place. Tricia moved, as she had long wanted, to Hebden Bridge in Yorkshire, and Iain to Ramsgate. He said they kept in touch, and I stayed up-to-date with edited forms of their life via my Facebook feed.

Ramsgate, a town on the Kent coast, was one of the great seaside towns of the nineteenth century; the twentieth did not treat it so kindly. Though now twitching with the first signs of gentrification, the town was still much as I remembered it from my intermittent trips there over the years – a once prosperous English coastal resort that had suffered from many years of decline. It reminded me of other such attractive and haunting places that ran the risk of fetishisation by those from the cities – Margate, Scarborough, Blackpool and Southend-on-Sea. Places periodically forgotten, then celebrated by visitors. Ramsgate had cheap accommodation, lacked job opportunities for its younger people who remained or couldn't leave; its Victoriana was scrubbed and scoured by saltwater and the coastal winds. Once it had been a member of the Confederation of Cinque Ports, under the Limb of Sandwich. Vincent Van Gogh taught there in the nineteenth century; Iain had pointed out the blue plaque to me on the first time I visited him after his breakup. Ramsgate had, like so many places, history. I have a photo of Iain grinning manically under that blue plaque.

There were pleasant Shepherd Neame pubs upgrading their décor in certain parts of the town to resemble restaurants or bars rather than a traditional public house. It was what current mainstream tastes craved; this was just something we had to weather, according to Iain.

But there was a more unpleasant side to the town too: in recent years, it had become the focus of various far-right nationalist groups attempting to stir up racial aggravation with the local Muslim population. This was a story all too common in the Britain I found myself living in. Perhaps, in their short-sightedness, the right-wing groups were attracted to the place for its role in both the Napoleonic Wars and the Dunkirk evacuations. I don't really understand the things I once thought I did, as if I now hover an inch or so from any grounded reality.

Iain and I maintained our friendship from childhood, through our university years and into adulthood, even if we perhaps saw each other only every eighteen months. He shared with me a love of folk music, walking the land when he could, and in days gone by, raving well into the deep dark of night and out the other side. I have fond recollections of sitting with him and Tricia as dawn crept through the windows of their Falmouth flat, the party over, nodding off to the disturbing sounds of Coil's Musick to Play in the Dark, Part 1 *and Can's* Future Days.

I have adapted his account of what happened at Pegwell Bay, just outside of Ramsgate, on 25 February 2015, and translated it into my own style, switching Iain's frantic first-

person account into what I hope is a more objective narrative. He said to me that I could have the story; he was keen to pass it on, as if he didn't want it.

He no longer lives in Ramsgate and no longer visits the bay. 'The place is too crowded,' he told me.

Gary Budden, Enfield, 2018

A few days before he fled the town of Ramsgate, Iain woke in the blank hours of the night in his newly decorated flat on Abbot's Hill, his heart thumping painfully, his throat parched, and his sheets soaked in acrid-smelling sweat. Ever since Tricia had announced, in her kind but firm terms, that their eight-year relationship had reached its natural conclusion, his sleep had been fitful and disturbed. Iain had moved from the south-west to the south-east, and the change had unmoored him, disquieted him, hurt him in ways he had not anticipated. This, he supposed, was normal. Banal, even.

How many people must be going through similar situations to this, at this very moment? he asked himself. His lack of originality was comforting, and he thought of himself as a pebble on one of Kent's beaches. Just one of many, weathered by time, buffeted and shunted around by tides he had little control over.

But amicable as it was, the separation from Tricia, after nearly a decade of relative happiness and security, lay heavier on him than he would have liked. He felt weighed down, pinned to the earth, as heavy and redundant as a menhir.

After a while staying with me in the quiet London suburb of Enfield, he secured work in the area he aimed to move to.

He found a decent and cheap flat in Ramsgate that he was able to buy with the modest amount he'd made on the flat sale in Falmouth, plus a small loan from his mother, his one surviving parent. Living here in this coastal town would allow him to be near family, but not so near that it might become a problem. And he had a few friends scattered across the county: Simon and Adrianna in the market town of Faversham, Jess in Canterbury. And he had many friends in London and its outer rim. There would always be the option to stay with people, head to other places for gigs and other cultural events. But the optional isolation Ramsgate offered appealed to Iain. He believed it would allow him to process and move on from the separation; a Victorian sense of the restorative power of the coast had always been in him, bone-deep and innate.

He packed up the van and drove from Enfield to Kent in the early autumn of 2014, as dark, heavy clouds hung swollen over the motorway. He listened at high volume to one of his favourite folk-rock records from the 1970s, *On the Shore* by Trees, as he drove. Iain imagined the purple and grey sky as skin bruised after a brutal underground fight, blood blooming under the surface. 'The damaged skin of heaven / Is ready to burst and split,' he said aloud to himself, as he overtook a middle-aged couple in a Land Rover. He noticed a kestrel hovering by the roadside, hunting for small rodents in the verge.

He arrived in Ramsgate just as the skies opened and the rain began. The gutters swirled with floating crisp packets and cigarette butts.

'Good luck, mate,' I said, as we shook hands on his doorstep. 'I'll be down soon to visit when you're settled in.

There's some good walks round there. We'll take a trip out to Pegwell Bay and the reserve when the time is right.'

Hope the move goes well xxx, texted Tricia. Iain couldn't bring himself to reply that day, but he did the next. *Thanks*, was all he texted back. Communication with Tricia then ceased for a long time.

Having arrived at the beginning of winter and the darkness it brought, then enduring the loneliness of his first Christmas as a single man, he had not yet acclimatised to this town on the Kent coast. He couldn't yet consider it the home he hoped it would become. These things took time, like anything, he told himself, but the streets felt uneven as he walked them, and he constantly took wrong turns down strange alleyways that felt desolate but conscious of his presence. He was disturbed by innocuous imagery in the town: a tidal paddling pool sat among the shining mudflats and dark swathes of stinking seaweed; an angled wooden post with the name 'Jodie' sprayed unevenly in black paint standing bent and purposeless by a footpath; the mural of a holidaying family rendered on a lift door in bright cheery colours and sharp angles. The family depicted in this mural had only eyes, no mouths and no noses. Their cartoon faces could not scream or shout or even smile.

He felt as if the old man in the newsagents regarded him with suspicion when he bought his pouch of tobacco and the occasional paper or music magazine. He felt like an impostor, someone looking from the outside in, a feeling he had never had in Falmouth or even London. Groups of the local schoolchildren filled him with unease – their conversation alien, conducted in a dead language of northern Europe – and mothers pushing buggies hurried past him. Old widowers with canes and white trainers smoked tarry cigarettes on the benches that overlooked the sea. They never registered his presence.

It took time to merge with a place, he knew that, but this teething period was tough nonetheless. So, he walked the streets of Ramsgate with herring gulls spiralling overhead and thought too much about Tricia, now in the green of West Yorkshire, posing in the ruins of Heptonstall Church with her sister Emily, or atop Boulsworth Hill with a male friend. Iain was aware that the area where she had relocated flooded often, due to years of soil degradation and abuse of the land. Every year the national news ran hysterical reports about a country sinking under water then all was forgotten until it all happened again. He wished her and her new life and all those people in the pictures to be flushed away, left in watery ruin.

What woke him to a pounding chest and sweaty panic was this: a dream, dim and retreating like the outgoing tide, of events out on the water. Tough, scarred men heaved oars through the brine aboard a Viking longship, their mouths sealed perfectly shut, only determined eyes in otherwise featureless faces. They were coming to Iain's new home, to land at Pegwell Bay and invade the town of Ramsgate. The words SWIFT and SURE were sprayed in black paint along the side of the longship, in lettering that had dripped and distorted before drying. These sailors were Norsemen of a kind, their hairstyles reminiscent of historical re-enactors, folk-metal groups and board game enthusiasts. At the prow of the ship, carved into the shape of a fearsome and degenerate emperor worm, stood a figure in inky black, his features obscured in shadow. He clutched a wet and discoloured plastic supermarket bag filled with items unknown. He was the leader of this expedition.

In the moments before Iain woke, he heard a droning noise, and saw a hovercraft approaching the longship from behind at high speed, with dead-eyed beings dressed as cartoonish Roman soldiers, like something from the *Asterix* cartoons he loved to read as a child, leaning over the sides and making obscene gestures at anyone who would notice. The Norsemen seemed oblivious to the oncoming collision.

And then Iain had woken, and could hear feral cats screeching and hissing in the back garden as they fought, and he ran to look outside and believed he saw an inky black figure clutching a plastic bag as a shadow among shadows. But there was nothing there: just the remains of the dream of an unhappy and anxious man.

For a while after, Iain sat at his small kitchen table, smoking a roll-up cigarette and drinking herbal tea that was supposed to calm him down. He thought about old mythologies, and a world-serpent devouring its own tail; of the endless loop of the M25 and traffic rumbling on the Great Cambridge Road near my house in Enfield. He doodled a sankofa bird on a crumpled post-it note as he smoked and sipped his tea; he thought of endings and beginnings.

>•<

The day Tricia had announced her plans – her confident pronouncement that time had run its course, as if she believed things could ever really begin or end – was an early summer's day with a first irritation of insects, and the smell of pollen and cut grass in the air. In the strained silence that followed, her words heavy like unearthed Saxon iron, Iain listened to the soft sigh of the sea. They lived so close to the coast. Tricia announced her plans and Iain had found himself mouthless, unable to speak.

Outside in the garden, he saw hoverflies among the flowers.

Down on the seafront, freezing wind whipped into Iain's face, causing his weaker left eye to leak in a constant stream. The tidal pool's surface rippled in the wind, and a middle-aged man threw a ball for a small grey terrier down on the sands. Scratched patterns of their passing were all over the shoreline. Iain paused to take a photograph of a battered sign in need of replacing.

ATTENT O PAD ING PO
Footwear should be worn
Strictly no diving.

Iain wondered what was submerged beneath the rippling water, ready to rip and lacerate, before the barking of the terrier pulled him out of his thoughts. The dog was growling and snapping at the waves, its ball forgotten.

Iain had decided to take a walk out to Pegwell Bay, not far from the town and his empty new flat. He'd send me some pictures, he knew I would appreciate them. The bay was a place recommended in his old copy of *Esoteric Kent*, an unusual guidebook printed in the late nineties by the defunct Malachite Press. It was in this book that Iain had discovered a striking photograph of one of his revered krautrock bands, Can, either arriving in the UK or departing after a tour back to the Continent. Standing in front of a hovercraft named *Swift* that ferried passengers to and from mainland Europe, the band were smiling and seemed slightly aloof. The photo was taken at Pegwell Bay.

The bay was once a place of happiness and sadness, filled with the joy of arrival and the pain of departure. The crossings were fast back then, taking just over twenty minutes to Europe. Iain would have loved to cross the water that way, hovering, with Tricia. But they were born too late. The hovercraft ceased their journeys in the eighties and the bay fell into forgotten ruin. No one had bothered to redevelop or regenerate the place, so all that was left was tarmac punctured by stiff grasses, a rusting stairway covered in old graffiti, car park markings shorn of all their meaning.

Others had arrived here too, of course. The Romans, under the leadership of Julius Caesar, landed here. Iain could see their logic.

Vikings too. A replica longboat, the *Hugin*, donated as a gift by the *Daily Mail*, standing in all its bright and gaudy colours in the picnic area above the bay, to commemorate a commemoration. Danes who had crossed the waters back in the 1950s on a replica ship, honouring their violent forebears who had done the same.

And Iain knew too that Saxon burials had been unearthed here. The bay had always been a busy place:

until now, perhaps. Was its status as a ruin, its wealth of cracked concrete and weeds, only of interest to people like himself? Iain realised what a cliché he might appear, but both recent ruins and deep time had always exerted their pull on him and that would never change. He was like that at the beginning and he would be at the end.

The thought crossed his mind that his interests had contributed to Tricia's decision that time had run its course. Iain, such a wanker in that moment, claimed he didn't believe in time, not in the way she conceived it. And Tricia, exasperated, told Iain that his views were cop-outs, justifications for not seizing opportunities when they arose and never fully taking responsibility for anything.

But Iain found solace in his ideas of circular time, even if he didn't fully understand. He felt it to be true, and for him that was enough.

It was in *Esoteric Kent* that he had discovered the strange stories about the county he was once again living in. The strange caves beneath Margate, that some attributed to the ancient Phoenicians. Strange beings of sackcloth and straw occasionally glimpsed along the Hollow Shore. The battle with a self-proclaimed messiah and his followers in the forest of Blean, near Hernhill.

He kept abreast of events after the book's publication too. Here, in Pegwell Bay, 2011, the washed-up body of a giant sperm whale appeared on the shingle by the nature reserve, hauled away at a cost of thousands. Online blogs dedicated to the exploration of ruin spoke of strange occurrences at Pegwell Bay at night. Lights out at sea, spied from the point where hovercraft left land to float above water. Songs sung in Latin and Norse, faint on the wind. Dogfights on the tarmac, out of sight of the town and prying CCTV. One message board was entirely dedicated to the continued sighting of a comet, visible only from a specific spot at Pegwell Bay.

'It is as if Donati's comet has never stopped blazing; blazing forever in a blazing world,' one commenter wrote.

The commenter referred to William Dyce's painting, one that Iain liked. He was thinking of getting a print of it to hang on the wall of his kitchen.

He wished that one day he could watch his family pick along the shoreline, hunting for fossils, happy. He pictured Tricia gripping a fossilised trilobite, the child they would never have covered in sand and wearing a red dinosaur T-shirt.

>•<

Iain discovered *Esoteric Kent* through his ongoing interest in the stranger occulted subcultures across the world, which had naturally led him to the Malachite Press, as well as his love of music like Coil and Current 93, the Vincent Harrier detective novels like *Saxifraga Urbium*, krautrock, psychedelia, strange antic fictions, the London canal network, once-obscure seventies TV shows, folk-rock and droning soundscapes. Iain loved the work of writers like C.L. Nolan, Hecate Shrike and Michael Ashman. Anything, he said, that helped him escape the mundane.

Their taste in music was always something that had

bonded him and Tricia, and Iain recalled fondly the days in Falmouth with their friends, microdosing mushrooms, letting acid dissolve on their tongues, and smoking thin roll-ups as they listened to work by The Haxan Cloak and Slow Moving Clouds.

>•<

What is a car park with no cars? What happens when the symbols we create lose their meaning? These were the questions Iain mulled over as he pulled on an old crimson fleece, laced up his muddied walking shoes and searched for his keys. The day looked clear and bright, cloudless, and he decided to leave his waterproof hanging on its hook. He opened the door, but hovered for a while at the threshold. He could have sworn he had forgotten something.

Iain walked down to the seafront and passed the mural of the mouthless family. They seemed to have moved position since his last visit and their eyes were frantic. The first stirrings of the new year were giving him a new hopefulness and desire to seize the day. Tricia would have been proud of him. He had his binoculars with him, a notebook, a few tins of Red Stripe he'd picked up from the off licence on the way down, a sandwich and fruit. He felt prepared, ready to rejoin the world and for his feet to touch solid earth again.

He checked his phone. Only a message from his network provider, and one from his mother he hadn't yet found the energy to answer. He thought about taking a photo, and perhaps sending it to Tricia. She would have liked it here, and he wondered why they had never visited in all their years together. But he decided against it. She was trying a new life in the gritstone of Yorkshire, attempting to take root in a different place. And here he was, on a different coast to the one that had been their home, but a coast that was comforting in its isolation. Iain would take root in the sandy, silted earth near to where he was born. And he had so much to explore still. The years had taught him to try and see the sights you cannot see.

Half a mile outside of Ramsgate, he stood on the clifftop, not close enough to the edge to risk an embarrassing fall, and looked out over Pegwell Bay. The reeds and coastal grass shimmered and trembled in a wind that gently moaned. Prickly sunlight bounced off the waters of the bay, illuminating a lonely landscape of virescent plants, sands ranging from flaxen to golden, and cracked concrete, shredded metal and tarmac that once formed the hoverport. He inhaled deeply, and the air smelled of salt as an oystercatcher flew noisily overheard. In the distance, like a piccolo played underwater, he heard the burble of a curlew.

A detectorist scoured a nearby patch of grass with his equipment, oblivious to him. Iain took what he hoped was a subtle and unnoticed photograph of him, and texted it to me.

Will you search through the lonely earth for me! I texted back almost immediately, with a smiley face after my words.

It was late in the February of 2015, when the evenings were finally beginning to stretch away from darkness and into the light but before the first flush of spring that would bring the birds and more walkers, dogs, buggies to these places. Iain knew this was the best time to be here. He knew that it was true what people said about the skies in this part of England. They were huge, transcendentally blue and cloudless, scoured only by flocks of dunlin and sanderling, and streaming chemtrails. People were holidaying using air rather than the water. There was no hovering now at the bay.

He headed away from the sandstone cliffs, and down to the bay itself. The land flattened out as he stepped on to the remains of the hoverport. A pair of carrion crows took flight at his appearance, leaving the decaying body of a gull, its eyes now gory red holes.

In front of Iain were white lines of painted information, long redundant and trying to spell the word CARS, cracked and faded and colonised by scrubby plants that he still didn't know the names of. Iain always said he liked ruins because they reminded us of our redundancy, our future uselessness. But now, in this moment, he just found it sad.

And then, as he crouched on his haunches on the cracked concrete, looking out to sea and imagining Roman soldiers running up the beach, the joyous arrival of hovercraft, the chants of long-dead Vikings as they hauled the *Hugin* into the shallow water, his phone rang. He looked at the number, and the number was Tricia's.

'You're at the bay,' she said. 'Thank you for the picture, Iain.'

Iain knew he had never sent a photo, and he told her this.

'You've sent me four or five now Iain.' Now she sounded unsure, tense. 'The bay. I've been dreaming of the bay.'

'You've been dreaming of the bay? Tricia, what are you

talking about?' Iain lit a roll-up cigarette and grimaced. There were no others on the bay, but as he squinted and looked up into the sky he could see the furious blaze of a comet.

'Iain, can you see the comet?'

'Tricia, how do you—'

'The comet blazes forever in a blazing world.'

'Tricia, are you feeling okay?'

'It's like you said Iain, nothing really begins and nothing really ends.'

Iain, as he flicked away his cigarette, noticed a fossilised trilobite by his right foot. He picked it up with his free hand, tossing it in his palm, feeling its roughness and its deep time.

'Tricia, I don't know what you're talking about.'

But as he said this to her, he knew exactly what she meant, and the bay was crowded, heaving, stifling, busy with life. Families dressed in the outfits of the early 1970s, tearful as their loved ones arrived. Fearsome battles fought by spectral soldiers from the days of Albion. And worse things too, things unrecorded in the history books. A young man drowned in the murk of the bay by a gang of bored bullies. An ancient whale, it's bloated body exploding in a ripe mess of gas and intestine. Ferocious dogs tearing chunks from each other's necks as dim-featured revenants cheered and threw down money. Norsemen with lank hair and blood-speckled metal. A dark figure with a Tesco bag, standing motionless in the reeds. And worse things too, things that Iain couldn't tell me when he arrived at my house in Enfield, couldn't vocalise as he sobbed on my sofa and tried to drink the vodka I handed him. Things I do not want to imagine into being on his behalf.

The residents of Pegwell Bay were all around him, crowding him, crushing him. And at Pegwell Bay, he wished for the possibility of an ending.

'Tricia, are you still there?'

But she had hung up.

THE HEADLAND OF BLACK ROCK

ROCK

ALISON LITTLEWOOD

There was a dead seagull at the foot of the cliff. It lay on its back, wings spread, white underbelly exposed and swollen. There was nothing but a bright red hole where its throat had been ripped out. I leaned over it, smelling only the sea, and saw tiny black insects wriggling in the wet. I grimaced. I couldn't guess what creature might have done it – killed it and left it there without taking another bite.

The cove was small and mercifully empty. The sea shattered against the rocks, sending up spume that dampened my skin and booming echoes that resounded around the cliffs. I was about to walk away when a smaller sound, a scraping of stone, drew me back. There on the cliff, its speckled down almost camouflaged against the rock, was a chick. It was large but ungainly, its feathers nothing more than fluff. I searched its bright black eyes for some expression I could recognise, but they were alien to me. As it shuffled along the rocks it revealed a malformed left foot, like a half-melted candle, and I knew then that it would die. It was probably always going to die, yet it peered down at what must have been its mother, no doubt hungering for some vile, half-digested fish. Had the gull died protecting her chick? It didn't seem likely. I imagined them to be cold, ravening creatures, no affection in them.

There wasn't much I could do about it either way. I took one more look around the cove: wild, smelling of brine and seaweed, too rough to swim, too pebbly for tourists to build sandcastles with their kids. Good. I fixed momentarily upon an odd arrangement of rocks just offshore – it looked a little like a seated figure – but there was nothing else to attract visitors. The guidebook had said that Cornwall's tourist hordes kept to Sennen Beach to the north and Land's

End to the south, leaving only a few hardy souls venturing along this stretch of coastline, fewer still troubling to scramble down the steep cliff path. I had found what I sought: isolation; nature; the simplicity of the world. The despoiled gull wasn't quite what I'd had in mind, but I pushed that thought away before I started the climb back up to Trevanann Cottage.

The holiday letting agent was waiting on the step when I arrived. I was gasping for breath, my sweat turning cold in the sea breeze. A few years back I would have jogged up and asked for more, another take maybe; I used to be as fit as my profession required. She only smiled, her eyes widening when she took me in – recognition? I sighed. She was grey and worn out and I wanted only to dismiss her, but she fumbled among her papers, found a bunch of keys and jangled them.

'I'm Sheila. Didn't like to go in without you.' She laughed as if she'd made a joke. 'I just called by to see if everything's all right. Brought a few things.'

I unlocked the door with my own key, wondering if she did this for all the guests or if she'd decided I was a special case, and she bustled in, pointing out the hob, the dishwasher, even the sink, as if a man on his own couldn't possibly have found them already. Trevanann was an old fisherman's cottage, retrofitted with everything I'd want for a month's stay – possibly longer, if I needed the time. She pulled a bundle from her bag, draped a fresh dishcloth over the tap, turned to the open-plan living area and withdrew a selection of magazines. I stared at the shiny pictures, the screaming fonts, recognising *Movie Scene*, its lead feature 'Forties and Fab'. The muscles in my jaw went tight. What did she want, an autograph? But she fanned them across the coffee table, a supply of well-thumbed paperbacks nested beneath.

'Anything else you need? You've found the cliff path, I see. Been to see the Irish Lady, have you?'

'The—?'

'It's the name for the rock just off the cove. There's a legend about it. You can read about it in the books.' She gestured towards the paperbacks and I barely glanced at them.

'Course, it can be lonely, too.' Her voice grew warmer, almost sympathetic, and I swallowed down my irritation. 'I'm always here if you need anything – anything at all, mind. If I'm not around I'll be helping at the pub in Sennen. You can find me there too, if you'd like. Any time. The Old Success.'

Again, I clenched my jaw. *The Old Success* – was she taking the piss? But I realised it was the name of the pub just as I took in her coquettish stance, her fingers combing back her wiry hair. *Anything at all*. She didn't imagine…?

Had she not realised who I was? I felt a sudden urge to flip through the magazine and show her, to point out that I'd been in a *movie*, for fuck's sake. How could she think I'd be interested in her? An image rose of my last girlfriend – and I remembered the blank adoration on her pretty face, her tiresome helplessness, her proclamations of love, and I forced myself to nod and smile as Sheila finally made her exit.

The first thing I did was pick up the magazine, though I'd sworn I was leaving all that behind, at least for now. My

PR had said I would be in it; I'd acted like I didn't care. The truth was, I'd been surprised. I hadn't had a decent role in too long, and I'd softened about the middle, lost a little hair. In certain lights, I might even look jowly.

I found the feature, which of course had lots of photographs and very little text, and saw that I'd been right: they'd bumped me after all. Then I saw the opposite page and my breath stopped.

'...And Not So Much,' the heading went, followed by more pictures: semi-remembered actresses' faces grown puffy, their bulk squeezed into the clothes of summers past, and in the middle, there I was. I'd been in the garden, my shirt off, my belly hanging over my shorts, the unflattering angle giving me multiple chins. *Bastards.* I'd never even seen the pap who took the picture.

I threw the thing across the room, knowing I shouldn't have looked. Should I fire my PR? Call the editor? Anything I did would only make it worse.

Instead, I went to the window and stared out. I looked beyond the cliff edge to the grey sea, the grey sky, all the miles and miles of nothing, and took deep breaths until I calmed.

The annoying woman was right about the book of legends, though it took a while to find it: an ancient, dog-eared thing called, somewhat misleadingly, *Popular Romances of the West of England* by Robert Hunt. The Irish Lady had a section of her own. A ship had foundered off Pedn-Men-Du, the Headland of Black Rock, during a storm. She was the only survivor. Daylight revealed the sight of her clinging to the rocks, but the sea remained too rough to reach her. Days and nights passed during which people could watch her dying, but do nothing; eventually, her body slipped into the water. Ever after – wasn't there always an ever after? – fishermen would catch glimpses of her when the waves were high, sitting on her rock, a rose in her mouth. They seemed to think the flower was to show her indifference to the tempest, though I hadn't heard of such a thing before; I always thought that roses meant love.

I imagined the local people, watching her die. It must have been quite the story, because Humphrey Davy had written a poem about her, dwelling on her tender age and her beauty. But of course: if she'd been old and ugly, I didn't suppose she'd have been worth the ink; she wouldn't even be in the book. The fascination in watching her light go out would have been all the stronger for how brightly it had burned.

I flicked through the book, pausing on a different legend, though I was struck at once by the similarity. Mermaid's Rock, a little further along the coast, was said to be the haunt of a Cornish mermaiden. She would make her appearance before a storm, and she sang most plaintively of all before a shipwreck. Young men, lured by her voice, sometimes tried to swim to her, but none ever came back.

That seemed a more obvious kind of yarn to tell, and I wondered why they hadn't assumed the Irish Lady to be a mermaid too – appearing when a ship was lost, so many sailors drowned. But what did it matter? It was only a rock, only a story. I tossed the book aside. Later, after lunch, I would go to the cove again. If nothing else, the walk would help me shift a couple of inches from my waistline.

>•<

The headland was indeed black, at least where the sea darkened the rocks. Again and again the waves threw a veil of white lace over them, and I blinked, because for a moment it seemed there was a woman sitting there – her legs twisted together, her hair long and wild, her face turned away from me, towards the horizon. Then I saw it was only a rock. I had been allowing things to get to me, I knew, allowing a series of images – mermaids, girlfriends past, my own ageing self – to circle around and around in my mind as the gulls now circled overhead, their cries like human voices, the sound of the wind and the waves the same.

The birds reminded me of the dying chick and I turned away from the sea, looking for its ledge. The gull was still there, its twisted foot held up and out – was it showing it to me, asking for help? Its eyes held only that same blank brightness. I wondered if it would be there again tomorrow, and the next day – like the Irish Lady, growing weaker, thinner, until it was gone.

But I couldn't feed it, couldn't save it. I imagined chewing up raw fish, spitting it onto a plate for this ravenous wild thing, and grimaced. I told myself it was impossible; I told myself there could be no fascination in watching it die.

Then I saw I was not alone on the beach after all.

She was caught in the perfect camera angle – a girl walking by the shore, long hair lifted and wrapped around her by the breeze, picking her way barefoot, a single gold thread gleaming about her ankle. She seemed unaware of anyone watching – and she was beautiful. She was the image of holiday romance, of youth, of carefree days filled with laughter and golden light, and she made me feel, suddenly and deeply, that life could be lived; that everything could start again.

I straightened, though she wasn't looking at me. She might have been the only person in the world, needing nothing other than the touch of sea-spray and the sound of the waves. I wished, at once, that I knew her name; I wondered what her voice would sound like. I wanted to run my hand across that taut young skin… but it felt as if the distance between us was a divide impossible to cross. I found myself wondering if she was real at all, or only another image conjured by my mind.

She turned and saw me. She smiled, and it was a real smile; I'd seen enough fakes in my time to know. Then she simply stood there, as if she was waiting.

The old questions arose – *an autograph hunter? A fan? A headcase?* – and were gone. I no longer cared. She surely wasn't like that; this girl was entirely natural and lovely, and I was walking toward her before I'd consciously decided to do so.

As I drew close she raised her head, revealing eyes that were perfectly blue, and gestured towards the sea. I called out, telling her my name, asking for hers, but she didn't reply. She gestured again – this time a finger-burst from her lips, as if to represent sound, and she shook her head.

'You can't speak?'

A shrug and another smile, as if a voice wasn't something she needed or even wanted. And maybe she was right; the silence – or rather, the sound of the sea all around us – said all that was needed. She reached out and caught my hand, pulling me towards her, stepped back towards the water.

'Oh – no, I...'

She mimed pulling off my shoes and I let out a sudden laugh. Paddling, at my age? But why the hell not? I tugged off my trainers and let them fall. Her fingers were slender and strong and sure as she led me into the surf.

The pebbles were sucked out from under my feet at once and I sank into them. She was light-footed, drawing ahead, her skirt floating on the water. She didn't fuss over it, didn't seem to care. When she turned to me again her smile was like a gift, beautiful and young but without all the things I'd grown so tired of seeing: the layers of meaning, the blind adoration, the recognition of who I was, and what; the *needing*.

Despite her muteness she spoke to me using her eyes and a twitch of her fingers, drawing me deeper, silently laughing. And I followed her, the water a shock of cold above my knees, gasping as a deeper swell reached my thighs. She kept looking at me, *into* me – and then she leaned towards me and kissed my lips. She tasted of iodine and salt; she tasted of the sea. I felt the pull of the waves and of her arms and I thought of simply letting go, of drifting with her, then I slipped and almost fell, one arm plunging into the water, meeting with nothing. I managed to keep my feet and staggered back towards the shore, though I still kept hold of her hand. When I saw the state of us both, I laughed, though the breeze set me shivering. I gestured towards the cliff top, mimed drinking coffee. I suppose I could have spoken the words, but somehow our silence felt right.

She withdrew her hand and I felt a pang of loss, but she cast a come-hither look over her shoulder as she walked ahead of me towards the path. My chest tingled. Was this really happening? It struck me that she was like me, on holiday alone and perhaps a little bored, but I didn't want it to be so prosaic and was glad I couldn't ask. It felt as if a little moment in time had opened, forming a bubble around us where nothing need matter.

She didn't turn again until we reached the top of the cliff. I was trying to gulp in air without letting her see how short of breath I was, but she didn't care. She kissed me again, long and deep, and then we were stumbling in at the door. I was enveloped in her hair; her arms were around me, then her leg wrapped mine, sand gritty against my skin, and I realised she must have left her shoes in the cove. I didn't take my lips from hers while I guided her to the bedroom.

>•<

When I awoke, the cottage was empty. The girl seemed as unreal as a dream but the sheets were damp with seawater and rough with sand, and I could still *feel* her, filling the empty spaces inside me, making everything new again.

I swept my hand over the bed as if I could conjure her shape, then pushed myself up and went in search of her. I already knew the cottage was empty. I could sense it in the still air, the silence an enemy now. I opened my mouth to call her name, realised I still didn't know what it was. But she had left a sign after all – a trail of wet footprints led across the floor from the bedroom, across the living area and towards the door. I tilted my head so that their gleam caught the light. I couldn't imagine how her feet had remained so wet, was sure I'd have heard if she'd taken a shower, but perhaps the moisture had come from her sea-damp skirts.

I made out the shape of her right foot, slender and elegant. And then I saw that the other print, the left foot, was shortened, as if the toes melted away into nothing. I wondered why that was, then realised that foot must simply have been partially dry. There had been nothing wrong with her form; she was flawless, and I felt the lack of her, the emotion stronger than anything I'd felt in months. I pictured her walking away from me, carrying the trace of my kisses on her salty skin, and something inside me twisted.

I shook my head. What the hell was wrong with me? I'd had women throw themselves at me before, proclaim their devotion, pursue me, but I hadn't felt anything except contempt. I felt a pang of guilt – but they'd been deluded, had *wanted* to be deluded. When they looked at me, they saw nothing but their own dreams.

This girl wasn't like that. Innocence like hers couldn't be faked.

A short time later I was on the beach, pacing the shoreline. I kept seeing her in my mind's eye – the turn of her head, the shifting of her hair, echoed in the tortured shape of the rocks. Was she a local? A holidaymaker? Would she even come here again?

I sat on a flat stone and waited, but the cove remained empty save for a rock shaped a little like a woman, its form mocking me now, and a dying seagull perched on the shelf of a cliff.

>•<

I spent much of that day at the cove, and the next. What else had I to do? I became used to the salt on my skin, my hair becoming lank. I told myself all the old lines – it was just a moment we had shared, nothing more – but I couldn't believe them. I waited and I watched. The Irish Lady bathed in the cold waves. The chick wasted away on the cliff. Nothing changed except the sea. I saw now that it held countless colours within it; ever-changing moods; innumerable faces. I couldn't take my eyes from it. I barely drank or ate and I'm not sure I thought of anything else, didn't care as time began to skip. A crab skittered across my foot and I picked it up without thought, crushing its shell between my teeth. I imagined the countless fish hidden beneath the waves, their cold bodies, gleaming scales, their viscid and staring eyes.

At night, when I returned to the cottage, I drank litres of water, though I found I wasn't hungry after all. I could settle to nothing until I found the book again, and I read of mermaids. I learned of the merry-maid of Padstow who choked its harbour with sand in revenge for some slight; of a man granted three wishes for saving a maid stranded in a rock pool. And I read of Honour Penna's daughter – stolen away as an infant, replaced by a mermaid changeling who lived as a human girl. Wronged by her lover, she pined away, but later she lured the wicked man to his death to repay his sins. Her kisses chilled his heart, kept him in her spell as he drowned in the cold waves. I found myself whispering the words of her song:

Come away, come away,
o'er the waters wild!
Our earth-born child
died this day, died this day.
Come away, come away!

I wondered again about the Irish Lady. If a woman could turn into stone, why not a mermaid or something else? An image rose before me: the girl walking naked through my cottage, every part of her perfect save her left foot, which ended in the twisted, malformed claw of a gull.

I shook my head. What the hell was wrong with me? It struck me that I might be having some kind of breakdown. The girl hadn't turned into anything. She was only a girl. She'd got into a car and driven away, or worse, been driven away by someone who actually mattered to her, and I would never see her again. Unless, that was, I looked so hard that I imagined her face everywhere, in the waves, in the rock...

I went into the kitchen and forced myself to eat, my throat gulping and convulsing over the dry mass of bread, and I grabbed my jacket. The girl had been real. That meant I had to be able to find her.

The Old Success was brighter and more modern than I'd imagined. A couple of bearded, grizzled locals sat in the corner exchanging yarns while a family complete with buckets and spades squabbled around a table. Sheila was standing behind the bar and when she saw me she waved with her whole arm, as a child might, and called, 'Yoo-hoo!'

When I went over to her she stared as if she'd never seen me before, then reached out and brushed at my cheek. I began to pull away, then felt the salt flaking from my skin.

She didn't comment, only let out her sputtering laugh, and I thought, with a stab of spite, that no one would ever write a poem about her. I pictured the girl on the beach, her lovely form, her golden hair, and even as I asked after her I wondered if my breakdown was so complete that I'd imagined the whole thing. It didn't help when Sheila's smile faded and she said, 'No, I don't think I've seen her. Sounds like a mermaid.' She sputtered again.

I tried not to show my dismay. 'I thought everyone here knew everybody else?'

'Oh, it's not like that now, love,' she replied. 'Not like it used to be. Some of the families go back a ways I suppose, but there's a lot of holiday lets now. A lot of strange faces.' She rambled on, telling me how she'd only moved down here a few years back, that she'd been quite the thing in the city in her day, and I tuned her out and made my escape.

The cottage couldn't hold me. Its walls were closing in, everything too small. I found myself writhing on the bed, burying my face in the sheets, grasping at grains of sand that slipped through my fingers. It had been real. *Real.* I pictured a mermaid on a rock, combing her lovely hair, perhaps even singing. And people watching her from the shore, so close but at an impossible distance; unable to see her for what she really was, seeing only what they imagined her to be. Was she wrecked by the storm or did she raise it?

Had the sailors truly perished in the tempest or had they leapt, despairing, into the waves?

Had they ever existed at all?

The words that came back to me were Sheila's: *strange faces.*

I went to the window, seeing my own pale reflection, my features distorted. The sky outside was already dark, gunmetal clouds roiling in from the west. In the far distance was the first flicker of light: a storm was rising.

I thought of the lonely cove, all the imagined glimpses of her face I had seen in its forms; and I thought of the gull trapped there, its leg useless, its body wasting. I had been watching it *die*. It seemed suddenly important, this thing I could have saved, some little good that I could have done with my life, and I started towards the door.

I half scrambled, half slid down the cliff path. The sky was monstrous, alive with movement and noise, as was the sea, as if something stirred within it. I had been warned that storms could whip the spray as high as the cliff top, and found my face damp; I blinked it from my eyes. Bright foam marked the meeting of wave and rock; moonlight formed a path into the sea, but all else was dark.

I made my way to the foot of the cliff where the chick had been and squinted up at the ledge. At first I could see nothing but shadows, then lightning flashed and I saw that the gull wasn't there. Perhaps it had flown after all, or had been taken by a predator. I was too late and I felt my eyes sting – salt water?

I cursed myself as a fool for venturing out, climbing down here for nothing, and then I turned and saw the girl, just as she had been, walking by the edge of the sea.

When she turned towards me, moonlight limned her hair, her face cast into shadow so that I couldn't make it out. And as I walked towards her I remembered another tale of a mermaid, one I had heard many years before, when I was young. That mermaid had been young also. She had given up her voice, her home in the sea, everything she had, in the attempt to gain love; but her prince hadn't really seen her, hadn't understood who she truly was.

She waited for me, the sea raging around her, and beneath its roar I heard the more plangent note of its echo resounding from the cliffs. For a moment, I was certain I heard her voice. It was as it had sounded in my dreams, ones I'd never wanted to leave; low and sweet, lulling my senses.

I realised she was smiling, holding out a hand towards me. Didn't she see how the waves seethed – wasn't she afraid? A wild comber lashed her to the waist, but she didn't flinch, only waited. I knew I had to reach her. I hurried down the beach, not pausing to remove my shoes, and glanced across the cove – black rock, moon-glitter striking the sea, cliffs etched against the sky – and the Irish Lady, where was she? I glimpsed only a sheet of flat rock, but that must be an illusion; the sea obscured everything.

Blinded by spray and drenched at once, I waded in, reaching for her. She must be deeper in than I realised, but then I caught sight of her, holding out both hands to me. She appeared calm; I made out the shape of her lips, curved into a smile.

The current's deep pull dragged at my legs, my flesh turning leaden. I told myself that if she could stand firm so could I, and I pulled in a breath, tasting brine on my tongue.

I tried to picture myself as she must see me: young again, strong and vital, full of life.

I took another step, felt the pebbles giving way beneath me, everything roiling and turning in the waves. Nothing was sure, nothing certain. And the words I'd read came back to me, as if carried on the freezing air:

Come away, come away...

I reached for her, flailing, and by some miracle felt the touch of her hand. Her skin was cold and pallid, almost like something dead. I had to get her out, to warm her – and I dragged her towards me and really saw her at last.

It was she – there were the same eyes, the same features, but subtly changed; and I saw that she wasn't young at all. She wasn't even beautiful. Her eyes weren't wide or welcoming; I wasn't sure she was entirely human. She made me think of things deep under the sea – pliant bodies, pale skin, creatures that lived without the knowledge of joy or mercy or love.

I tried to make out the expression in her eyes, hoping I was wrong. I tried to see the love in them. They were unknowable and alien and bright. Suddenly my arms were without strength and I felt all the passing of years, the way I was failing, and instead of pulling away she drew me in until the sea was up to my waist. She wasn't even looking at me any longer – she was already tired of me. There was no fascination in watching me die, not when my light had already half gone out. I thought of the girls I had dallied with, taking my pleasure and casting them aside, heard again their entreaties ringing in my ears. But the words they whispered had changed, becoming lines from a story I'd read in a book: the mermaid's song as she lured the lover who had scorned her into the waves:

His corse shall float
Around the bay, around the bay...

I shook away the words but I couldn't fail to hear as she opened her mouth to speak at last. I saw her white teeth, the red inside of her mouth; her voice was a raw, plaintive cry from the back of her throat. Her laughter was the cry of a gull and in her eyes was not innocence, but a terrible knowledge: a hunger as endless as the sea.

THE DEVIL IN THE DETAILS

RAMSEY CAMPBELL

'We oughtn't to go if young Brian will be bored. It's his holiday as well, Barbara.'

'You won't be, will you, Brian? There'll be plenty to see in the house and the park.'

'It's your day, Aunt Leonie. It's your turn to say what we do.'

'He's a credit to you both. I wish I knew more like him. Now, Brian, don't make that face.'

'Your aunt wants to see the paintings while she has the chance. It won't hurt you to look at them as well.'

'Jeff, I think the face was just embarrassed. Maybe they'll help you with your art at school, Brian. You can tell your teacher what you saw. So long as you don't mind…'

Brian did his best to seem enthusiastic despite wondering how much more he might have not to mind. Because his aunt disliked flying they'd gone not to Turkey but to St Brendan on Sea, which wasn't quite northern enough to be close to mountains and lakes. Supposedly the town was famed for its murals three centuries old, but Brian kept being told there was plenty to occupy him. His aunt had to be considered because she'd lost her husband Quentin recently, though only by divorce. Even the activities Brian's parents chose for their days seemed to be mostly for her. In case he wasn't sufficiently uncomfortable his mother told him 'Do what you have to do and we'll be off.'

Though he was twelve he had to share the family room while his mother's sister had next door all to herself. His father had told him off for dislodging the toilet seat, though it had already been askew. Brian dabbed at the results of his inefficient aim with toilet paper and wiped his hand on his trousers on the way downstairs, past a kind of china totem pole composed of sleepy cats. His aunt produced a laugh every time she saw it and waited until Brian manufactured one, so that he couldn't help feeling relieved that the family was waiting outside the Seeview. Even from upstairs the only view was of the whitewashed hotels opposite.

The family clambered into the Clio, which his aunt frequently called Cliopatra. Five minutes' drive past tearooms and antique dealers and Victorian shopping arcades took them out of the small town. While Brian's mother drove through country lanes his aunt pointed out sights she appeared to think he would otherwise have missed, not that he would have cared too much. Twenty minutes of this brought them to Foliant Hall. The stone lions guarding the gates put Brian in mind of the china cats in the boarding house, but it seemed this time he wasn't meant to laugh.

A guide half his aunt's age was leading a party of visitors out of the sandstone mansion. 'You won't mind waiting for us, will you?' Aunt Leonie appealed to her and hastened into the lobby, miming a search for her credit card until Brian's father overtook her to buy tickets. When the party was complete at last – Aunt Leonie enacting comical haste rather than achieving actual speed – the guide said 'We'll start in the chapel. The Soulous ceiling is being restored.'

Brian made a manful effort to anticipate a treat as everyone trooped along an avenue to the ruddy chapel. A man was perched on scaffolding underneath a mural full of angels, though for the moment he was busy drinking from a mug. 'Good morning, Charlie,' the guide said as though to prompt him to demonstrate his skills, but he only raised the mug in a salute.

'Maurice Soulous has made our little town world-famous with his paintings…' The Foliant family had taken up the painter and commissioned his work for the hall as well as the chapel, and he'd provided murals for both the Catholic churches in town. He'd become a painter and a convert late in life, one reason why the Foliants had supported him. In return he'd painted images of their acceptance into heaven, and you can see them there and there. As Brian peered up at the solemn well-fed faces of the white-robed figures being borne away by angels, his aunt said 'He wasn't such a saint himself, was he?'

'No photographs, please.' Having waited until all the offenders lowered their phones, the guide said 'That's why he converted. Charlie, when you're ready—'

'Don't they say he painted angels to disguise himself?' Aunt Leonie said.

'I hadn't heard it put that way.'

'To disguise his nature, and maybe his conversion was meant to do that too. Maybe it let him end up thinking he hadn't been a monster to his wives.' For just the family to hear, Brian's aunt murmured 'Like someone I won't name treated his wife.'

'I was meaning to come to that later.' In the same tone of muted reproof the guide said 'Charlie—'

'You'll be saying how he put himself in every mural but those details were all painted over.'

'I was coming to that now. In fact Charlie—'

'Only nobody knows who did it. They aren't sure Soulous did even though it's in his style.'

'Well, you've told the people everything I would have.' As though retrieving triumph from defeat the guide called

'Charlie, have you found him?'

'Could have.' The man set down his mug with visible reluctance and used a tool to point at the cluster of angels directly above him. 'He could be under them.'

Brian squinted at the flaking section of the mural until the outline of a white-winged figure seemed to shift. The rest of the party had finished admiring the interior and were wandering out of the chapel. Perhaps the restorer disliked having so large an audience, because he abandoned the mug to pick up a tool. Brian was backing towards the exit while he watched when the heavenly vista seemed to light up from within.

It was the flash of a camera. Someone had lingered to take a surreptitious photograph. The glare made a figure appear to lurch out of the mural above Charlie's head. Presumably the restorer was twisting around to remonstrate with the photographer, however much he looked as though he was recoiling, but his left foot slipped off the platform. In a moment the rest of him did.

Brian hadn't realised how long a second could last: long enough for the man to finish a wordless cry that might have been aimed at the photographer, and to flail all his limbs as if trying to swim in the air, and even make to clutch at his head with both hands to protect it. The gesture ran out of time, and the back of his head collided with the stone floor with a thud like the fall of a stuffed sack. Brian couldn't turn away until the floor around the twitching figure began to look as if someone had spilled paint, and then he dashed out of the chapel. All the visitors, even his family, were retreating along the avenue. 'Mum, dad,' he cried, 'he fell. He's hurt.'

His aunt was the first to look back. 'What are you saying, Brian?'

'Someone took a photo and made him fall. It wasn't me.'

Was the culprit retreating through the trees towards the house? The guide and her party crowded around Brian, and he was distracted by a woman saying 'I'm a nurse.'

She and the guide hurried into the chapel, followed by a thud – the door. As the rest of the party loitered near the entrance Brian's father said 'You didn't do anything, son.'

It wasn't quite sufficiently unlike a question. Brian took out his phone to display the lack of evidence, and was surprised to find his fingers weren't as steady as they ought to be. In his mind the man's fall had begun to resemble a scene from a film with half-hearted effects, while his surroundings – blue sky, green trees, red church, variously coloured faces – seemed unnecessarily vivid. Telling his mother he was all right only prompted her sister to ask if he was sure. Before he had to say so yet again, the nurse reappeared. 'I'm afraid there's been a fatality,' she said.

The guide emerged paler than when she'd gone in. 'I'm sorry, I'm going to have to cancel today. Please go back to the desk for a refund or reschedule.'

'Could you have a look at our son?' Brian's father asked the nurse. 'How do you think this may affect him?'

The nurse performed a swift examination before ruffling Brian's hair. 'How are you feeling, old fellow?'

Brian felt further embarrassed by saying 'Sad for the man.'

The nurse pronounced him fit, and the family made for the mansion, where Brian's father obtained tickets for the day after tomorrow. On the way to the car Brian saw an ambulance arriving at the chapel. The flicker of the roof lights plucked at the shape of a man who slipped into the building, though at that distance the door looked hardly even ajar. During the drive back to town Aunt Leonie devoted herself to pointing out views she would have put on canvas if she hadn't left her painter's equipment at home. 'It would only bore young Brian,' she'd said.

St Brendan's was ten minutes' walk from the Seeview, up a hill ribbed with terraces of white cottages. 'The walk will do us all good,' Brian's mother said, but he thought she mostly meant him. No doubt the church had been built on the hill for sailors to see from their ships. The interior walls were a mass of angels, which might have swarmed out of the stained-glass windows, and on the ceiling another flock raised a saint to heaven. 'Look behind the angels,' Brian's aunt told him as if he needed some diversion from his thoughts. 'Maybe you'll see the man himself.'

'Aunt Leonie, what did he do that was so bad?'

'He tortured his wives, all of them. They said it excited him. He nearly killed some of them, but he had too many friends in high places to be put in prison.' As Brian's parents showed signs of intervening she said 'These days men have other ways of abusing us. Make sure you're never like that, Brian.'

'I believe we can guarantee that,' his father said and told him 'Just look at what we've come to see.'

Brian didn't know if he was being directed to search for the artist or advised against doing so. He peered at the relentlessly holy faces so hard that the edge of his vision quivered, which made figures that he wasn't looking at directly seem to inch aside, as if another figure needed room. Whenever he glanced at them, the impression subsided. He was quite glad when his aunt let everyone leave, though only to visit another church.

St Mary Magdalene's faced a shop that sold fishing tackle on the main street. Once again the interior was overrun with angels, a cluster of which were lifting a saintly woman under the roof. Brian looked for signs of torture, but presumably she hadn't been a martyr. Near a table that he gathered was an altar, though he thought it could have passed unremarked in a florist's shop, he saw a booth with two doors. 'What's that for?' he said and felt childish.

'It's a confessional,' his aunt said. 'People tell the priest their sins in there and that's supposed to make it right. That shouldn't be how it works, though they let Maurice Soulous think it was. Some things you shouldn't be forgiven just because you own up.'

'Leonie,' Brian's mother said, 'I don't think we need that in church.'

Brian felt compelled to search for the artist without feeling sure that he wanted to find him. Some angels appeared to have shadows, but whenever he looked closer the dark addition dodged back. Could the confessional be in use? If he was hearing a whisper, it could hardly be behind the booth, where a section of mural was flaking away. Perhaps the booth was meant to hide the damage, unless it was the cause. As he tried to focus on the peeling shadow his mother said 'What's wrong, Brian?' Though he moved away at once, she didn't stop watching him until they left the church. 'Let's get some fresh air on the front,' she said.

The bay was strewn with fishing boats, and nets lay on the stony beach. The promenade offered a bingo hall, a coin arcade that he'd been warned was a waste of money, a fairground where the rides were too young as well as too antique for him, a ballroom with posters for performers apparently determined to resurrect celebrities by imitation. A salty breeze ruffled Brian's hair as the nurse had, inspiring his aunt to tell him 'This should give you an appetite,' and he wondered if she felt responsible for the shock everybody thought he must have suffered in the chapel.

His appetite could indeed have done with stimulation. Dinner at the Seeview consisted of a feebly international menu, far less varied than his parents made at home. The curry he'd tried last night was half the strength of his mother's, though his aunt had pronounced it too fiery for her. The fish of the day appeared to be that of the week if not the month. Brian opted for a cheeseburger, which arrived in a bun competing for softness with eight chips that lent it a presumably inadvertent resemblance to a crab. Afterwards the family joined others in the lounge to watch a television smaller than the one in Brian's house. Aunt Leonie was among the guests who called out answers to quiz shows while Brian sent phone messages to friends. When his mother chided him for distracting the contestants, he took his embarrassment to bed.

The photograph above it, of men in hats and women in long dresses on the promenade, didn't trouble him. All the same, he fell asleep with a sense that some unwelcome presence was above him, or would be. As he climbed the ladder to the platform on the scaffold he craned back to take in the whole of the ceiling mural, but none of the angels acknowledged him. He did his best to balance on the platform, which consisted of a solitary plank, but his antics unbalanced the ladder, and he made a desperate grab for whatever might save him. When a hand seized his from overhead, he was so reluctant to see the rescuer that his protest wakened him. His father's disgruntled mumble fell short of words, and Brian lay not much less still than a painting to be sure his parents stayed asleep.

At breakfast they seemed heartened by how much he ate. 'You'll need a good walk after that,' his aunt said, which gave him an idea for his day. 'Let's see how far we can walk,' he said, 'and see what else there is.'

Yesterday he'd noticed a cliff path leading from the promenade. The walk brought views of an increasingly rocky coast peopled only by birds, and he felt pleased with his choice until his aunt began saying 'Keep away from the edge, Brian' and 'Be careful, Brian' and 'Don't go too close.' Eventually she said 'Your uncle used to do that. He knew I hated heights.'

'You didn't when we were Brian's age,' her sister said.

'That was how someone I won't mention worked on me. I'm getting my confidence back.'

'Was that how he tortured you, Aunt Leonie?'

Before she could respond Brian's father said 'Do as your aunt says and stay clear.'

The walk led them to a clifftop pub in time for lunch. Brian thought his parents would have sat outside if his aunt hadn't met the prospect with a shiver. Among the brochures for local attractions in a rack next to the entrance he found one for Foliant Hall. A photograph of the interior of the chapel bothered him enough that he took it to the table. How was the ceiling mural different? It felt like trying to solve one of the picture puzzles he used to enjoy – looking for a hidden face – but he hadn't succeeded by the time his aunt said 'Can't you wait to go back, Brian?'

'I was just seeing if he's there.'

Perhaps this hinted at aversion, because his father said 'We all have to make sacrifices. Your aunt has come on a walk she doesn't like.'

'I do like it, Jeff. Don't make Brian feel guilty when there's no need. You're helping me get over my fear, Brian.'

Brian stuffed the brochure into a pocket and concentrated on his fish and chips. Afterwards his aunt insisted on walking further along the cliff, perhaps because his father kept him well clear of the edge. The evening brought another burger, followed by another clutch of the quiz shows Aunt Leonie never seemed to tire of. Brian gave the brochure his attention and was disconcerted to find that however long he stared at the murals in the chapel, they didn't stir. This was among the issues that lingered in his mind when he went to bed.

He used to like his uncle Quentin, who'd been fond of wrestling with him and telling jokes the other adults disapproved of and letting him watch films the boxes said he was too young to see. Should Brian feel guilty for having liked him – for persisting in it now? Another source of confusion was his father's remark about sacrifice, although until he was close to sleep Brian didn't realise why it stayed with him. Of course, the death of the restorer would have functioned as a bloody sacrifice in several of the films Uncle Quentin had put on while the rest of the family were elsewhere. They were only films, and so Brian didn't dream, though in the morning his aunt asked if anybody had. 'We don't, Leonie,' his father said.

'I don't think you can speak for everyone.' For a moment she seemed about to say something other than 'Are you sure you want to go to the Hall again, Brian?'

His parents seemed to feel he should make the effort, and so he said 'Course I do.'

Too late he wondered if she'd wanted an excuse to call the visit off. 'Everybody does, Leonie,' his mother said.

'Thanks for all your trouble with the tickets, Jeff.'

Might Brian's aunt feel constrained to revisit Foliant Hall? He was about to admit reluctance, whatever the cause, when his mother sent him to the bathroom with no chance to argue. On the way to the Hall his aunt was so determined to distract him if not herself that she kept drawing attention to sights they'd already seen. When Brian saw the gates bore a notice, he thought the tours were still cancelled until a man bustled out of the drive to remove that hope.

The guide was back at her job. She gave Brian's aunt a sharp look and him a sharper one. The chapel remained shut to visitors, but the rooms of the main house were painted with angels too. Crowds of winged figures guided children through life, or helped shepherds in the fields, or stood behind personages the guide identified as members of the Foliant family, to advise or guard them. Brian was busy searching for Maurice Soulous, whatever the artist might look like. That must be why he saw a figure dodge behind an angel who was ushering a child into a church, and drop to all fours to hide in the midst of a flock of sheep. He even thought one angelic face, which was intent on the Bible a man was reading at a desk, had begun to slip askew. He assumed the painted face was flaking until he came close enough to find it was intact. In a bid to finish looking for the hidden presence he said 'Have you seen him yet, Aunt Leonie?'

'I'm not looking very hard today, Brian.'

'I thought you wanted to find him. I thought that's why we came.'

'We've never turned him up,' the guide said, explaining to the other visitors 'The self-portraits of the artist. They may be just a myth.'

Brian spoke before he was aware of thinking. 'Maybe your friend uncovered him.'

'Who?' Without waiting for an answer the guide said 'What do you mean?'

'The man who fell.'

'Brian,' his father warned him, but the guide had more to say. 'He wasn't there to do that. He wasn't looking underneath.'

Brian found he was anxious to learn how the accident had affected the mural. As he tried to think of a way to ask, his father said 'Enough. Nobody wants to hear.'

Brian felt as if he'd been left alone with all the paintings in the house. Each bedroom sported angels overhead, and he kept thinking that one of the radiant faces was about to fall awry like a mask. Was his aunt troubled by some impression of the kind? They were in the last bedroom when he thought he glimpsed a spidery intruder scuttling behind a rank of angels up above, peering over every shoulder at him. By the time he dared to look directly up there was no sign of movement, and yet he had a sense that part of the mural was remaining unnaturally still so as not to be noticed. He was desperate to speak to his aunt about it, but as they left the house she spoke first. 'You didn't need to look for him for me, Brian. Let's forget about him now.'

She and his father seemed to have left him nothing to say. He was silent on the way back to town, where the family strolled around the antique shops and bought not a single item, and throughout dinner, ignoring how the burger and its attendant chips resembled a dormant spider, and the quiz shows even when he knew an answer. 'Don't sulk, Brian,' his mother eventually said. 'We'll go for a drive tomorrow.'

He still had to face the night. In bed he found he wished the room were lighter, or else so dark he couldn't see the photograph on the wall. He had an unpleasant fancy that one of the vintage holidaymakers was about to raise not just his hat but along with it his face. Squeezing his eyes tight didn't shut out the impression. 'Don't want to see,' he mumbled. 'Never did.'

'Go to sleep now, Brian. Your mother wants her rest before she drives.'

Brian must have slept already, since he hadn't realised his parents were in the room. Their presence ought to let him feel safe while he reassured himself that nothing had happened to the photograph, and he opened his eyes. As the dim arrested figures set about reclaiming their outlines from the gloom he could have imagined one of them had stirred – the one that was craning over a woman's shoulder. It was resting lanky fingers there – indeed, it appeared to be digging them in. Now it was clambering out of the picture like an insect emerging from a chrysalis. Its face resembled a swollen blister in paint, and gazed at Brian with peeling eyes while it thrust its crumbling grin at him. 'Go away,'

Brian begged, burying his mouth in the pillow while he hid under the quilt. 'Go somewhere else.'

When he heard scrabbling above him he tried to believe it sounded more like a mouse in a wall than nails scraping at glass. He held a breath that would have come out as a scream if he'd heard the glass give way or the noise emerge around the frame of the photograph. He found it hard to breathe even when the sound receded and dwindled and was gone, but at last he managed to sleep.

He would rather not have gone back to the chapel even if his aunt believed they hadn't seen enough. She ventured in ahead of him, and when he followed he couldn't immediately locate her. Someone had spilled paint again, for it was dripping from the platform overhead. No, it was coming from the mural, where the restoration must have recommenced, although Brian couldn't see who was doing the job. Instead he saw his aunt, pressed flat to fit into the mural and by no means yet dry. His mouth was still pressed against the pillow, and his muffled shriek failed to rouse his parents.

Was his protest echoed? He could even have imagined his cry had been the echo. He peered nervously at the photograph in the twilight before dawn until he managed to establish that the glass was unbroken. He could see no intruder among the antique figures on the promenade. He couldn't help listening for his aunt, whose bed was against the far side of the wall and closer to his than to his parents, but there was no sound apart from running footsteps in the street. They vanished into the distance without wakening his parents, and surely any other noises had been part of Brian's dream, though he wasn't sure how the slam of a door fitted in. The reassurance let him go back to sleep.

His mother had to waken him. He felt eager for breakfast and for a day of driving, even if Aunt Leonie devoted herself to directing his attention. When he left the room he found his parents outside her door. His mother knocked on it again, and then harder. 'Leonie,' she called and raised her voice. 'Leonie, it's time we got going.'

'Try her phone, Barbara.'

Brian heard the bell trilling in his mother's mobile but no sound from the room. 'I'll fetch Mrs Mason,' his father declared and marched down the corridor.

The landlady looked flustered and doubtful about unlocking the door. Once Brian's mother took all responsibility Mrs Mason let her into the room. The bed was violently rumpled, but that was the only sign of life. As Brian's mother opened the inner door to find the bathroom just as deserted, the landlady demanded 'What's happened there?'

The glass of the photograph above the bed was splintered, erasing the face of a Victorian holidaymaker. There was blood on the shards and on the quilt beneath. Brian's mother was making to speak when her phone rang. 'It's Leonie,' she said with relief.

'Barbara?'

Brian's mother faltered, because it wasn't her sister's voice. 'Who is this?'

'I was walking on the beach. I'm afraid there's a lady who's fallen.'

'The beach,' Brian's mother said with what might have been hope.

'Yes, the rocks. It's her phone. You're the top name on it. I've called emergency.'

'How is she? How's my sister?'

Brian was already dashing into the corridor, faster when his father called his name. He was almost at the front door when a woman with a vacuum cleaner emerged from the dining-room. 'Don't say you're running off as well.'

'As well as what?' Brian had to ask.

'As the lady in the room by yours. She went out hours ago. She must have wanted to be somewhere in a hurry. You'd have thought she was being chased. I nearly thought I saw someone.'

Even more reluctantly Brian asked 'Who?'

'I told you, nobody. It must have been a shadow.' With some defiance the woman said 'Nobody looks like that.'

Brian didn't care to hear any more, and his parents were on their way downstairs. He ran out of the Seeview and past shop after shuttered lifeless shop to the promenade. He was trying to hope his aunt had managed to conquer her fears, whatever they might be. He hadn't sprinted far along the cliff path when he saw his aunt lying face down on the rocks, where a woman was keeping a dog clear of her. However close he ventured, the sight didn't change for the better. His aunt's limbs were splayed like an explosion of flesh, and her flattened shape simply appeared to spread larger. When he heard his parents catching up with him he turned to them, though he had to cover his face. 'I didn't see,' he pleaded. 'I didn't want to see.'

SWIMMING WITH HORSES

ANGELA READMAN

The lights of the Ferris wheel made chalky trails on the sky in the distance. On this side of the bay, it was just us and the waves. Kiera walked ahead clutching the bundle close as a bag of chips. I stared at the lights of the fairground over the water. Girls swirling on the waltzers seemed a planet away.

'Are you sure?' I asked, my teeth chattered, though it wasn't that cold.

Kiera nodded and I followed her across the beach. She slipped off her shoes and waded into the water, tucking her skirt into her knickers. The tide was roaring in. Horses galloped to the shore, carrying the moon on their backs.

I held Kiera's shoes and the towel. There was a small torch on my keyring I flicked on and off, on and off, like the North Star. I looked at the light glowing orange in my jacket pocket. And when I looked up, the horses were closer. Kiera kissed the bundle, lowered it into the ocean and let go.

I held the torch high for her to make her way back to me. My eyes were so watery the light broke and burst, but Kiera wasn't crying. She stood still, watching the waves for a while and finally said, 'I'm freezing! Pass me that flippin' towel!'

She smiled, drying her legs, squishing her feet into shoes without undoing the laces. Or maybe, she was only trying to smile, and smiling was a habit she didn't know how to break. It's hard to say. I've never really understood the whole thing with her and the kelpies. I barely understand *her*. Before last year, Kiera and I weren't even friends.

We both had jobs we hated, and would have loved to last longer than until September. In the cafe in the arcade, I served soggy chips and orange tea in polystyrene cups to tourists and silver-haired ladies who loved the slot-machines. Kiera strolled past the cafe wearing a cap with a fluffy puffin on the peak, dishing out flyers for boat trips to the island. She'd come in at lunchtime and sit by herself most days. I served her the same as anyone else, barely paying attention, jangling coins and the squall of video games dragging me elsewhere. I was only half there, and half dreaming of being anywhere else. I suppose she was the same.

'You've ran out of forks,' she said.

I wiped the counter and inspected the box of disposable forks. It was empty, but the caddy of cutlery for sit-in customers was full to the brim. 'You're eating in,' I said. 'You can use the steel cutlery. The forks are right there.'

'I like the wooden ones,' Kiera said.

I replaced the box and saw her take out two forks. She used one to shovel down her chips and snuck the other one into her coat. Later, she told me she liked the feeling of the wood on her fingers, the smooth surprise of it whenever she put her hand in her pockets. She was the strangest of girls. I never met anyone like her.

She wore an oversized jacket with *Island Tours* printed on the front, and sturdy shoes she didn't bother changing after work. Ida and Jen would call her a loser, if they were here. I hadn't heard from either of them since they left for uni, but the three of us were friends all through school. It was just me and Ida sometimes. Or just Ida and Jen. Or Jen and me. We were all faithless, and tight. Our friendship was a carousel spinning around and around, someone was always jumping on, or hopping off.

I'd never have bothered with Kiera if they were here, I don't think. Kiera lacked Ida's spikiness, or Jen's sparkle like a holiday girl with sun on her legs and mermaid streaks in her hair. Kiera was just there. Dipping her chips into gravy, looping her ponytail out of her anorak, and, somehow, unbelievably, snogging the most beautiful man I ever saw.

He appeared from nowhere. It seemed like he wandered into the cafe one drizzly day and woke us all up from the slumber of killing time until the end of our shift. They called him Corin, and I'd decided I'd probably marry him. Quietly, without really speaking to him, I cleared his table, willing him to look up and see into my soul or something.

It wasn't just me though, *everyone* loved him. He was dark-haired, honey-skinned, and spoken for. Just looking at him made us all think of the folklores about selkies and kelpies we'd heard as bairns, stories of men so handsome a girl's sense sails away.

His girlfriend was beautiful too, slender and pale. She came in with him, red ponytail swinging, one arm around his waist and one hand in his jean pocket. Often, when they reached the cafe, she kissed him and let him wander off on his own until they met up late afternoon. The girls were all over him when she wasn't there. They rushed into the cafe, ordering burgers and chips, blowing bubbles into their Cokes, just to sit opposite him and gawp. It was worth clogging up an artery or ten just to watch him sip coffee and look us up and down. Did he wink when we smiled? Did he notice us? We thought so, then again it was impossible to say.

He noticed Kiera, that's for sure. They met at the claw machine. She described it to me afterwards as one of those slow-motion moments you don't think will ever happen to you in life. She caught his gaze through the glass case and a shiver rippled down her spine. She knew he was different right away.

'You're too jerky,' he placed his hand over Kiera's on the lever of the claw machine, showing her how to drop the fluffy octopus into the prize slot.

I saw them often when I finished my shift, holding hands, lips locked outside the bingo, leaning against the plastic chairs that filled up when it rained. I also saw his girlfriend. Once, I even saw her show up to meet them both, red hair flickering around her face in the wind. She looked Kiera up and down, Kiera looked at her, and then, suddenly, they all laughed. I saw them head off to the sands – all three of them, as if they were pals. Except they couldn't be pals, could they? Not really. I didn't know Kiera well enough to ask.

We didn't really speak until the day I caught her on her knees in the Ladies. The soles of her shoes facing me under the stalls like a girl saying her prayers.

'Are you all right?' The cistern whispered. Kiera walked to the sink.

'Well, since you ask…' Kiera lifted her anorak and showed me her belly, so much firmer than the rest of her. Round.

I didn't know what to say. I mean, babies are cute and that, but…

'No one knows yet,' Kiera pumped liquid soap, 'I'm keeping it quiet.'

Even her ma would never guess, she reckoned. She was so aware of Kiera being self-conscious about her size she was always telling her, 'Kiera, you have a beautiful face, like Botticelli. You're not fat, you just have a shape that isn't fashionable right now.' If she noticed Kiera getting bigger, she'd never breathe a word.

I nodded, unsure what just happened. Kiera Hunter had

no reason to tell me a secret. I had no loyalty to keep it. I didn't envy anything about her enough to be her friend.

And yet, we were friends after that, as if a secret is a key that locks people together. I kept noticing Kiera around work – huddled under an umbrella, straightening the puffin on her hat, cheerily doling out flyers. She zipped her oversized anorak to the chin, dressed for permanent winter. No one would notice her belly, not even if they looked. Kiera gave no one any reason to. She was so ordinary, except when we went swimming between shifts.

There were no rides across the other side of the bay, only birds, and an abandoned outdoor pool full of pondweed and rain. We took off our uniforms and wriggled into our bathing suits behind our towels.

'What you scared of?' she called. 'Getting your hair wet?'

I got into the pool, keeping one hand on the side. Kiera swirled in the water, so gracious if anyone saw her swim they'd be sorry she wasn't a dancer on land.

'You never asked about my boyfriend,' she called. She was the only person I ever saw float and laugh at the same time.

'I thought you'd tell me when you're ready, or not. Whatever,' I replied.

This was why she chose me to be her friend, I suppose. I was someone who *never* asked. Not about her boyfriend, his girlfriend, or anything. It used to drive my pals mad. Honestly, Ida and Jen said, I was like a lad sometimes. I never had any gossip. I let the juiciest stories drift over my head without looking up. I denied it, but it was sort of true. I never felt I needed to know everything. I've been that way ever since my dad left, I suppose. Kiera laughed and rolled in the water, it seemed she didn't want to tell me much anyway.

She wanted me to ponder. She wanted to get dressed and go for a fried Mars bar and chips.

It was a Friday when she told me. The season was almost over. I was learning to knit. I'd started a jade blanket I was planning to give Kiera when the baby was born. For now, I gave her a velvet seal from the bingo full of old ladies who seemed to spend all day staring out at the waves, calling 'house'. Kiera stroked a flipper and handed the seal back to me.

'I'm not keeping it you know,' she said. The wind whipped her hair, a strand stuck to her lip gloss. 'Corin and Brook are going to raise it. You must have seen his wife? The red-headed lass? They're both dead excited about it! They love the baby already.'

It seemed like she'd been dying to tell someone, and suddenly, she told me it all, about how she'd known Corin had someone else, and it didn't matter for long. 'Once I met her it was like we'd known each other all our lives,' she said. 'You ever met someone and felt like that? I loved her. She loved me. We all loved each other. It felt right.'

Girls our age stepped off the waltzers, laughing and organising their hair. I wished I knew them. I wished we were them. It looked so simple to be those girls. While they swirled around every night, flirting with fairground fellas they didn't dare give their numbers, Kiera was involved in something so complicated I couldn't get my head around it. And yet, I couldn't blame her. I'd been bedazzled by beautiful faces sometimes myself. Somedays, I looked around the arcade and thought I could fall in love with almost anyone, just to make another work day more bearable. Kiss the boredom away.

The burger stalls brought in their drizzly condiments and shuttered up for the night. Kiera dragged me to the beach before the last bus. 'Come on, I've got something to show you.'

It was dark, other than for the moonlight on the water. Several couples were wandering onto the sand, looking around to check they were alone. I crouched behind the bins next to Kiera. She placed a finger on her lips, 'Ssssh'. Together, the couples stripped off their clothes and strode into the ocean, waves crashing against their shoulders, flanks, hair, manes soaked in moonlight. Where people once made sandcastles, horses ran. They raced into the ocean and swam, smashing the moonlight on the water into grains.

'They're all around us,' Kiera whispered, 'the kelpies. They mate for life, but they love our company. Aren't they beautiful? They come ashore, but the land doesn't own them. Nothing does. They come and go as they like.' Kiera put her arm around me, leading me off the sand. 'You see? It's okay. That's the life he'll have out there, wild, loved,' she said. 'What could beat that?'

Kiera gave birth a few weeks later, alone. It didn't look like she thought it would, she told me afterwards. The baby came out covered in a milky sac, she could see him underneath like morning through cloud. He was beautiful, she said, all legs, covered in hair from his crown to his ankles, neither foal nor human. His tail was soft and silky. Kiera said it was the colour of her hair when she was small.

'They say if he never touched the ocean he'd look more like me every day,' Kiera said.

We sat on our coats under the arches, surrounded by cans and the graffiti of couples who'd loved there.

'You don't have to do this,' I said.

'I know.' Kiera ran her finger over a soft hoof-shaped foot. 'Can you imagine it though? Walking when he could be swimming, never feeling he's in the right place. I've spent my whole life that way.'

I was too sad to say anything. She knew her mind more than I'll ever know mine. 'It's almost time. Come on, they're coming.'

There was a small window for her do this, she said, if she missed her chance her boy would be locked on land and become more ordinary every day. I didn't know if I believed her. If I'd believe anything.

The tide was riding in. The horses swam close to the shore. Two, side by side. One was so dark it was almost black, one a blood bay. I held the small star of my torch and flicked it on and off. Kiera waded out, dropped the bundle in the water and watched the foal swim out of sight.

THE **AUTHORS**

JENN ASHWORTH was born in 1982 in Preston, where she still lives. She studied at Newnham College, Cambridge and the Centre for New Writing at the University of Manchester. Before becoming a writer, she worked as a librarian in a prison. Her first novel, *A Kind of Intimacy*, was published in 2009 and won a Betty Trask Award. On the publication of her second, *Cold Light* (Sceptre, 2011), she was featured on the BBC's The Culture Show as one of the UK's twelve best new writers. Her third novel, *The Friday Gospels* (2013), is published by Sceptre. Ashworth has also published short fiction and won an award for her blog, *Every Day I Lie a Little*. Her work has been compared to both Ruth Rendell and Patricia Highsmith; all her novels to date have been set in the North West of England. She lives in Lancashire and teaches Creative Writing at Lancaster University.

GARY BUDDEN is a writer, editor and the co-founder of Influx Press. His dark book of uncanny psychogeographies and landscape punk, *Hollow Shores*, was published in 2017 by Dead Ink, and his dark fiction novella *Judderman* (as D.A. Northwood) is published in 2018 by the Eden Book Society. His short story 'Greenteeth' was nominated for a 2017 British Fantasy Award and adapted into a short film by the filmmaker Adam Scovell. His work has been published widely, including *Black Static*, *Structo*, *Elsewhere*, *Unthology*, *The Lonely Crowd*, *Gorse*, and *Year's Best Weird Fiction (vol. 4)*. www.newlexicons.com.

RAMSEY CAMPBELL lives on Merseyside with his wife Jenny. His pleasures include classical music, good food and wine, and whatever's in that pipe. His web site is at www.ramseycampbell.com.

The Oxford Companion to English Literature describes Ramsey Campbell as 'Britain's most respected living horror writer'. He has been given more awards than any other writer in the field, including the Grand Master Award of the World Horror Convention, the Lifetime Achievement Award of the Horror Writers Association, the Living Legend Award of the International Horror Guild and the World Fantasy Lifetime Achievement Award. In 2015 he was made an Honorary Fellow of Liverpool John Moores University for outstanding services to literature. Among his novels are *The Face That Must Die, Incarnate, Midnight Sun, The Count of Eleven, Silent Children, The Darkest Part of the Woods, The Overnight, Secret Story, The Grin of the Dark, Thieving Fear, Creatures of the Pool, The Seven Days of Cain, Ghosts Know, The Kind Folk, Think Yourself Lucky* and *Thirteen Days by Sunset Beach*. He recently brought out his Brichester Mythos trilogy, consisting of *The Searching Dead, Born to the Dark* and *The Way of the Worm*. *Needing Ghosts, The Last Revelation of Gla'aki, The Pretence* and *The Booking* are novellas. His collections include *Waking Nightmares, Alone with the Horrors, Ghosts and Grisly Things, Told by the Dead, Just Behind You, Holes for Faces,* and *By the Light of My Skull*, and his non-fiction is collected as *Ramsey Campbell, Probably. Limericks of the Alarming* and *Phantasmal* are what they sound like. His novels *The Nameless* and *Pact of the Fathers* have been filmed in Spain, where a film of *The Influence* is in production. He is the President of the Society of Fantastic Films.

DAN COXON is part of the editorial team at Unsung Stories, as well as owning the editing and proofreading company Momus Editorial. His book *Being Dad* won Best Anthology 2016 at the Saboteur Awards. He currently edits *The Shadow Booth*, a bi-annual journal of weird and eerie fiction.

RICHARD V. HIRST is from Manchester. He is the co-author of *The Night Visitors*.

ANDREW MICHAEL HURLEY's first novel, *The Loney*, was originally published in 2014 by Tartarus Press and then John Murray a year later, after which it won the 2015 Costa 'First Novel' award and the 2016 British Book Industry awards for 'Debut Novel' and 'Book of the Year'. His second book, *Devil's Day*, was published in October 2017 and was listed as one of the books of the year in *The Times*, *Financial Times* and the *Mail on Sunday*. It went on to jointly win the 2018 Royal Society of Literature Encore Award for best second novel. Hurley's short fiction has appeared in *Granta*, *Best British Short Stories*, *The Spectator* and in the English Heritage anthology, *Eight Ghosts*. The author lives in Lancashire with his family and teaches Creative Writing at Manchester Metropolitan University's Writing School.

TIM LEBBON is a New York Times-bestselling author of over forty novels. Recent books include *The Folded Land*, *Relics*, *The Family Man*, *The Silence* and the *Rage War* trilogy of Alien/Predator novels. He has won four British Fantasy Awards, a Bram Stoker Award, and a Scribe Award. The movie of his story *Pay the Ghost*, starring Nicolas

Cage, was released Hallowe'en 2015. *The Silence*, starring Stanley Tucci and Kiernan Shipka, is due for release in 2018. Several other movie projects are in development in the US and UK. Find out more about Tim at his website www.timlebbon.net.

ALISON LITTLEWOOD's latest novel is *The Crow Garden*, a tale of obsession set amidst Victorian asylums and séance rooms. It follows The Hidden People, a Victorian tale about the murder of a young girl suspected of being a fairy changeling. Alison's other novels include *A Cold Silence, Path of Needles, The Unquiet House* and *Zombie Apocalypse! Acapulcalypse Now*. Her first book, *A Cold Season*, was selected for the Richard and Judy Book Club and described as 'perfect reading for a dark winter's night.'

Alison's short stories have been picked for *Best British Horror, The Best Horror of the Year, The Year's Best Dark Fantasy and Horror* and *The Mammoth Book of Best New Horror* anthologies, as well as *The Best British Fantasy* and *The Mammoth Book of Best British Crime*. They have been gathered together in her collections *Quieter Paths* and in *Five Feathered Tales*, a collaboration with award-winning illustrator Daniele Serra. She won the 2014 Shirley Jackson Award for Short Fiction.

Alison lives with her partner Fergus in Yorkshire, England, in a house of creaking doors and crooked walls. She loves exploring the hills and dales with her two hugely enthusiastic Dalmatians and has a penchant for books on folklore and weird history, Earl Grey tea and semicolons. You can talk to her on Twitter: @Ali__L, see her on Facebook or visit her at www.alisonlittlewood.co.uk.

KIRSTY LOGAN is the author of the novels *The Gloaming* and *The Gracekeepers*, the short story collections *A Portable Shelter* and *The Rental Heart & Other Fairytales*, the flash fiction chapbook *The Psychology of Animals Swallowed Alive* and the short memoir *The Old Asylum in the Woods at the Edge of the Town Where I Grew Up*. Her books have won the Lambda Literary Award, the Polari First Book Prize, the Saboteur Award, the Scott Prize and the Gavin Wallace Fellowship, and been selected for the Radio 2 Book Club and the Waterstones Book Club. Her short fiction and poetry has been translated into Japanese, Spanish and Italian, recorded for radio and podcasts, exhibited in galleries, and distributed from a vintage Wurlitzer cigarette machine. She lives in Glasgow with her wife.

JAMES MILLER is a novelist and academic. He has published the acclaimed novels *Lost Boys* (Little, Brown), *Sunshine State* (Little, Brown) and *UnAmerican Activities* (Dodo Ink), as well as numerous short stories and the collaborative poetry collection *Strays* (HVTN), written with Julia Rose Lewis. He currently runs the MA in Creative Writing at Kingston University and can be found at @jmlostboys and www.jamesmillerauthor.com.

ALISON MOORE's short fiction has been included in *Best British Short Stories* and *Best British Horror* anthologies and broadcast on BBC Radio. Her first novel, *The Lighthouse*, was shortlisted for the Man Booker Prize and the National Book Awards, winning the McKitterick Prize. Her latest novel is *Missing*, and her first book for children, *Sunny and the Ghosts*, will be published in November. Born in Manchester in 1971, Alison lives in a village on the Leicestershire-Nottinghamshire border. She is grateful to her son Arthur for the gift of Slimo. www.alison-moore.com.

JEANNETTE NG is originally from Hong Kong but now lives in Durham, UK. She has an MA in Medieval and Renaissance Studies. She runs live roleplay games and used to sell costumes for a living. *Under the Pendulum Sun* is her debut novel.

ANGELA READMAN's short stories have won the Costa Short Story Award, the Mslexia Story Competition, and the National Flash Fiction Award. Her debut story collection *Don't Try this at Home* (And Other Stories, 2015) won The Rubery Book Award and was shortlisted in The Edge Hill Prize. She also writes poetry. Her latest book, *The Book of Tides*, was published by Nine Arches in 2016.

GARETH E. REES is the founder and editor of the website *Unofficial Britain* (www.unofficialbritain.com), author of *The Stone Tide* (Influx Press, 2018) and *Marshland* (Influx Press, 2013). His work has featured in anthologies including *Unthology 10* (Unthank Books), *An Unreliable Guide to London* (Influx Press), *Mount London* (Penned in the Margins), *Acquired for Development By* (Influx Press), *Walking Inside Out: Contemporary British Psychogeography* (Rowman & Littlefield), *The Ashgate Companion to Paranormal Cultures* (Ashgate), and the spoken word album *A Dream Life of Hackney Marshes* (Clay Pipe Music). He awaits the apocalypse in Hastings with his two daughters and a dog named Hendrix.

ROBERT SHEARMAN has written five short story collections, and between them they have won the World Fantasy Award, the Shirley Jackson Award, the Edge Hill Readers Prize, and three British Fantasy Awards. He began his career in the theatre, and was resident dramatist at the Northcott Theatre in Exeter, and regular writer for Alan Ayckbourn at the Stephen Joseph Theatre in Scarborough; his plays have won the Sunday Times Playwriting Award, the World Drama Trust Award, and the Guinness Award for Ingenuity in association with the Royal National Theatre. A regular writer for BBC Radio, his own interactive drama series *The Chain Gang* has won two Sony Awards. But he is probably best known for his work on *Doctor Who*, bringing back the Daleks for the BAFTA-winning first series in an episode nominated for a Hugo Award. His latest book, *We All Hear Stories in the Dark*, is to be released by PS Publishing next year.

STEPHEN VOLK is best known as the writer of the BBC's notorious 'Hallowe'en hoax' *Ghostwatch* and the award-winning ITV drama series *Afterlife* starring Andrew Lincoln and Lesley Sharp. His other screenplays include 2011's *The Awakening* starring Rebecca Hall and Dominic West, Ken Russell's *Gothic* starring Gabriel Byrne and Natasha Richardson, *The Guardian* (co-written with William Friedkin), and *Midwinter of the Spirit*. He won a BAFTA for *The Deadness of Dad* starring Rhys Ifans. His novellas and short stories have been selected for *Year's Best Fantasy and Horror*, *Best New Horror*, *Best British Mysteries*, and *Best British Horror*, he has been a Bram Stoker and Shirley Jackson Award finalist, and is the author of three collections: *Dark Corners, Monsters in the Heart* (which won the British Fantasy Award in 2014), and *The Parts We Play*. 2018 sees the much-anticipated publication of his *Dark Masters Trilogy* – 'Whitstable', 'Leytonstone' and 'Netherwood' – two novellas and a short novel featuring luminaries of the genre, Peter Cushing, Alfred Hitchcock and Dennis Wheatley.

CATRIONA WARD was born in Washington, DC and grew up in the United States, Kenya, Madagascar, Yemen and Morocco. She read English at St Edmund Hall, Oxford and is a graduate of the Creative Writing MA at the University of East Anglia. Her debut novel, *Rawblood* (W&N, 2015) won the August Derleth Prize at the 2016 British Fantasy Awards, was shortlisted for the Author's Club Best First Novel Award and was selected as a Winter 2016 Fresh Talent title by WHSmith. *Rawblood* is published in the US and Canada as *The Girl from Rawblood* (Sourcebooks, 2017). Catriona's second novel, *Little Eve*, was published by W&N in July 2018. She lives in London and Devon.

ALIYA WHITELEY's last two speculative fiction novellas, published in the UK by Unsung Stories, have been shortlisted for numerous awards, including the Shirley Jackson Award and John W. Campbell Award. Her next novel, *The Loosening Skin*, will be published in October 2018. She has a website at aliyawhiteley.wordpress.com, and can be found on Twitter as @AliyaWhiteley.

The Backers

THIS BOOK WOULD NOT HAVE BEEN POSSIBLE WITHOUT THE SUPPORT OF ALL OUR GENEROUS BACKERS ON KICKSTARTER. THE NAMES LISTED BELOW MAKE AN INSPIRING COMMUNITY OF PEOPLE, THE KIND OF PEOPLE THAT DREAM OF BETTER WORLDS.

A.B.E. Kristiansen
A.K. Wallace ~ Twisted Writer Chic
Abi Hynes
Adrian Spink
Adrien Palladino
Alex Burton-Keeble
Alex Herbert
Alexander Coles
Alexis Wolfe
Amanda Merritt
Amy Griffiths
Andrew Campbell-Howes
Andrew Cook
Andrew Hatchell
Andrew Saxby
Andy Perry
Anna Chapman
Anna Kay
Anne Scott
Anthony Self
Ashley Hamm
Ballad Of Scum
Barbara Matzner-Volfing
Becca Read
Ben Cartwright
Ben Webster
Benjamin Hausman
Benjamin Judge

Bethan Evans
Björn Prömpeler
Boudicca Press
Brett Kay
C Geoffrey Taylor
C&M Putnam
Cat Vincent
Catherine Baker
Catherine Hargrave
Catherine Spooner
Cato Vandrare
Cavan Scott
Celia Guerrieri
Charles Prepolec
Charlotte Organ
Chris B
Chris Bekofske
Chris Chastain
Christian Rennie
Christine Garretson-Persans
Christine Slade
Christo
Christopher 'Vulpine' Kalley
Christopher Stanley
Claire Harvey
Clifton Roberts
Connar Fyfe
Cullen 'Towelman'

Gilchrist
D Franklin
Daniël Verhoeven
D.J. Cole
Dagmar Baumann
Dan Grace
Dan Hanks
Dan Hess
Daniel Broadbent
Daniel McGachey
Danny Barker
Darren and Hannah Coxon
Darryll smith-walker
David Gullen
David Harris
David Hartley
David Maciver
Dead Ink Books
Debbie Phillips
Dennis D'Ooghe
Duncan Lawie
Dy Booth
Dylan T Robertson
Edward Drummond
Elder Carrie
Eleanor Walker
Eley Williams
Elizabeth Ciancio
Elliott Finn

Emilio Francischelli
Emily Louise Parsons
Emma Jackson
F Scott Valeri
Fat Roland
Fenric Cayne
Fred W Johnson
Gina R. Collia
Hassan Ali
Hazzlebee
Heather
Heather Valentine
Helen Kemp
Howard Blakeslee
Howard Wong
Hugo Godfrey
Iain Rowan
Ian Chung
Ian Hill
Ian Mond
Imran Mohamed
Jack James
Jack Wheeler
Jacob West
Jaide Wilson
James Cleaveley
James Shaw
Jamie Hardwick
Jane Roberts
Jared Morrison
Jennifer Elizabeth York
Jennifer Martinez
Jennifer Woods
Jeremy Day
Jeremy Wasik
Joakim Waern
John
John Grillbridges

Jonathan K. Stephens
Jonathan Mackenzie
Jonathan Pinnock
Jonathan Thornton
Joseph Camilleri
Joseph Gustafson
Josh S. Talley
Joshua Engle
Jules Fattorini
Justin Davis
Karli Watson
Karolina Lebek
Kenneth SkaldebÃ,
Kevin
Kevin Eddy
Keyne Day
Kieran Wood
Kim McGreal
KT Wagner
Kurt
L George
Lark Cunningham
Laura Elliott
Leon Hitter
Liz Xifaras
Lloyd Thistle
Lorraine Phipps
Lucie McKnight Hardy
Luke Brason
Lydia Gittins
M Knight
Marc Stigaard
Mariam
Mariam Pourshoushtari
Marian Womack
Mark Clerkin
Mark Featherston
Mark Gerrits

Mark Newman
Mark Weisgerber
Martina Zvantje Hofmann
Mary Jo March
Matt Gamble
Matt Hill
Matthew Adamson
Matthew Beckham
Matthew Craig
Matthew Fadling
Matthew J Shaw
Matthew Lee
Melanie Flynn
Melinda Gramnaes
Melissa Harrington
Micah Israel Thomas
Michael Dean
Michael H Bullington
Michael Hirtzy
Michael J. Dalpe, Jr.
Michael Krawec
Mike Vermilye
Mike Whiteman
Mikkel Rasmussen
Nancy Johnson
Nici West
Nikki Brice
Nikolas Isensee
Noel Johnson
Oliver Isbell
Oliver Langmead
Olivier Vergnault
Olwen Lachowicz
Paul Childs
Paul M. Cray
Paul Ramage
Paul Watson

The Backers

Paul y cod asyn Jarman
pete sutton
Peter Burton
Peter Curd
Peter Haynes
Peter Koller
Phil Exon
Phil Shipley
R.S. Konjek
Ralph Robert Moore
Ray Bradnock
Reggie Chamberlain-King
Richard Grainger
Richard Hing
Richard Kerridge
Richard Raghoo
Richard Sheehan
Richard Wells
Robby Thrasher
Robert Dex
Robert Hood
RODNEY O'CONNOR
Ronald H. Miller
Roy Rosales
S.A. Rennie
Sam Reynders
Sam Spencer
Sam Wood
Samantha Squires
Sarah Dodd
Sarah Garnham
Sarah Kohtz
Scarlett Parker
Scott Maynard
Simon Bowie
Simon Hardy
Soror Somnia Clare

Spike Searle
Stark Holborn
Stefan Von Blon
Stefan Wertheimer
Stephanie Wasek
Stephen Livingston
Steve Birt
Steve J Shaw
Steve Walsh
STORGY Magazine
Stuart Forbes
Tammy Sparks
Tania
The Franklin Design Forge
Thomas Jager
Thomas Keith Stone
Tim Cooke
Tim Foley
Tim Stretton
Timothy J. Jarvis
Tom Atkinson
Tom Hardy
Tom Wojciechowski
Tomek Dzido
Tyler
Verity Holloway
Vicki Jarrett
Victoria Hoyle
Vince Haig
William C. Pike
William Fecke
Yosen Lin

PSEUDOTOOTH

BY VERITY HOLLOWAY

Aisling Selkirk is a young woman beset by unexplained blackouts, pseudo-seizures that have baffled both the doctors and her family. Sent to recuperate in the Suffolk countryside with ageing relatives, she seeks solace in the work of William Blake and writing her journal, filling its pages with her visions of Feodor, a fiery East Londoner haunted by his family's history back in Russia.

But her blackouts persist as she discovers a Tudor priest hole and papers from its disturbed former inhabitant Soon after, she meets the enigmatic Chase, and is drawn to an unfamiliar town where the rule of Our Friend is absolute and those deemed unfit and undesirable disappear into The Quiet...

Blurring the lines between dream, fiction and reality, Pseudotooth boldly tackles issues of trauma, social difference and our conflicting desires for purity and acceptance, asking questions about those who society shuns, and why.

Get a free extract
www.unsungstories.co.uk/trypseudotooth

Follow Verity @Verity_Holloway

DARK STAR

BY OLIVER LANGMEAD

The city of Vox survives in darkness, under a sun that burns without light. In Vox's permanent night, light bulbs are precious, the rich live in radiance and three Hearts beat light into the city. Aquila. Corvus. Cancer.

Hearts that bring power to the light-deprived citizens of the city of Vox whilst ghosts haunt the streets, clawing at headlights. Prometheus, liquid light, is the drug of choice. The body of young Vivian North, her blood shining brightly with unnatural light, has no place on the streets.

When Cancer is stolen, the weaponisation of its raw power threatens to throw Vox into chaos. Vox needs a hero, and it falls to cop Virgil Yorke to investigate.

But Virgil has had a long cycle and he doesn't feel like a hero. With the ghosts of his last case still haunting his thoughts, he craves justice for the young woman found dead with veins full of glowing. Aided by his partner Dante, Virgil begins to shed light on the dark city's even darker secrets.

Haunted by the ghosts of his past and chased by his addictions, which will crack first, Virgil or the case?

Get a free extract
www.unsungstories.co.uk/trydarkstar

OR SCAN THE QR CODE

www.oliverlangmead.com

THE BEAUTY
BY ALIYA WHITELEY

THE ARRIVAL OF MISSIVES

BY ALIYA WHITELEY

"Stark, poetic, forthright and live with the numinous. One of the most original and haunting stories I have read in recent years."
Nina Allan

☆ **2016 JOHN W. CAMPBELL AWARD FINALIST**
☆ **2017 BFS AWARDS FINALIST**
☆ **2016 BSFA AWARDS FNIALIST**
☆ **2016 JAMES TIPTREE JR. AWARD LONGLIST**
☆ **2017 SABOTEUR AWARDS SHORTLIST**

From Aliya Whiteley, author of the critically-acclaimed *The Beauty*, comes a genre-defying story of fate, free-will and the choices we make in life.

In the aftermath of the Great War, Shirley Fearn dreams of challenging the conventions of rural England, where life is as predictable as the changing of the seasons.

The scarred veteran Mr. Tiller, left disfigured by an impossible accident on the battlefields of France, brings with him a message: part prophecy, part warning. Will it prevent her mastering her own destiny?

Get a free extract
www.unsungstories.co.uk/trymissives

Follow Aliya @AliyaWhiteley